Awak

The Gaia Series

Book 2

Chris Ord

For my family - thank you for giving me the wings

Cover design: Steven Walker of 50 Foot Long Horse

Copyright © Chris Ord, 2019

The right of Chris Ord to be identified as the author of this work has been asserted by him in accordance with the Copyright, Designs and Patents Act 1988.

Further information on the author and his work can be found at:
http://chrisord.wixsite.com/chrisord
or on Facebook at:
https://www.facebook.com/chrisordauthor/

ISBN: 9781709462344

All rights reserved. No part of this publication may be reproduced, stored in a retrieval system, or transmitted, in any form or by any means, electronic, mechanical, photocopying, recording or otherwise, without the prior permission of the copyright owner.

'Now is the time of monsters'

(Antonio Gramsci)

1

The village was bathed in darkness and the night birds had returned. On the island they were elusive, a shadowy threat; in the village, numerous and bold. Gaia had seen their black wings and bodies sweeping through the night sky, flashing past the moon. She had heard the menacing clicks, much louder and piercing than before. Whatever the night birds were, they were many. The villagers feared the creatures, and few would speak of them. Yet, there was a greater terror; something lurking beyond the walls, beasts far more menacing and dangerous. They also came at night; seldom seen, always heard.

Gaia sat at the wooden bench by the stream, shivering in the icy night air, the cold nipping at her cheeks. She stared into the frozen water, shimmering as it caught the moonlight, saying a silent farewell. She had spent many hours here, hidden amongst the trees, her connection with nature, another reality, the world she had almost lost. She would study the patterns in the icicles for hours; each unique, its own shape and size, random, transient, a moment of existence while the world carried on regardless. Gaia always felt compelled to look at them. It gave them value, validated their presence. Their silent beauty touched her, left a soft footprint in the sands of her mind, giving even the smallest fragments of her life meaning. She knew this was what she was searching for too. All she ever wanted was to matter.

The water reminded her of the sea, of the island, and the hours on the beach, her beach, her special place. This was where it all began. Only a few weeks before she had sat on the golden sands dreaming of escape. Now she longed to be on those sands again, to feel the island and its beauty, gaze at the eerie light in that magical hour before sunset. The light like no other, a fiery red blanket wrapped in a strange, fuzzy haze. Gaia knew she would never see the island again. This world was gone, a chapter in her life ended, a new one about to begin. The island seemed like a dream to her now.

Something caught Gaia's eye. Across the stream, beyond the trees by the wall surrounding the village two men were wrestling with someone, dragging them through the snow. Black hoods covered the captive's head, hands tied behind their back. Gaia edged round the green and followed them, using the trees for cover. She couldn't see their faces, but they were well-built and the prisoner was small, and despite attempts to struggle, looked weak. The men snaked round the perimeter, hugging the wall until they came to a gate, a small side entrance Gaia was unaware of. It was manned by two tall, thickset guards, wrapped in heavy clothing, and wearing masks. They unlocked the gate and led the hooded captive out, closing the gate behind. Several minutes passed, before the men returned, alone. One of the guards locked the gate and the two men headed off towards the main part of the village. Gaia watched as the guards joked and chatted, jumping up and down in the snow, banging their gloved hands together, as puffs of icy vapour billowed from their mouths. Gaia slipped back through the trees towards her lodgings.

There was a howling in the distance. The dogs were on their way. Each night, as the last rays of winter sun disappeared, their howls could be heard.

Chilling, terrifying cries ripping through the silence of the night, shattering sleep and turning dreams into nightmares. So far the walls of the village had withstood them, but it had not always been this way. Stories were told of the early days, the time The Community first occupied the village, the time before the wall and defences. Soon after The Community arrived the beasts picked up the human scent and began their raids. The dogs were giant, monstrous mutations that had sprung from the time before. They were vicious, relentless beasts and many villagers had been taken. The rats of the island and lowlands were a strong predator and foe, creatures to fear, but they could be defeated. The dogs were different. Their strength and savagery was at a level few could match. Even with the best of weaponry, a team had little hope. The Community's only chance was to defend and avoid, to keep the creatures out at all costs. In seeking freedom, they had become trapped.

The dogs were intelligent, and knew the defences were strong. Still they came each night to make their presence known. The beasts were searching for a weakness, a breach in the wall, some act of foolishness leaving a victim exposed. Most nights they left without prey, but their visits were a reminder, a warning: the hills belonged to them. This was their domain and the night was their playground. Whoever the men had cast beyond the walls there was little chance they would survive the night. The men knew this, as did Gaia. The prisoner had been condemned to die. This was how The Community worked, a web of silent and unspoken truths, wrapped in a veil of lies.

As Gaia walked through the village, the howling continued, drawing nearer, familiarity and frequency never dampening its chilling impact. All light had gone now, and the village was deserted. Apart from the howling, all Gaia could hear was the whistle of the arctic wind and the crunch of her boots in the snow. Soon her lodgings came into view. Set on the far edge of the village, she was housed in an old cottage two storeys high, made of local stone and with a pitched slate roof. The house was encircled by a low wall protecting the small rose and flower garden within. The garden was cared for by the old woman, one of the elders who shared the house with Gaia. This was her last goodbye, a loving memento before she was taken for her reckoning.

Gaia entered the cottage and removed her damp, outdoor clothing. Placing her boots to the side, she hung the icy wet clothes in the nook by the door. The flakes of snow still clinging to her overcoat melted into droplets in the warmth of the cottage. Gaia watched as they trickled downward, forming patterns of tiny streams on the fabric. She brushed herself down and rubbed her hands together, clasping them tight and blowing air into them. The heat of the room began to seep into her frozen pores as her hands thawed. Gaia's face was pink and raw, and her body shivered. Stamping her feet on the door mat, she made her way through to the lounge.

The room was small and cosy, with an open fire roaring from fresh logs. The flames leapt up the chimney and hurled comforting waves of heat into the room. Gaia felt a blast of fiery air strike her face as she took a seat on the sofa. Stretching her feet, her toes reached for the fire. Old paintings lined the walls; a bookcase hugged the corner peppered with long forgotten classics and cooking books no-one read. Two ancient, high backed sofas dominated the centre of the floor. One was pushed against a wall, the other pulled forward by the rug in front of the fire. The fireplace was cast iron, and either side stood two armchairs, similar in antiquated style as the sofas, each a different colour. Flowered tiles adorned either side of the fireplace, which was topped by a magnificent wooden mantel. A long mirror hung on the wall above, encased in an ornate brass frame. The room had a quaint, aged feel, as if everything had been thrown together from fragments across the decades. It was comforting and inviting, if a little neglected. Gaia loved it, especially when she was alone, but this evening there was company.

Hannah sat in the armchair by the fire, pencil in hand, diary on her lap. This was her evening ritual, peering down at pages through narrow spectacles teetering on the end of her nose. Her hair was short and greying, her face and hands dry and gnarled. Her tiny, hunched frame looked lost in the tall armchair, the gaunt face always with the same thoughtful, grave expression. She reminded Gaia of Jack, who she had thought of often these past few weeks. Gaia wondered what the old man was doing, if he was still alive, and tending the herd of cattle. Jack had been frail, with the look of someone resigned to his fate. He knew what was about to happen, his reckoning was of a different kind. Not the promise of The Community, but one determined by nature. She thought of his words about The Community, how they never knew the wonder of being young, how they had forgotten because *'they are never allowed to get old.'* His words echoed through Gaia's mind when Hannah looked up from her diary and spoke.

'Good evening dear. You look chilled to the bone. Would you like me to make some tea?'

'No, I'm fine.'

'Are you sure? I was just about to make one for myself.'

Hannah smiled and waited, her spectacles looking as though they would fall from her nose at any moment. Gaia resisted, but knew she had no choice.

'Well, only if you're making one.'

Hannah leapt to her feet with the energy of someone half her age. There was little that could lift her soul more than the opportunity to make tea. She made her way towards the kitchen with a spring in her step while Gaia remained to soak up the soothing warmth of the fire. Staring into the roaring flames, she traced the changing shapes as they flickered and danced. Smoke billowed up the chimney, the red embers of the logs glowing a deep orange. Gaia was mesmerised by fire. It was powerful, destructive, but also cleansing. In the wrong hands it could devastate, but with care it was as essential as food or water. Most of the time the people of The Community took it for granted, but not in times like these. These hardest and bitterest of winter months were a reminder of its comfort, safety, and reassurance. Fire was life, and The Community cherished it. In this new world they had come to realise the things of true value.

Gaia thought about her journey the following day. This was the last time she would feel this comfort for several days; the last evening she would stare at these flames. It was the last night Gaia would spend in this house, her room, the first room of her own.

Other than her times in isolation on the island, this was her first taste of privacy. Most likely, it was the last time she would see Hannah too. Gaia had been in the village a short while, but had grown fond of the old woman and the small comforts of the house. Hannah had been kind and attentive during Gaia's recovery. She wasn't wary of their young prisoner like the others. Few in The Community saw Gaia as a person, and none but Hannah trusted and treated her with respect. Only the old woman saw beyond the suspicion and saw the scarred and vulnerable girl, someone who mattered, and needed help. Gaia would never forget that.

Hannah returned with a tray filled with two teacups, a teapot, a jar of honey and array of fresh, homemade biscuits. There was no milk, as such luxuries had gone in recent weeks. The remaining cattle had been slaughtered as the village had become more and more stranded from the rest of The Community. The biscuits would now be scorned upon by the others, a selfish extravagance. For Hannah they were a final small act of defiance from someone resigned to their fate. The old woman placed the tray on a small table by the armchair and poured tea into the two cups. Adding a spoonful of honey to each cup, she stirred, placing a couple of the biscuits on a saucer and passing it to Gaia.

'This'll warm you through. There's nothing in this world a good cup of tea can't sort out.'

'Thanks. You and your tea, Hannah. What am I going to do without you?'

There was an awkward silence, each of them not wanting to catch the other's eye. Hannah sat in the armchair and began to stir the tea. Taking one of the biscuits, the old woman dipped it into her cup, waiting just the right length of time until the liquid was absorbed without the biscuit crumbling. She had mastered this art over many years. Smiling, she placed the biscuit in her mouth, and washed it down with a large gulp of tea. Hannah looked across at Gaia who was still gazing into the flames.

'Penny for your thoughts, my dear.'

Gaia shook herself from her daydream, focusing on Hannah's words.

'I'm leaving,' she said.

Hannah raised her eyebrows. Placing the cup and saucer on the table, she clasped her hands together resting them on her knees. The old woman waited, anxious for Gaia to continue. There was a long pause, and after a sip of tea Gaia obliged.

'They're taking me to The Haven.'

Hannah's expression changed, and the look of grave concern returned. This time it was more intense. The old woman remained silent, waiting for Gaia. Age and wisdom had taught Hannah the power of silence and listening, and the precious value of words. She would speak once she had gathered her thoughts, and would choose her words with care.

'We're leaving at first light tomorrow. Kali left instructions that as soon as I was well enough I had to follow her and Freya there. I have to go. I need to be with Freya.'

Gaia was choked, the papered cracks of her fragile spirit were opening again. Her throat was tight, her mouth dry. She struggled to force out her words.

'I guess this is it. The time for goodbye.'

Gaia stared at Hannah, trying to read the old woman's expression, but only the worried frown remained. Gaia sipped her tea and nibbled one of the biscuits, the ginger mixed with the hot tea and honey giving a sharp, spicy flavour. Hannah spoke, her voice calm and reassuring, the frown evaporating from her face.

'I'll be sorry to see you go. You know how fond I am of you. You're a special girl.'

Hannah composed herself, fighting back the tears.

'Take good care of yourself out there.'

There was a long moment of silence before the old woman spoke again.

'You know this will be the last time we see each other.'

Gaia shook her head.

'Please don't say that Hannah. I don't know how long I'll be there, maybe I'll come back soon.'

Hannah's face darkened with a scowl, a dark expression Gaia had never seen from her before.

'My days are coming to an end. It'll be any time now.'

'What do you mean?' Gaia asked.

Hannah eased herself from the chair and walked to the living room door. It was ajar. She slipped into the hall, looked up the stairs, and returned, closing the door behind her. The old woman shuffled back to her seat and perched on the end, her body leaning forward, elbows on her knees. She whispered, her voice stretching out each of the words, one by one.

'This is the end Gaia. There's nothing for me after here. Whatever you've heard, it's all lies. There is no promised land, no paradise where we grow old with dignity and grace. Someday soon they'll come and take me into the hills at nightfall.'

The old woman waited, took a deep breath and continued.

'They'll leave me there, for the dogs.'

Gaia was stunned. She had questioned all The Community had told them, always doubted their truth, but to hear this from the lips of Hannah was still a shock. The old woman's tone and choice of words were unusual. This was not the warm, carefree friend Gaia had come to know. It was a lonely, frightened old woman knowing she was about to die a brutal death. Silence and tension enveloped the room as Gaia thought of the incident earlier. After a while, Hannah spoke.

'I'm going to show you something, but you mustn't tell anyone. I know all about you Gaia, what you've done, and why you are here. There has been a lot of talk amongst the leaders about you and Freya. You're both special, and Kali knows it. There is a purpose for you both and Kali has plans. She wouldn't have let you live otherwise.'

Questions raced through Gaia's mind, her head tumbling, slipping into chaos and confusion. She needed a moment to pause, take control, make sense of what Hannah was saying, but the old woman continued.

'I know you have doubts about The Community. You don't trust them, or how things are done. That's good. Don't lose it. Stay cynical. You're young, and you don't like what you see. It's important you question everything. You're right to, and it's how it should be.'

Hannah waited, studied Gaia's face, waiting for a reaction.

'They'll try to break you. They'll keep trying until you give in, til they're sure you are theirs. Don't let them win. Keep fighting it. You were made for something bigger. One day you'll realise what that is, but now is not the time.'

There was a fire and passion in Hannah's voice that surprised Gaia. These words were forbidden, and if anyone heard them it would mean certain death. The old woman spoke with the spirit of someone who no longer cared. Hannah leant forward, moving much closer to Gaia, lowering her voice to barely a whisper. Her voice sounded frail, on the verge of collapse.

'I'm sorry.'

Gaia gazed into the eyes of her friend as a single tear trickled down her cheek.

'There's no need to be sorry,' Gaia said.

The old woman lowered her head.

'The leaders told me to keep a watch on you. They wanted me to report anything suspicious. They've been using me as I'm one of their spies.'

She paused, raised her head and gazed into Gaia's eyes, a look of pleading in her face.

'I've told them little, nothing that could hurt you. I promise. I care for you Gaia. Please, I want you to know that.'

Gaia took the hand of her friend and smiled.

'Don't worry. I know. You mean the world to me. You're one of the few who has ever shown me any kindness in my life. I'll never forget that.'

Hannah returned the smile, and for a moment their eyes remained locked together.

'And what about Aran?' Hannah said.

Gaia looked away, staring into the flames as they raged in the hearth. She spat out her reply.

'He means nothing to me now.'

'There are things about Aran you don't know or understand. Don't be too hard on him.'

Gaia continued to gaze into the fire. Hannah continued.

'There are things many don't know. The Community is filled with secrets.'

Hannah paused, waiting for Gaia to respond, but she kept looking away, her eyes fixed on the fiery glow in the hearth.

'There's something I need to show you.' Hannah said.

Gaia frowned as Hannah edged further forward and lowered her head. Lifting her arms, the old woman began to play with her eyes. First her left, removing something and placing it on her lap, then repeating the action with her right eye. The old woman raised her head, opened her eyes wide, and directed a piercing stare at Gaia. At first Gaia was shocked by the severity of Hannah's look, her face was manic and contorted. So much was her alarm that she failed to notice the most important change in Hannah's appearance. Then she saw them, and a look of horror crept across the young girl's face. Hannah's eyes were no longer blue, but had transformed into a dark hazel colour. Gaia looked closer, but there was no mistaking the deep brown hue. She looked on aghast, and before she could speak Hannah whispered.

'I wear lenses to make them think I'm one of them.'

Gaia's mind was racing, full of a thousand questions. The old woman waited until Gaia was calmer, then gripped her hands and continued, her voice the same fragile whisper.

'There are others among us. You can seek them out in The Haven. Find them and speak with them. They have some of the answers you're looking for.'

Hannah lowered her head and placed the lenses back into each eye. She turned and took her cup and saucer, sat back in her chair, and sipped at the tea. The old woman was relaxed, as if nothing had happened, while Gaia struggled to take in Hannah's words, trying to make sense of them. The young girl's head was spinning, she wanted to know more, needed to.

'What answers? What do you mean? What should I be asking them?'

Hannah nodded, the faintest of smiles on her lips.

'You will find out my dear. Especially once you reach The Haven. You have a chance to make amends. Make things right. Build a different future, free from this. There are others who will join you. Young people like yourself. Find them.'

There was a noise outside, the faint creak of a floorboard in the hall. Hannah sat up, alert and put a finger to her lips. Rising to her feet, she tip-toed to the door placing her ear against it. Gaia listened, but there was nothing. Hannah placed her hand on the door knob and turned it, easing the door open. Pushing her head through the gap, she scanned the hall outside while Gaia looked on and waited. After what seemed like an age, the old woman stepped back and looked at Gaia with a puzzled frown, shaking her head. Hannah spoke, her voice still a cautious whisper.

'There's no-one there, but they may have been listening. It's not safe to speak here. I can take risks, but you need to be protected.'

Hannah shuffled forward and stretched out her arms to Gaia. The young girl got to her feet and they embraced, old and young together, the past and the future. Both remained locked together for a while, arms wrapped in a warm and tender hug. They both knew this would be the final time they would see one another, though Gaia longed to think they might meet again. The old woman began to tremble, her body overflowing with emotion. She whispered in Gaia's ear, and they were the last words she would ever hear from the lips of her dear friend.

'Goodbye Gaia. Trust no one. Nothing is ever as it seems.'

2

Gaia heard the crunching of footsteps, stopping just behind her. There was a voice, a cold, chilling voice, one that had become familiar to Gaia, that haunted both her waking hours and her dreams.

'111. We meet in the hall in an hour.'

Kali trudged off in the crisp, fresh snow. There was a burning inside Gaia's chest as she focused on the gentle wind through the trees, and the silence beyond. Staring at the snow by her feet, she could almost feel the flakes melting together. She concentrated on the patterns etched in white, gazing at one small area, trying to pick out each tiny, individual shape. Everything around her was hazy, seeming to dissolve, leaving only the myriad of icy patterns. Her mind began to empty and the pain eased. Kali's steely grip was still upon Gaia, crushing and suffocating her, but the suffering was over. This was Gaia's refuge, her sanctuary, deep inside the protective walls of her mind where Kali could not reach her.

She was woken from her dream by the sound of banging on her door. She got up and dressed. The bitter chill in the bedroom stung her skin, her breath puffing icy vapours of steam into the room. This was the cruelest winter for many years. Blinding snow had enveloped them in a prison of ice. The snow had fallen for days with no remorse. Sometimes it was gentle and delicate, slowing and almost threatening to end. Then dark clouds would move in and the brutal blizzard would return. Each morning The Community would wake hoping for a glimmer of warmth, the start of the thaw. Only the thick white blanket remained. On occasion, piercing rays of sunlight would puncture the clouds, smiling with golden shafts of hope. It was another false dawn, the beams of warm comfort soon severed by cruel blades of ice and bitter arctic gusts sucking every fragment of heat from the air.

Weeks had passed since Gaia's capture. Countless days in which she had recovered piece by piece. The wounds of her broken body mended, but her spirit was still destroyed, her will to fight shattered like shards of a thousand fragments of glass. It would take time for her to rebuild. Kali thought she had saved Gaia, pulling her back from the brink of certain death. Broken, but alive, Gaia belonged to her now. Kali had dragged Gaia kicking and screaming from the precipice, back to the world, The Community. She had persuaded the other leaders it was safe, that in time Gaia would heal, that she would come round. Kali would make Gaia whole again, return her to the path chosen by The Community - her destiny. The leaders believed Kali, trusted and feared her, and granted her the time she needed.

Gaia had wandered The Community for days, a shell without words or expression. In the old years this wilderness of hills and moors had been known as the Cheviots. The name of the village had been long forgotten, wiped from memory and history like so much else. The old houses remained, now occupied and converted by The Community. It had been a village of character and charm, with a large patch of green dominating its centre surrounding an open pond. There was a small square from which the village cascaded. In its centre was a monument to soldiers of the past. Dead and long forgotten. On top of the tall, shiny marble obelisk stood a statue of a man in uniform, head bowed, one arm in a sling, a rifle resting in the other. A metal plaque at the base of the monument once held the names of the fallen men, those that had sacrificed their lives in some distant war. The names could no longer be read, defaced in an act of dishonour and disrespect, a sacrilege typical of the chaos before The Community. This was the new world now, a place where history was reborn and rewritten, where the old world no longer existed.

A stream ran along the edge of the green, and several stepping stones and small walkways crossed it at various points. It reminded Gaia of the village on the island, but while that lay desolate and lost, this was lived in. The island of the young was a prison of the becoming, this was a village of the awoken waiting for their reckoning. There were no children here. They were somewhere else, scattered in pockets across the desolate landscape, being programmed and prepared, made ready to become. The majority were trapped on the islands of the far north, and on the Holy Island from which Gaia and the others had fled. Islands made the perfect prisons, only the few managed to flee and survived. Despite the fragments of character that remained, the village was sterile and soulless. Much of what made it special had gone. There was no laughter, no play, and no joy. The village had people, but no life.

It was just after dawn when they woke Gaia. As the days were short they had to squeeze every moment from them if they were to reach their first destination on time. As instructed by Kali, Gaia had packed light, taking only warm clothing. Her personal things, those precious items had gone, taken when she was captured. All that remained were the functional items, things of need and use. There was no place for sentiment or nostalgia in the new world.

Gaia paused at the door of her room, stealing one final look around before leaving, knowing she would never return. This small space had given her some comfort, the rarest feeling of safety in the sea of darkness. Creeping down the stairs, the creak of the floorboards was the only sound that filled the house, echoing throughout the hall as she made her way towards the door. She waited, hoping Hannah might come and bid her a final farewell, but her friend did not appear. Slipping through the door she made for the centre of the village, through the morning haze, not seeing the lone figure standing at a window and looking on, wiping tears from her eyes. The old woman waited until Gaia slipped out of view, then let the curtain fall.

Joe was waiting for her in the village square. At his feet were some rucksacks and a wooden box filled with weapons. Savas, the other leader tasked with taking them to The Haven had not yet arrived. As Gaia approached Joe looked up.

'You're late,' he said.

'I came as soon as…'

'I said you're late. Now put your things in here and leave that bag behind. You won't be needing it.'

Joe passed Gaia a larger rucksack which she filled with her clothes, discarding the smaller bag in the snow. The rucksack was filled with blankets, jumpers and socks. It was light and more than manageable. She looked at Joe, waiting for the next order.

'Weapons. We can't let you go out there unprotected. There'll be just the three of us so we'll need to work as a team. But be warned, one false move and we'll have no hesitation in killing you. Do you understand?'

Gaia had no doubt of his intent. He was not one to make idle threats. Of all the leaders in the village Joe and Savas were two of the strongest and most capable. She knew this was why they had been chosen to take her. Kali would not take any risks. She nodded and looked on as Joe rifled through one of the bags. The leader was tall and thick set with sharp features that gave him a natural menace and fierce intent. His calm, methodical manner masked a ruthless streak. Joe was a survivor, someone who would take any means available to protect himself. He was not the kind of man Gaia would chose to confront, unless it was necessary. At the same time he was someone you would be glad to have watching your back on such a perilous journey. Savas was a different matter. Gaia had heard many rumours about him, and knew he was someone who could not be trusted. Joe looked up at Gaia.

'Let go of any stupid ideas now. I want to get there in one piece. Kali wants you there as soon as possible. I don't know why, but it must be important. You're lucky to still be alive. Not many get second chances with her.'

Gaia looked back at Joe, his cold blue eyes piercing through her, a mocking grin on his face. Pulling free of his gaze she stared at the ground, as he continued to lock eyes on her, his face filled with threat.

'So what do you prefer? I've been told you like an axe and dagger,' he said.

Gaia nodded, taking the weapons from Joe as he fished them from a box, and passed her a belt to carry them. Putting the belt on, she placed the dagger in the sheath and slipped the axe through a strap on the rucksack. She adjusted the belts, making sure it was comfortable. The journey was no more than thirty miles, but the conditions were treacherous and would prove one of their biggest enemies. Food was scarce and the creatures would be desperate. Even those that would most often avoid humans might attack in desperation. The cold weather, stiff joints and thick clothing would hamper movement and weaken their defences. Gaia knew they would all need to be on their guard and extra vigilant if they were to survive.

Joe looked up the street for Savas. He was jumping on the spot and rubbing his hands together, puffing steam from his mouth. Gaia watched him as they waited, listening to the crunch of his boots in snow. The leader was growing more edgy and impatient. It took a lot to stir his emotions, but Savas could test the patience of most.

'Where the hell is he? Why is he never on time for anything? We need to get going soon. At last!' Joe said.

Joe noticed Savas heading towards them from the top of the street.

'Get a move on!' Joe shouted.

Savas trudged towards the square, his steps laboured with a combination of the deep snow and the last remnants of sleep. He soon reached them, flustered, but not appearing too concerned. Joe made no attempt to disguise his disdain, spitting his words at the other leader.

'Get your rucksack and weapons and let's get a move on. We can't afford to lose any more time.

And we'll need to keep up the pace as best we can. Come on.'

Savas twisted his face, mocking, with the look of a scorned, but indifferent child. As leaders Joe and Savas could not have been more of a contrast, and their mutual hatred was well known. It made the choice of both for the trip a surprise to Gaia. While they both excelled on their own, together there could be problems. She was sure Kali would have a reason for the choice, a bigger agenda, but she could not fathom it for now. Savas was well aware of his reputation and the contempt he drew from many of the other leaders, including Joe. Savas would be wary of both his companions. Joe would be cautious too, but for different reasons.

Savas filled the rucksack with his clothes, and threw it on his back. Grabbing a dagger and spear he stood upright and alert, looking at the other two as though they had been the ones causing the delay. Joe looked as though he was about to chew Savas up and spit him out. Clapping his gloves together, Joe turned and led them to the gates, where two guards let them through. Despite their thick clothing, the faces of each of the guards looked raw and ravished by the blades of the icy wind. Both gazed at Gaia as she passed, one with a mocking sneer on his face.

As the group were leaving, Joe hung back and whispered a conversation with one of the guards. From a short distance Savas looked on, the two men exchanging awkward glances as Joe approached and ushered them on. Soon they had left the protection of the village walls and headed over a nearby hill. The snow was just short of knee high and the going was heavy and slow. Joe led the way, setting a brisk pace and rarely checking to see if the others were keeping up. Gaia tucked in behind Joe followed by Savas covering the rear. They soon entered into a steady march, with heads lowered, and no conversation.

The beautiful green landscape that had captivated Gaia on their escape from the island was now gone, replaced by a different kind of beauty. A blanket of the purest white stretched as far as the eye could see. At first it dazzled, but the novelty soon melted away as monotony and tiredness took hold. The sky was a clean, light crystal blue, the sun hanging low just above the horizon, casting a cold, hazy glow. Any faint glimmers of warmth were struggling to fight their way through the wall of icy air. In the distance bulging clouds rolled towards them, slow, ominous and threatening. The wind was light, but at some point Gaia knew the clouds would reach them and unleash another deluge of snow. They had to reach their first stop before the clouds caught them, and before nightfall. Without shelter they were at the mercy of both the weather and the creatures.

The group trudged ahead all morning, through mile after slow mile of the white wilderness. The honeymoon of its pristine splendour had been crushed by the relentless biting cold. Gaia's legs were leaden, each step growing more difficult. They passed some animal footprints in the snow. Large but alone, they left a meandering trail that snaked into the distance over a hill. She wondered what the creature might be, hunter or hunted? Not that it mattered. All living things were vulnerable and hungry, desperate and exposed, and there was nowhere to hide in this bleak desert of ice.

They ate as they walked, picking at small regular snacks of fruit and nuts. Joe was keen to press on while the sky was still clear. The clouds were drawing nearer, growing more menacing with every passing hour. They would be lucky to make it to shelter before it engulfed them. Gaia could see Joe's concern, as he surveyed the sky, then turned and barked out orders for the others to hurry. She couldn't move any faster. Her legs were numb and heavy as though liquid concrete had seeped into every muscle and set around every sinew. She was beyond aching, and past the point of caring. Staring at the deep footprints in front, she tried to place her legs into each of them as best she could. The templates of compressed snow made the going easier, and any effort saved was welcome. Joe pushed on regardless with an endless stream of energy and dogged determination. He never slowed, nor seemed to tire, fuelled by his endless supply of simmering anger.

Crossing the brow of a hill, they paused and gazed down into a wide valley stretching out below. A thin line of snow topped trees traced a line along the valley's centre. Joe instructed them to move towards the trees, and soon they came to a river which was frozen solid. Testing the ice with his boots, Joe eased onto the glassy surface, step by step, edging towards the other side, using the tips of his toes to test the strength of the pathway ahead. With his awkward and cautious approach Joe managed to make it to the other side where he turned and ushered Gaia across. She followed, mirroring Joe's delicate movement, as though she had memorised the choreography of the leader's steps. Reaching the centre of the river, Gaia could feel the ice groan. There was a crack. Pausing, she held her breath, studied the ice, listened and waited for any further signs of it weakening. After a moment, she eased forward across the remainder of the frozen surface. With each step she could hear the ice creaking, feeling sure it was about to collapse, but managing to shuffle to safety without it giving way. Joe grabbed her as she leapt onto the riverbank beside him. Staring across the icy divide, he shouted a warning to Savas who was about to cross.

'Go easy and don't do anything stupid. The ice is starting to give way.'

Savas thrust a menacing look at his fellow leader.

'Thanks for the advice. I'll manage.'

He stepped onto the ice, trying to be delicate, but looking clumsy and ungainly. Gaia looked on with growing concern, and could hear Joe cursing under his breath with every step.

'Idiot!' Joe said.

Creeping onward, the other two watched and waited in anxious anticipation. As he progressed he seemed to grow in both confidence and indifference to any danger. Each step became less cautious as his boots hit the ice. Gaia winced as she expected the ice to collapse at any moment, and just beyond the centre of the river it happened. There was a loud crack and in an instant the ice gave way. Savas stumbled and fell as it subsided, waving his arms at his side in a futile attempt to keep balance. Within seconds he had plunged into the icy water, and though the river wasn't deep enough to submerge him, he was standing just over waist deep. The strong currents tugged at his feet below, dragging him into their bitter depths, while the searing cold sliced through his clothes, pulling him towards a hypothermic shock. He scrambled in panic and looked around him, but there was nothing to grab onto, only the fractured sheets of ice. As his limbs froze, he struggled to maintain any footing, fighting against the strong currents and the impact of the freezing water. Joe flung off his rucksack and slid onto the ice, barking instructions at Gaia as he moved.

'Snap a branch from one of those trees and pass it to me.'

Lying flat on the ice, he began to shuffle towards Savas, sliding across the ice like a cobra, as Gaia ditched her rucksack and scanned the trees behind. Spotting a suitable branch within reach, she scrambled up the slippery bank towards it. Jumping onto the end, she hurled her body back so all her weight was pulling down on the branch. Snow fell from the other branches as the tree rocked and swayed. Gaia kept swinging, legs in the air tugging at the branch. She could feel the wood creaking as it wrestled with her, and with each jerk felt the branch weakening. There was a sudden jolt as it snapped and she was flung onto the snow. Leaping to her feet, she grabbed the branch and dragged it to the river. She lay on her belly, and slid towards Joe who was now flat against the ice near the centre of the river, holding onto Savas with his outstretched arms. Savas had a pained expression, looking pale, almost blue. With lips shuddering, he leant forward, and clung to Joe's arms, still fighting the strong currents trying to drag him under. It was a battle against time and certain death, as Gaia passed the branch to Joe. He slid back a little, holding onto one end and stretching the other towards the stricken leader. Joe looked over his shoulder at Gaia.

'Move back and hold my legs. We need to form a chain and you'll need to pull us.'

Gaia sat up and took hold of Joe's ankles, leaning her body back and pulling, using the heels of her boots for traction. Joe checked Savas had a firm hold of the branch.

'Lean forward slowly, keep tight hold of the branch and we'll pull you out,' Joe shouted.

Savas could only nod, his lips trembling, his face now blue. He was still lucid enough to make sense of the orders and did as Joe instructed. Gaia began to tug at Joe's legs, as they edged backwards feeling the weight of Savas as they eased him from the icy waters. She continued to creep towards the riverbank, bit by bit, for what seemed like hours. She pulled, watching as Savas slid onto the ice. Together Joe and Gaia hauled him in, edging ever closer to the comfort of the riverbank, the heels of her boots still gripping the ice. She felt her back touch the river's edge, and soon Joe was upright sitting alongside her. They dragged Savas the short remaining distance to safety.

Joe rolled the rescued leader onto his back. Savas was shivering, his face now a far deeper and more alarming shade of blue. His lips and chin were quivering, and his whole body shook, the cold seeping through him like a poison devouring every drop of warmth within. Moving without hesitation, Joe took some dry clothes and blankets from one of the rucksacks. He stripped off the leader's wet garments, and clothed Savas in fresh dry ones, then wrapped him in fresh blankets. In the meantime, Gaia assembled and lit the camping stove and began to boil some melted snow. Joe helped Savas to his feet, wrapping his arms around him, stamping up and down on the spot, and barking orders.

'Come on! Move! We need to get the blood flowing again.'

Savas struggled to remain upright, his limp body slumped against Joes. After a while, he began to sway on the spot, small tentative steps at first which soon became more determined and assured. The two leaders rocked in an almost comical dance, still wrapped together, Joe continuing to shout orders. The water on the stove boiled and Gaia prepared some tea, watching her companions all the while. She stood and passed cups to Joe and Savas who unlocked from their odd embrace and began to sip at the hot tea. Both men stood awhile enjoying the glimmer of warmth as it trickled back through their veins. Joe was the first to speak.

'You were lucky. I knew it was a mistake them sending you.'

Despite his frozen limbs Joe could still ignite a fire in Savas who was in no mood to be lectured.

'Do you think I want to be here anymore than you do?'

Savas glanced at Gaia.

'I don't know why we have to risk our lives for her anyway.'

Joe looked at him and sneered.

'The quicker we get this over with the better. We'll be safer at The Haven if we can manage to get there in one piece.'

'We have to get there. They won't hold out much longer in the village. They're going to need help soon,' Savas said.

There was an awkward silence, each waiting for the other to respond.

'We need to make the best of this and not take any more risks. Let's just get there as quickly as we can and deliver the girl to Kali,' Joe said.

He paused while Savas tried to avoid his companion's stare. The shivering had eased and some colour was beginning to return to Savas' face. Joe continued.

'Do you feel up to moving? We need to get going. We've still got a bit to go and those clouds are nearly on us now. We can rest when we get to the house.'

Gaia looked at the skies where the wall of thick, black cloud was moving in. It was now a matter of minutes before they were swept within the storm and trapped in a blizzard of snow. The others stared at the clouds too, scowling with the realisation of the imminent danger. Whatever doubts Savas had about his strength to continue, they were crushed by the threat of this incoming storm. Savas looked at Joe.

'I'll be OK. I owe you both an apology and…'

He paused.

'Thank you.'

Gaia and Joe looked at each other and then Savas, both offering unspoken acknowledgements. After packing away their things, Joe bundled the wet clothes in a plastic bag. Gaia looked up at the incoming clouds.

'We're not going to make it,' she said.

Joe glared at Gaia.

'Well then let's quit talking and get a move on.'

Joe grabbed his bag and set off, and the others followed. As they headed up through the woods and across the brow of the hill into the other side of the valley, none of them realised they were being watched. Crouched in foliage on the other side of the river the lone follower looked on and waited. As soon as Gaia and the leaders had disappeared over the hill the shadow made their move and continued in pursuit. Trudging through the fresh footsteps, they moved a little down river to where the ice remained firm. After tiptoeing across the glassy surface, they snaked towards the top of the hill, a safe distance from their target. They would wait until the time was right.

Gaia found the going even tougher now, but the clouds were almost upon them, adding extra drive and purpose to their steps. Joe pushed the pace even harder than before, while Savas seemed to have recovered enough to struggle on behind without any fuss. Gaia moved up alongside Joe.

'How much farther is it to the house?' She said.

'We're close now. Two, maybe three miles, but if the storm catches us, it'll feel double that at least.'

Gaia could sense Joe's concern. He knew the dangers in this frozen wilderness. They had all focused on the storm, but this was just one of many threats. If darkness set in before they reached the house, the weather would be the least of their worries.

'The light's fading. We must get to the house before it gets dark.' Joe said.

Joe caught Gaia's eye, before looking up at the storm clouds. The wind was picking up and further down the valley swirls of snow were being whipped into the air, twisting and twirling like dervishes dressed in white. Joe stopped and looked back at the others.

'We're not going to out-run this storm. The house is a couple of miles away and we need to get there soon. One final push and we'll make it.'

Joe and Savas exchanged glances. There was something in their eyes, something they knew but weren't saying. Gaia could see a look of fear, a look she seldom saw with leaders. Joe rummaged through his rucksack and passed out some lines of rope.

'Tie these to your belts. If the blizzard thickens we won't be able to see. These'll make sure we won't lose each other. Tuck in behind and follow me.'

They tied the ropes to their belts, joining together in a human chain, their fates now entwined. Joe was the head of this human snake, dragging itself through the white desert. At its tail was Savas, still weak from the chill that had seeped into his bones, while Gaia formed the body. The three of them weaved through the thick snow, the wind building all the time, and the black clouds breathing down upon them with every lumbering step. It was only a matter of time now.

Savas was the first to feel the storm's savage assault. The snow at his feet began to lift in fine strands of icy dust, thrusting into the air like lashes from a whip of cold steel. The razor sharp threads ripped at Savas' cheeks and eyes. Within seconds the storm enveloped the others, snow and wind dancing between them, searing at any exposed flesh. At first Gaia could feel every stroke of the icy gusts, then the raw skin on her face became numb to the pain, only her eyes continuing to endure the torment. Every swish and every flick burned, like acid being sprayed into her face.

The stinging lacerations of the wind were only the beginning. Soon they were struck by a thick wall of snow, so intense it filled the space in the sky and smothered every inch of air. Gaia struggled to breathe, suffocating in the swirling blanket of white.

The group pressed on, step by step, dragging one other onward. Joe the most determined, fighting the storm with every ounce of remaining strength. Every now and then Gaia would feel the rope behind her tighten as Savas stopped or stumbled, or the one in front slacken as she edged closer to Joe. She could see little but white, and beyond that an eerie grey darkness had descended on the world. Her lungs burned with every gasp of air, pumping harder with each step, searching for any remaining oxygen. Joe forged ahead, drawing on years of experience honed by The Community. There were no milestones or pointers to be seen, only the blizzard and the roar of the storm.

There was a change in the light ahead, a large black shadow was looming, and growing as they pushed forward. They were nearing woodland, a dense canopy of trees, the promise of some shelter. Joe stopped and untied the ropes. One by one, they scrambled over a fence and entered the protection of the pines. Packed together, the branches of green had caught much of the snow, the white carpet on the ground within was much thinner, the air clearer. Gaia felt able to breathe again. Joe stopped, turned and beckoned them together. They huddled close, each covered in a blanket of white, speckles of coloured clothing peeking through. The raw pink flesh of their faces glowed, highlighting the crystal blue of their eyes. Joe wiped his face with his gloves, spitting snow before he spoke.

'We're not far now. The house is just down the hill. We'll stay under cover of the trees all the way. We still need to push on though, we're losing the light.'

Joe looked at Savas who didn't respond. He was wiping snow from his clothes, and trying to fight the shivering spasms. The visibility was better in the woods, and there was no further need for the ropes. They would only hamper their progress through the trees. Just as they were about to set off a distant sound punctured the sky, even more chilling than the shrill whistle of the wind. It was some way off, almost an echo, but it was unmistakable. It was the howling. The group all stood upright, alert, their expressions filled with alarm. All eyes were searching for the direction of the sound, their brains trying to calculate the distance. Gaia paused, paralysed by fear, hoping there would be no further sounds, hoping the threat would move off into the growing darkness. It came again. This time louder and what seemed like nearer. Maybe it was just the wind playing more cruel tricks. Joe was the first to shake himself from the crippling fear. He spoke, his voice simmering with panic.

'We need to move now! They're heading this way. Run!'

Joe shot through the trees and down the hill at a swift pace. The others followed in turn, Gaia with Savas close behind. The terrain had changed, the snow was thinner but disguised hidden perils underneath. As she ran, Gaia could feel the crunch of logs, fallen branches, and the thick vines that formed a spiky uneven carpet. The group kept moving at a brisk tempo despite the awkward obstacles, veering off down an incline which soon became more acute. Gaia led with the heels of her boots, thrusting them into the ground to stop her from stumbling. The howling came again, even closer than before. The dogs were coming and gaining ground all the time. Joe quickened his speed with all three now running as fast as they could. Each of them was weaving and darting their way through the trees, ducking under branches, and leaping over snow drenched fallen boughs.

Another set of howls ripped through the grey dusk, this time from a different direction, while more came from behind. The terrifying sounds were drawing nearer. The group had left a trail of footprints, and both their scent and the sound of their fleeing had been picked up by the beasts. The dogs were fast, strong, and vicious, and hunted in packs. If they caught the group they would stand little chance. Gaia knew their main hope lay with Joe. He knew the way, and the safety of their destination would soon be upon them. The house would be well chosen, and strong enough to withstand an onslaught from the dogs. They had to keep running and hope they could reach it in time.

She kept up the pace despite her aching limbs and burning lungs. They followed Joe who was zipping in and out of the trees, and hurtling down the hill. The howls kept coming, more and more of them, all from different directions, drawing nearer with every second. The path ahead was clear for now, and Joe pushed on with the others close behind. His head was down, looking at the ground, seeking the clearest path, checking for any obstacles, knowing the slightest stumble would mean death. He lifted his head for a moment, a look of alarm on his face, as though he had seen something. Switching direction, he moved to the left, and Gaia saw it up ahead, the silhouette of a large building bathed in darkness. There was no light coming from the old, lead lined windows, its roof and walls were covered in clean fresh snow. Perched on the side of a valley, it looked over a small river flowing below. They were almost there, well within its welcoming reach. Just behind, the crunch and crack of the beasts could be heard now, as they leapt and darted through the trees. The hounds were almost upon them and gaining with every leap.

Just seconds from reaching a side door, there was a wall of terrifying noise behind as the howling came again, much louder and more frenzied. Gaia could hear the rabid clamour of the creatures, a hunter sensing its prey, the final cry before it was about to pounce. She knew they would be caught soon. The building was within reach now, and Joe was at the door already. The trees thinned and a narrow stretch of open lawn opened up before Gaia. She sprinted across it, followed by Savas, hurtling towards the door and leaping upon it. Joe tugged on the handle and picked at the lock, while the others were pressed against the stone walls alongside, looking back up the hill for the first glimpse of their pursuers. There were more frenzied howls, and a thunder of noise as the beasts' legs pounded through the trees. Gaia strained her eyes, reaching into the darkness, but she couldn't see them yet. Savas had a look of panic while Gaia continued searching - her head sweeping across the panorama of the trees seeking out the dogs. Hands pressed against the weapons in their belts, both were poised to attack. Savas kept casting looks at Joe, urging him on in his attempts to unlock the door. Shuffling along the wall, edging closer to Joe, Savas spoke, his voice quivering with fear.

'Hurry up!' he shouted.

Joe tried to remain calm, concentration etched on his face, tussling with the frowns of frustration and fear. It was as though he was pleading with the lock, willing it to click open. He knew what he was doing, had sprung many before, but his confidence was being devoured by the impending danger. Ignoring Savas' looks, Joe tried to cover his sense of alarm.

'I'm almost there. Just focus on those dogs,' Joe said.

'They're here!' Gaia shouted.

The first of the dogs had burst through the trees less than a hundred yards up the hill. It was far larger than she had imagined, huge compared with the rats and other mutant creatures she had encountered before. The beast was covered in black fur, its jaws and razor sharp teeth were slavering, and a long, pink tongue hung from the side of its mouth. Gaia could see the eyes of the creature as it neared. They were red, burning with anticipation, enflamed with the smell of its victims, tasting their raw flesh in its mind already. The beast was starving and the scent of the humans was intoxicating. The thought of the kill driving it delirious with excitement.

Two more dogs sprung from gaps in the trees, just as huge and fierce, and covered in the same jet black coats. Gaia moved off the wall and stood in front of Savas and Joe. Her axe was drawn, as she crouched low, preparing for the onslaught. She knew a lengthy encounter would mean death. She would have one chance to strike, one attempt to land a fatal blow, or injure the beast as much as possible. Savas moved alongside her, spear raised and ready to launch. Gaia glanced back at Joe who was still struggling with the lock. She saw the look of horror on the face of Savas willing Joe on, with the first of the beasts just yards away.

'Got it!' Joe cried.

The door burst open and he dived inside. Hearing his fellow leader's words, Savas turned and lunged towards the door while Joe looked back into the night and shouted:

'Come on Gaia! Get inside.'

Gaia froze. Part of her knew she should turn and dive through the door, but something stopped her. The black dog was hurtling through the air towards her. Any second its jaws would lock on her throat, but she remained crouched, her axe poised. Time seemed to slow as the beast approached, mouth wide open, ready for the kill. A strange serenity washed over Gaia, her face without expression as her mind cleared. All her focus was on the beast, watching and waiting for the perfect moment, her one chance. As the jaws were about to reach her, she whipped her body to the side and dropped to her knees. In the merest glimmer of a second she thrust the axe in the air and plunged it into the beast's chest. The creature let out a blood curdling whine as it kept hurtling forward. Now its target had moved there was nothing to break its fall, nothing but the wall of the house it hurtled towards and smashed into. The dog struck the cold stone with a crunch, sliding to the ground with a thud, the axe still in its chest. It lay on the snow covered earth, helpless now, whimpering like a child, oozing dark crimson blood which stained the white carpet around it. The beast lay crippled, its only movement those final gasping pants and a series of manic spasms.

On instinct, Gaia pounced, ripping the axe from the dog's body and slitting its throat with a single swift stroke of her dagger. Lying dead at Gaia's feet, its ravenous jaws were wide open, tongue hanging out, blood oozing from its neck and chest. It was all over in seconds while the two other dogs moved in for the second wave of attack. She turned to see them about to lunge towards her. Knowing they were too much to tackle alone, the mist lifted from her mind and she shot through the door just as they launched their attack. She stumbled onto the floor inside, while Joe and Savas slammed the door shut.

The two leaders slid down, backs against the door, both still panting, gasping for air. Gaia lay on the cold stone of the floor, listening to the thud and scratching of the dogs behind the door, their frenzied barks and frantic whimpers. They lay in the pitch black for a long while, each wrestling with their thoughts, pondering what might have been. None of them were under any illusions as to how close they had come. Gaia tried to regain her breath amidst the frenzy of the pack outside and the panting of the leaders in the dark.

There was the sound of someone fumbling with a bag, then the fizz of a match being struck. Joe's face lit up in the faint orange glow of the flame. He lit a candle, then another, and passed them to Gaia and Savas in turn. The faint flicker of light spread across the darkness, unveiling a narrow passage. Gaia was lying on a red carpet that lined the centre of a stone floor. Savas and Joe were still pressed against the door. Savas had his head bowed while Joe got to his feet, the light of the candle casting a sinister glow on his stern features. He looked down at Gaia, an odd look on his face. There was a long pause before he spoke.

'They told me you were crazy, but that was something else!'

Shaking his head, he continued.

'Don't ever do anything like that again. Do you hear me?'

She looked up at the leader and nodded.

'Good. We should be safe here for the night. Those things will move on when they realise they can't get in. Are you OK?'

He looked across at Savas who raised his head.

'I've felt better. I just need some dry clothes and some rest.'

Gaia noticed Savas' hands were trembling. She felt a sharp pain in the pit of her stomach. The fear and adrenalin had masked their aches and hunger. The release they now felt in refuge was unleashing the shock of what they had just been through, how close they had come. She felt her heart steadying to a regular beat, but could still taste the last bitter remains of fear. Joe turned towards the doorway.

'Let's find a room, get a fire going, eat and rest.'

3

They made their way into a large hall, the light from their candles catching images of imposing faces on paintings lining the walls. Gaia gazed at the sombre expressions, as Joe led them up a grand, open staircase. They ascended several flights before reaching the top of the house. Joe ushered them into a vast, cavernous room, littered with an assortment of extravagant furniture. A giant four poster bed stood against the far wall looking out through tall windows draped in thick, heavy curtains. Ornate panelled walls were covered with an odd mixture of paintings, mirrors, and lamps, and a grand stone fireplace lay to the right of the bed. Shelves were filled with a multitude of books, while the floors were covered with an array of carpets and rugs. A couple of huge leather sofas dominated the centre of the room, surrounded by random armchairs of different sizes and design. It was as though layers of history had been packed into this one room.

Gaia wandered, in awe of the unusual items. She stopped in the corner where an unusual object was perched on a wooden stand. It was ovular, made of wood with a hole in the centre, and a long wooden neck with metal strings stretched along it. Laying down her rucksack and bag, she took a closer look, brushing her hand across the metal strings, which made a strange but pleasant sound. Savas approached and stood watching at her shoulder. He had a grin on his face, intrigued more by Gaia's actions than the object itself.

'Do you not know what it is?' he said.

Gaia looked over her shoulder and shook her head.

'No.'

'It's called a guitar.'

Gaia shook her head again, a quizzical look on her face.

'What's it for?' she asked.

Savas looked across at Joe who was sorting through one of the packages for food. He seemed cautious, reluctant to continue, but Joe stopped rummaging and stood up straight, looking across at Savas and Gaia standing by the guitar.

'It's an instrument for playing music,' Joe said.

Gaia gazed at both men with a confused expression.

'What is music?'

Savas lowered his head as Joe continued.

'It's something from the old world. It's not something that is encouraged in The Community anymore. It's an unnecessary distraction. We realise time is precious, and it's important to focus on what needs to be done.'

Gaia stared down at the guitar as Joe returned his focus to the bags again. Savas leant in close and whispered.

'Don't believe him. We do need music and it's the most wonderful thing. It's still there, if you look for it. Just be careful.'

Joe caught Savas from the corner of his eye, and jumping to his feet, he edged towards them.

'Have you got something to share with us Savas?' Joe said.

The leader stood in front of them, glaring at his fellow leader who smirked and shook his head. Joe spoke, his voice calm, but menacing.

'The world survives perfectly well without music. It isn't productive and it encourages dangerous thinking. Our survival as a community is all that matters. That's our only purpose, anything else is time wasted. The Community is far more important than the whims and pleasures of individuals, whatever they think we need. If The Community ends so do the people within it. Survival comes first.'

There was a long pause before Savas spoke, his voice little more than a whisper.

'But without music and culture we are nothing more than beasts.'

Joe lowered his face towards Savas and spat out his words.

'What did you say?'

Savas lifted his head and looked back in defiance. It was the first time Gaia had seen Savas behave in such a way. This was dangerous, and tantamount to treason to challenge The Community with such talk.

'We've gone too far Joe. We all know what happened and where it's left us. We're all struggling to deal with the consequences. I know that more than anyone. No-one has lost as much as me, but it can't just be about survival, not at any cost. There has to be something more. There has to be a reason for living. We've lost sight of that. We need to find what makes us human again. We've created a world without joy. We exist, but we no longer live.'

There was a silence, though his whispered words seemed to echo around the room. Joe looked down at the guitar, his face smeared with a sneer. Lifting his hand, he began to stroke the handle of the machete by his side. He spoke, his voice filled with a latent threat.

'It's the way it has to be. You don't get to decide. We all do. Don't think I don't know what you get up to in The Haven. Just be thankful those of us who do know have turned a blind eye to it for now. Don't worry. Your secret is safe with me. At least for now.'

The leaders glowered at one another, before Joe turned and made his way back to the centre of the room, crouching to sort through the food items again. Gaia could feel the tension in the air, but was still curious and desperate to hear more of the strange sounds. Stroking the strings had triggered something in her head, a distant memory of a sweet voice. Someone was reciting words to her, but they weren't speaking. It was as though they were crying, but in a soft, enchanting way. It was a woman's voice. Gaia couldn't see the face, but could hear the words, their rise and fall as the woman recounted them. The sounds in her head were warm and comforting. It made her feel safe. Lost in her half-dream she heard herself speak.

'Can I hear it?'

Savas stared across at Joe. There was a silence as they waited for his response.

'What about it Joe? One song? What harm will that do? Who knows if we'll get through this journey alive.'

Joe remained silent. He was not a man to back down, but it had been a long, tiring day, and he was not in the mood to fight with Savas. There were more important worries, and the prospect of more dangerous fights ahead. Despite his warnings Joe knew the rules of The Community were fragile and often broken, especially in The Haven. Without speaking, Joe left the room.

Savas picked up the guitar from its stand, made his way over to one of the empty armchairs. Gaia moved to a sofa, while Joe continued sifting through the bag. Laying the guitar across his lap, Savas rested his right arm over the main body, grabbing the neck with his left arm, and forming a shape on the strings with his fingers. Gaia looked on, mesmerised by this strange sequence of movements, almost a ritual. She was rippling with excitement as Savas spoke, his voice softer than usual.

'This song is a very old one. A friend of my family taught me it when I was young. He used to work in a grand house like this. He said that despite all his employer's money it still couldn't save him from the end when it came. 'Death is the great leveller' he would say. It's called 'The Song of the Lower Classes.' It has a beautiful melody, but listen to the words. In the best songs the words are always important.'

Nodding at Gaia, the stern expression on the leader's face eased as he began to move his hand across the strings of the guitar. When she had stroked the strings earlier the sound had been soothing, but this was different. It was enchanting, and she could feel the music washing over her body, tingling as the soothing sounds floated by. He began to sing, his eyes closed, lost in the melody and words, his voice delicate and tender. This was a different Savas, someone she had never seen before. There was a glow to his face, a tranquility, a humanity. Gaia watched him as he drifted in the music, clinging to the tune, helpless as it led him away. She listened to the words as he sang. They spoke of the rich, and the poor men and women that worked for them. Labouring hard, ploughing and sowing the fields, making bread, digging the mines - all so those who had more than enough already would have more. The words were powerful, moving, and stirred an anger deep inside Gaia. The song ended with the verse:

We're low, we're low our place we know
Only the rank and file
We're not too low to kill the foe
Too low to touch the spoil

Gaia noticed Joe standing in the doorway. Savas stopped singing and caressed the strings a while longer, his fingers changing shape, new sounds coming from the guitar all the time. They were magical sounds triggering memories and emotions in all of them. Memories buried deep inside for many years. For Gaia, it triggered feelings that were new. For Savas, it was something he had longed for and missed. Even inside the cold shell that Joe had wrapped around himself, hidden depths of emotion stirred inside, of his father long since gone, taken when The Poison first came. In this briefest of moments, they all shared something. As the song had played they had become connected, each in a different way. The sounds had rippled through the air, weaving their magic and now Gaia understood what Savas meant. This magic was something The Community had lost, a common thread that bound them together. This couldn't be found in rules and regulations, or purpose alone. There had to be something more than just survival. In living they had to find happiness, the one thing that elevated them above the creatures they feared and fought.

Savas placed his right hand against the strings and the music ended. Lifting his head, he opened his eyes, and spoke in a gentle whisper.

'History is written by leaders, the people who govern and control. But songs and stories are written by those who are led, the people who build communities. If you want to hear the truth about what happened before The Poison then find the old songs and folk tales, listen and learn them, tell them to your children. Never let them die. I always remember something the old man said to me, 'Blessed are the poets and the misfits, the artists, the writers, and the music makers. Blessed are the dreamers for they force us to see the world differently.' You're still young Gaia. Whatever happens, see the world differently and make the world you want to see.'

Joe lurched towards Savas. Lowering his head, he pressed it close to his fellow leader. His voice was calm, but the simmering anger and threat was clear.

'You've had your fun. Now it's over,' he said.

Joe lifted his head and began to ease away. He stopped and spoke again.

'Tell me this Savas. How would your artists and poets fare against those dogs outside? Come on! How? The world's different now. It's no place for dreamers and romantics. They die and the strong survive. This is the time of monsters.'

Savas locked eyes with Joe. Grinning, Savas spat out his reply.

'But who are the real monsters, Joe?'

There was a long pause and silence as the two men continued to glare at one another. It was Joe who broke the silent deadlock.

'We'll see Savas. We'll see. Now make yourself useful and get some more candles lit. The night's setting in and we need to get a fire going and eat.'

Joe grabbed the neck of the guitar and tugged it from Savas' lap. Dragging it across to the stand, he slammed it down, the strings letting out a discordant groan as he turned and barked out instructions.

'Come on. Let's get to work!'

....

Gaia had taken up the second watch, and was sitting in an armchair by the tall window. The thick, heavy curtains had been drawn, with a gap at the side so they could see down into the courtyard. The leaders were both sleeping, each on one of the sofas, while Gaia had made do with the rug in front of the fire. Joe was the first watch, and handed over to her about an hour ago. She hadn't managed to get much sleep, her mind racing with thoughts of Freya, Kali, and Aran, and haunted by the words and music of the song.

The snowstorm had lifted and the sky outside was clear. A full moon lit up the still night world, the trees, fields, and valley beyond. Moonbeams glistened as they spread across sheets of silvery snow. Gazing at the blazing white orb in the sky, she searched for shapes on its surface, soaking up the pure, dazzling light. The silence was almost suffocating. Only the crackle of the fire could be heard, and the occasional shuffle of one of the leaders. She tried to stay alert and vigilant, but was struggling to stay awake. Scouring the woods that encircled the house, and the trees and bushes that lined the courtyard, she could see nothing - no sound or movement, no lights, only an eerie stillness. The world was frozen. The night was dead.

The day had exhausted her, and the lack of sleep didn't help. She fought the urge to give in, but could feel herself drifting in and out of consciousness. She was lost in the dream world, the shimmering space between the woken and the dead. Her head bobbed back and forth, jerking forward and waking her with a start. She lost all track of time, and with it any sense of whether she was now awake or dreaming. Then she saw it. At first it seemed like a trick of the mind, the tiredness toying with her. Shaking herself and rubbing her eyes, she forced herself to focus on the spot in the garden. There it was again. In the trees that lined the courtyard there was a movement. Shadows, black and hidden, but there was no mistaking them. This was no animal. They were human and several in number. Edging closer to the window, and straining her eyes she locked them on a small area below. It was a clear patch in the trees, where the light from the moon had broken through a gap, to reveal a wall beyond. A shadow flashed across the opening, then another, and another. Branches of the trees nearby fluttered as the dark figures rushed past one by one.

She jumped from the armchair and moved to where Joe lay. Leaning over she shook him. Sitting upright with a startled look, Joe's hand reached for his weapon. Realising it was Gaia, he eased off.

'What is it?' he asked, his voice cracked and unsteady.

Gaia replied, little more than a whisper, but still charged with alarm.

'There are people approaching the house, through the trees by the courtyard.'

Joe leapt to his feet and woke Savas. In an instant they were all bustling into action, booted and armed, and huddled together in front of the fire. Savas and Gaia looked at Joe awaiting his instructions. The leader was calm and precise.

'Did you see how many there were?'

'Not exactly. The light wasn't great and they were in the trees, but there are quite a few of them. I counted at least six.'

'Let's hope it is just six. It's safe to assume they're armed and they know we're here. There are groups of 'Others' scattered all over this area. My guess is it's one of those. They might have seen us approach the house earlier. If they're creeping up on the house they probably know we're in here, but they don't know where we are. We stay here, sit tight, and wait for them to come to us. We'll cover the doors and hit them one by one as they enter. We'll have surprise on our side. They won't be as well trained, but they will be fearless. Savas and I have fought many of them before and they're desperate, and driven by their hatred for The Community. Three of us is worth a good few of them though. Are we good?'

Gaia and Savas nodded and after blowing out the candles and smothering the dying embers of the fire, they all took up positions as Joe directed them. Gaia and Joe were either side of the main door, while Savas slid the sofa opposite the door and crouched behind it. Joe looked to see they each were ready, and then waited.

Seconds drifted into minutes, which dragged into what seemed like an hour. The room remained cloaked in an eerie, grey darkness, the glow of the moonbeams pushing through the gaps on the edges of the curtains. The burst of energy and adrenalin they had felt at first had begun to dissolve, replaced by a nervous restlessness. Joe's approach to wait was sensible, but the anticipation was crippling. Gaia had too much time to think, speculate, fill in the gaps. Her growing anxiety turned to fear and flashes of momentary panic. She began to doubt herself, thinking she may have imagined what she saw. Were they really there? Perhaps she was dreaming, or the tiredness had been playing tricks on her. Maybe she had seen them, and they had moved on. Savas was growing restless and impatient, shuffling and sighing in the darkness.

'Maybe we should make a move. See if we could find them first,' Savas said.

Joe's reply was swift and abrupt.

'We stay put and together. The last thing we do is split up. If they come to us we can take them by surprise. That's our best chance.'

The drifting time stretched out and began to smother them in despair. Just when Gaia thought it was all over and any threat had gone she heard a sound on the landing. It was the creak of a floorboard. She recalled the same sound on the way in. Pricking up her ears, she reached into the darkness for a trace of another sound. There was nothing. Then they came, the light, muffled sound of footsteps approaching. She could feel them drawing nearer beyond the door, step by step, the growing threat. In her mind she pictured a shadow in the corridor, waiting, listening, poised to enter and pounce. The creak came again. Someone else was following the first set of footsteps.

Raising her hand to alert the others, she took a deep breath. She looked down at the door handle, watching and waiting. It began to move. Slow, tentative, beginning to creep downwards. Joe was concentrating on the gap in the door, machete clasped in his hand, pointing at the opening, ready to thrust the blade into whoever appeared.

The handle clicked and the door began to edge open. Gaia watched the line of the door and saw a head peep round and begin to ease its way into the room. There was a jolt, and a crunching sound, as the head jerked forward and the body fell into the room onto the floor with a thud. Wasting no time, Joe had thrust his machete through the neck of the shadow, the incision clinical and exact.

No sooner had the body hit the floor than the door burst open and a number of attackers piled through. Gaia and Joe reacted in an instant. Leaping from behind the door, she grabbed the hair of one of the assailants, pulled back their head and slid the blade of her machete across their throat. The body slumped to the ground, and Gaia could just make out it was a young girl, not much older than herself. With no pause, she dived onto another shadow and plunged the blade into its chest. Meanwhile, Joe had slaughtered another and was wrestling with two more. Even in these opening seconds, they were making swift work of the assailants, Joe plunging a spear through the chest of one and slashing his machete across the neck of the other. Gaia dodged a lunge and the swish of a blade and stabbed her attacker through the temple. She felt something warm spray across her face as one of Joe's victims lurched back and fell, and tasted a bitterness on her lips.

Savas had moved to join them now, leaping from behind the sofa and felling two attackers with a series of swift, merciless movements with his knife. Arms and bodies were flailing everywhere, the majority were those of the shadows feeling the full impact of the precise blows and plummeting to the floor. The speed of Gaia and the leaders counter-attacks, coupled with the element of surprise had caught their attackers off guard. As Joe had said, they were frenzied, but less skilled, and despite their superior numbers were no match for three trained assassins. Within a few minutes seven corpses lay on the floor. All the shadows lay dead, the attack was over.

Joe inspected the bodies, and with boots and clothing splattered in fresh blood, he kicked the corpses, pressing their faces with his boot heel looking for any response. The floor was littered with an array of weapons, such as knives and axes, effective in the right hands, but not this group. They had been weak and vulnerable, something Gaia and the leaders were quick to exploit. It was difficult to see in any detail in the poor light, but they were all dressed in the same uniform, clothing of dark clothes, high boots, and what looked like long black trench-coats. They were a mixture of ages, with a couple only young, too young to die in this way. Satisfied their work was complete, Joe spoke.

'Are you both OK?'

They nodded.

'Do you think we got them all?' Gaia asked.

Joe stepped through the open doorway, and looked up and down the hallway, listening for any further sounds. Gaia looked on, sensing something was wrong. Turning to the others, he put a finger to his lips, then eased back into the room, stepping over two of the corpses. Reaching down, Joe dragged aside one of the bodies blocking the doorway, while Savas moved the other. Gesturing to Gaia to close the door, Joe signalled to both to take up the same positions again. Savas crept back behind the sofa, and all three readied themselves for another wave of attacks.

This time there were no tiptoed footsteps, but a stampede along the corridor. The door burst open, swung back and hit Gaia in the face knocking her head against the wall. For a moment she was stunned, but the sound of the fresh attack jarred her back to consciousness. Pushing the door back, she kicked it as it swung round, and there was a jolt and a thud as the door battered against one of the attackers. Black shadows were pouring into the room, and it was clear they were outnumbered already.

Knife in one hand and axe in the other, with lightning quick and precise movements Gaia ploughed through the dark, slashing and felling the faceless assailants. What they offered in numbers they still lacked in co-ordination or skill, and both Gaia and Joe were hurtling through them with clinical efficiency. Savas had been forced back, and was now in the centre of the room, with a mountain of a man launching a brutal assault on him. Savas was no match for his attacker's strength, but the leader's speed and agility meant he could avoid the frantic attempts to bludgeon him. With each wave of hammer-like blows the man was edging Savas backwards with presence and determination alone. Gaia saw Savas was struggling and after claiming another victim with a sweep of her axe she leapt from the arm of the sofa and plunged her dagger into the back of Savas' opponent. At first even that only slowed his giant frame, but it distracted him long enough for Savas to deliver two huge blows to his head and throat with his machete. The giant teetered and swayed, then dropped to his knees like a felled oak, as Gaia crunched the blade of the machete through the top of his skull.

Shadows fought shadows, and bodies tumbled to the floor. The stream of attackers were no longer entering the room, and Gaia and the leaders were ripping through those that remained one by one. Six or seven remained and fought on, the survivors, the strongest, most agile and skilled. They were putting up a much stronger fight now, each seemed stoked with an added burst of anger and venom. Gaia's opponent was manic and his speed and strength were testing all her skills. She could feel herself creeping backwards with each wave of blows, and was soon pressed against a wall with nowhere to go. In one final act of desperation, she swept her axe towards the side of the head, but the assailant blocked it, knocking the axe from her hand. Seizing his opportunity, the man lunged forward and pinned her arm against the wall with a knife, thrusting his free hand against her throat. She felt his long, thick fingers lock around her neck, crushing her windpipe. Gasping for air, she was kicking and flailing with all her strength trying to break free. She knew he was too powerful and was boosted by the intensity of his rage. In the dim light of the moon she saw the attacker's face press close to hers and felt his warm, foul breath on her skin. Saliva dripped from his mouth, smearing his bearded chin, as droplets splattered against her face.

She could feel consciousness slipping from her, the screams and clatter of the fighting all around was drifting off into the distance. The pain eased and the pressure lifted. The muscles in her throat began to stretch and air seeped through again. She attempted to swallow and gasp, but only fragments of air were reaching her lungs. It was enough though, enough to bring her back round. Dropping to her knees, still dazed, she noticed the body of her would-be executioner slumped on the floor beside her, a spear lodged in his back. She looked up, the moonlight through the curtains cast a glow on a face staring down at her. At first her heart jumped with relief, but her instinct was soon swept aside with a burst of vitriol and hatred. She knew the face, but it was not a welcome one. Grabbing her machete, her impulse was to attack her rescuer, but something held her back. Reaching out a hand, she took it and let him help her to her feet. Dazed and stunned from the attack, she heard the voice whisper in her ear.

'If you want to stay alive, you need to come with me. I'm going to get us out of here.'

4

Grabbing her by the arm, Aran led Gaia from the room, stumbling over the injured bodies and corpses strewn on the floor. Joe and Savas were still locked in combat with the remaining attackers, too preoccupied to notice them slipping away. They sped along the passage and down a different staircase, narrow and winding it led to a small side entrance. Aran paused a moment, before darting across the courtyard into the thick canopy of the woods. Gaia's heart was pounding, her head spinning, fresh from the fight, adrenalin and questions hurtling through her mind. All the while she scanned the few yards she could see ahead, searching and listening for any signs of danger, any movement. It was the dead of night, when only the foolish or the desperate dared to travel. The only light to guide them was the moon, but even this was dimmed by the canopy from the evergreen pines. She tried to stay close to Aran who pressed on at a brisk, unrelenting pace. Stumbling several times, her feet became snared in the dense undergrowth.

They kept running, though Gaia was desperate to stop and confront Aran. She knew if Joe and Savas managed to overcome the attackers they would soon realise she was gone and would follow. If the attackers had prevailed they too would be on their trail. Then there were the creatures, the night birds and the dogs. The night was their time. The dog's acute hearing could pick up movement from some distance, and Gaia and Aran were anything but delicate in their frantic escape. The sounds of their boots crunching on the undergrowth seemed to echo throughout the cavernous valley and still night.

Aran kept pushing on, with Gaia following as best she could, though even she was tiring now. They reached a narrow gulley forged by the flow of a bustling stream. Aran paused and listened, a gap in the trees allowing the moonlight to bathe them in its brilliant white light. Gaia watched him, his face pale in the ghostly glow, a wound of several days was spread across his cheek. He looked exhausted and worried. Gaia listened for any sign of impending threat, but all she could hear was their panting.

'We need to head downstream. I know a place we can take refuge for the night,' he whispered.

'Is it safe?'

Aran frowned.

'Nowhere's safe at night, but it's the best we can hope for.'

They set off alongside the frozen stream, the moonlight reflecting off its grey, glassy surface. Aran's pace was brisker now, though the going was easier as the undergrowth thinned and they no longer had to weave through the dense trees. Every now and then he would stop, pausing to listen, alert to any potential sounds or incoming danger. Satisfied they were still alone for now, he pressed on until they reached the brow of a ravine where the stream snaked off and tumbled down the side of a steep incline. Aran took a sharp left, leaving the stream behind and following the brow as it edged upwards. The trees thickened again, and as the canopy returned the light dimmed and Gaia struggled with her footing once more. Pausing once more, Aran scanned the area as Gaia leant on her knees, grasping the freezing night air for breath.

'Is it much longer?' she said.

'Ssshhh. Listen!'

His voice was still a whisper, but his expression was stern. Gaia could see something was worrying him. She listened, but could hear nothing other than the roar of silence and the faintest of breezes playing with the treetops. Then she heard them. They were some way off, but there were voices, faint, muffled, but unmistakable. Aran darted ahead.

'Come on. We need to move quickly.'

She struggled to keep up with him now as he darted through the trees. Despite his haste, he was nimble and precise, cutting through the various obstacles in their path as though they weren't there. Gaia was less assured, as she tried to match his pace and movements. Her body was aching after the exertion of the attack, and her lungs burned with every icy breath. They pushed on for what seemed like an age until Aran began to slow. They had reached the edge of the woods, the point where the trees met the acres of moorland that on summer days were drenched in a carpet of purple heather and green ferns. Tonight it was a blanket of white, glistening with the caress of the moonbeams. The sky was crystal clear and beyond the moon's glow the dark blue night was sprinkled with millions of tiny pinpricks of twinkling lights. As they paused for a moment, both of them gazed at the vast arc of darkness and light dancing together overhead. The distant voices had gone, and only the deafening sound of silence remained. A streak of light flashed across the sky, hurtling towards earth, and disappearing in an instant. There was another, and another. Soon a myriad of momentary strips of white light streaked across the canvass of dark blue. Gaia was mesmerised, overcome with wonder.

'What are they? They're beautiful,' she whispered.

'I've no idea. I saw the same thing once on the island. It was the night before the sky turned green and danced with strips of red and purple light. Do you remember that?'

'Yes. We thought the world was going to end and The Poison had spread to the sky.'

Aran looked at Gaia and smiled.

'This is why the ancients believed in gods. They must have been as terrified as us.'

Gaia caught Aran's eye, and she felt a rush of blood through her cheeks. For the briefest of moments she felt like it was before, with a warm, soothing sensation in her chest. Then the image of him in the room flashed in her mind. He was her betrayer. Aran saw the sharp change in her expression, and sensed the shift in her mood.

'Come on. We need to get going,' he said.

The trees had ended and the way ahead was clear, stretching out across the moor to the silhouette of the horizon, where the land met the moonlit sky. The moorland was vast and dotted with a smattering of snow capped, rocky outcrops. Mounds of ancient grey stone that in daylight were decorated in patterns of green lichen and moss. Aran weaved a route across the moors using the rocks to provide cover. Their destination was some distance from the trees, and he knew they were exposed as they swept across the snowy landscape. As they pushed forward, something else flashed across the sky: shadows crossing the moon and sweeping low past them as they ran. Gaia heard a chilling and familiar clicking sound. She called to Aran,

'Night birds!'

Lifting the pace, they darted across the moorland as the night birds dived lower, each time swooping closer to their heads. She felt a blast of cold wind as one flew across her path, narrowly missing her face. They scrambled through the snow, which seemed to be getting deeper and heavier with every step. All the while wave after wave came upon them, swooping and clicking over their heads. She tried to look down, concentrating on each few metres ahead, focusing on every step, one foot after another, pressing forward, ignoring the danger overhead. Her lungs and muscles were burning, all her energy had gone, only desperation kept her moving.

They reached a large lump of rock and stopped. Aran crouched on his hands and knees, crawling around the edge of the stone, feeling the earth beneath the snow for something. Gaia looked on, all the while flashing looks up at the sky, where the shadows continued to swoop and soar. Then she noticed their movements change as the night birds shifted and began to move towards the woods. Staring across the grey blanket of snow stretching back towards the trees, she saw shadows moving on the edge of the woods and heard the echo of distant voices.

'Hurry! They're coming Aran.'

He peeled back a square slab of mossy earth at the base of the rock to reveal a hole, just wide enough for someone to squeeze through. Looking up at Gaia and then back across to the woods, Aran ushered her inside.

'Get in quick.'

Gaia squeezed her legs into the opening and lowered her body down into a short tunnel. Moving her arms in the darkness she felt the arc of stone and earth curving all around and overhead. It was pitch black, but with her fingertips against the wall she could guide herself as she shuffled through the small, underground cave. She heard Aran behind her as he followed her into the passage. There was the sound of him fumbling through his bag, then the fizz of a match, and a small glow of orange light. He lit a candle and passed it to Gaia who was sitting cross legged, her back pressed against the wall of the cave. The space was tight with only just enough room for two, and it was freezing cold, the light of the candle catching the icy steam of every breath. Aran rummaged through his rucksack, and passed a blanket to Gaia who wrapped herself in it.

They waited and listened in silence. Minutes drifted into what seemed like hours, each of them too nervous to speak for fear of being found. They heard nothing, and eventually Aran broke the silence.

'We'll stay here till morning and then move on,' he whispered.

Gaia's lips were dry and cracked, the skin on her face numb. Her jaw ached as she replied.

'Do you think it was the leaders or the group that attacked us?'

'I don't know. It could be either. There were still four or five on two when we left, but the leaders are well trained. I wouldn't be surprised if they got out.'

'The ones left were strong fighters. The one who attacked me knew what he was doing. I've never come across anyone as powerful as that.'

She paused a moment, her expression changing, as the memories flashed through her head again.

The pain and bitterness of his betrayal returned, and she leant forward, her voice colder.

'What are you doing here, Aran? Why were you following me?'

He pressed his back against the wall, trying to ease away, but there was no room to escape. Nervous and uncomfortable now, there was a long wait before his reply.

'I know I've got a lot to answer for Gaia, and you have no reason to trust me, but things will become clearer if you let me explain. I had little choice with the escape from the island. Kali forced me to do it.'

He paused then continued.

'It's a lot more complicated than it looks. Things aren't what they seem.'

Gaia shook her head, a look of disdain on her face. She spat out her words.

'Why should I believe you? The escape, the whole thing was a set up. You led us into a trap. People died because of you, Aran. Yann died because of you. The girls, they've gone, and no-one knows what has happened to them. Why, Aran…?'

Gaia's voice faded, while Aran lowered his head. He took a long time to answer, thinking through his words, measuring his response, knowing how much what he said mattered.

'I'm sorry, but please let me explain. Do you remember I told you about the boy who asked me to escape with him? I showed you his letter.'

She nodded.

'It was true. There was a boy who had tried to escape before me.'

Aran took a deep breath and cleared his throat.

'He was my brother.'

Though little more than a whisper, the words echoed around the stone chamber. Aran waited for Gaia to respond. Sitting in silence, she was soaking up his words, wary and confused, still not knowing if he could be believed. The silence remained, and after a while he continued.

'I was meant to go with him, but I couldn't. I got caught on the night. One of the leaders saw me as I was leaving the dorm. The next morning he was gone and there was no mention of his disappearance. It was as if he had never been there. From then on, I knew the leaders were watching me. You could tell. Everything was more intense. Everywhere I turned they were there. Months went by and I heard nothing. Then, one day I was summoned by Kali. She told me my brother had been captured and was being held at The Haven. She said she knew I was part of the escape, and made it very clear if I didn't co-operate with her she'd see to it my brother was killed. From that point I was hers. I had to do what she wanted. I had no choice Gaia, can't you see that?'

He began to take slow, steady breaths, before continuing again. His voice was now cracked, wavering, heavy with emotion.

'I know what you think, but I was desperate. I couldn't risk him being killed. He was all that I had in the world. Surely, you understand that now.'

He stared at her, waiting for a reaction, some kind of acknowledgement, however small. She remained silent, her face blank, refusing to respond, waiting for him to continue.

'At first she wanted me to spy on people. It was just little things at first. Then she told me to watch you, tell her everything, especially when you went to the beach on your own. I had to tell her what you were up to. Then it became all about you and things got more intense. It was like she was obsessed, paranoid that you were up to something.'

Gaia broke her silence.

'So it was you watching me?'

'Most of the time, yes.'

'And did you know about my things?'

'What? Your secret stash? Yes.'

Gaia thrust a dark look at Aran who looked down at the floor. He continued.

'I wasn't the only one. Kali had a network of spies and usually found out what she wanted. If it hadn't been me, it would have been someone else.'

Gaia clenched her fists, feeling the mist drawing in, taking all her strength to control it. Her head was pounding as she seethed with rage. She spoke, her words fizzing with simmering rage.

'What about Freya? Was she one of Kali's spies too?'

He shook his head.

'No. Kali asked me to watch Freya. You can never tell with Kali, but I think she knew Freya was playing her. Freya is smart, but Kali had a hold on her. Someone told me things had happened between them.'

He paused, catching Gaia's eye while he continued.

'Kali will go to any lengths to get what she wants.'

Gaia replied.

'I know. Freya told me.'

He frowned and continued.

'Kali controlled everything on the island. The other leaders were just her puppets. She got what she wanted from the leaders and from those of us she had manipulated in some way. I don't know what it was about you and Freya, but you were always of particular interest to her. You especially. There was something about you that Kali knew. You were different.'

Taking a water bottle from his bag, he took a long drink. He passed it to Gaia who took it and drank. The water was ice cold as it swept down her throat, but its refreshing flow dissolved the dry, bitter taste in her mouth. She returned the bottle to Aran as he continued.

'Kali told me she wanted me to lead an escape. It would be a set up, and it had to involve both Freya and you. I was surprised when she asked me. And confused. She never told me why she wanted it to happen, just how and when. This is the way with Kali. You never get to know what is going on in her mind. She never explains why. It's only ever orders, never reasons or explanations.'

Gaia interrupted.

'Did you know Freya was my sister?'

'No! I had no idea. Not until we got to the village and the room. I only found out when you did. It was a shock to me too.'

There was a moment of silence, each mulling over what the other had said. Gaia was trying to make sense of everything, while Aran was gauging her reaction. She still felt so much anger towards him, but part of her could she why he acted as he did now. Whatever his reasons, he had lied, deceived, and betrayed her.

'Trust no-one. All is not what it seems.'

Those words had been a constant warning, and now they rang out over and over in her head. The escape had been her becoming, but this journey was different. It was the start of her awakening. All that she had thought she had known was unravelling. Every layer of knowledge and experience was disappearing to reveal a different truth. So many of the things she now knew, she wished she had never known.

'How did you know he was your brother? That's not how The Community works. The young aren't allowed to know their family. We're all part of the same family, The Community is our family,' she said.

Aran shuffled, edging forward, his face drawing closer to Gaia as his voice softened.

'Some of us know. The Community takes who they want when they're young. They strip them of their identity, take away their names, their memories. They steal everything. But there are a few of us who know the truth.'

He waited a moment, gazing at the puzzled look on Gaia's face. She shook her head.

'Who?'

'Not everyone in The Community is as they seem, Gaia. There are some of us who are different. We know the truth about The Community, the lies they spread. We're waiting for our moment, but our time will come soon. Their days are numbered.'

Her head was beginning to spin now, but he wasn't finished.

'I know you spoke with Hannah, didn't you?'

She gave him a menacing look, as their eyes locked.

'What about her?'

'She's one of us.'

Gaia leant back against the wall of the cave. His words were racing through her head, and it was all too much for her now. She was tired from the long journey, bruised and aching from the fight. She was trying to make sense of what he was saying, another layer peeling away, more lies exposed, another truth revealed. She sat forward again.

'You said Hannah is one of 'us'. Prove it.'

A puzzled look crept onto Aran's face. She continued.

'If what you say is true, then you know what I mean.'

He frowned, then nodded. Lowering his head, Aran began to play with his eye. It was a routine Gaia had seen before, and thought she might see again, except not this soon, and not with Aran. Lifting his head, he drew close while she focused on the eye glaring back at her. She could see it in the flickering glow: it was confirmation. The colour had darkened, the pale, steely blue of before, now replaced with the deepest hazel. She looked at his other eye which was still the familiar crystal blue. Easing back she raised the candle and gazed at both his eyes in turn. He looked odd, almost alien. He remained still, his face without expression, waiting for her response. She kept scanning him, checking over and over, not wanting to believe, but knowing it was true.

'You can put it back now,' she said.

He dipped his head forward and replaced the coloured lens, then they both sat, deep in thought for some time. They were so close, yet felt so distant, maybe further apart than ever before. Aran wanted her to speak, to say what she felt, but he broke the silence.

'I know how this seems, how you feel. I understand you feel betrayed. I've had a long time to come to terms with this, but for you this is all happening very quickly. I'm sorry.'

He gazed into her eyes, and saw a softening, a tenderness, a look he had seen before.

'So what do we do now?' she said.

'I think we want the same thing, but I need to know it's what you want. I can't ask for your forgiveness, but at least try and understand why I did what I did. We need to work together if we're going to get through this.'

Gaia looked puzzled.

'What do mean?'

'The leaders were taking you to The Haven. What is it you would have tried to do when you got there?' he said.

She thought for a moment.

'I wanted to find Freya, and know if she's alive. I have to save her. She's my sister and she saved my life. It's my turn to help her now.'

He nodded.

'I want the same thing. For all I know Kali still has my brother a prisoner there too, and I still believe he's alive. Like you, I have to save him.'

He waited, took a deep breath and continued.

'We want the same thing and stand a much better chance if we work together. There are others there who can help us. I know where we can find them and therefore you need me. You won't be able to save Freya alone.'

Gaia fought her emotions. Part of her wanted to strike him, and the clenched fist of her right hand sat poised and ready. Something held her back, the realisation in side that what he said was true. She could not do this alone. Together they were stronger. He continued.

'You might think you could never trust me again. But in time I'll show you, and you'll understand what it's been like for me. You know now what it feels like to have a sister, how important it is, how much it changes you. I've had to live with that for a long time, and the pain and guilt of knowing I let my brother down. You know what that feels like now. Kali gave me no choice, but we both have a chance to take our revenge and make her pay for what she's done.'

Gaia closed her eyes, and all she could see was Freya's face. The image was clear, as though she was in the cave beside them. It stayed in her mind as she opened her eyes again.

'Maybe we do need to work together, for now. But don't think this changes anything between us,' she said.

He reached out his hand.

'I understand.'

He paused, his hand still outstretched, with Gaia looking down at it. Her head was spinning, a mixture of adrenalin, shock, and confusion. The world she knew was gone again. Nothing was certain, everything was changing. He waited for her to respond, to take his hand and confirm their agreement, but she remained silent, leaving his hand hanging there.

'I know it'll take time, but you don't belong with The Community, Gaia. You aren't one of them. You know that and you'll find the truth soon, see them for everything they are.'

She looked down at the outstretched hand, as he lowered his eyes and withdrew it.

'I'm sorry. That's all I can give you for now.'

There was a long silence before she replied.

'Let's get to The Haven and find Freya and your brother. You help me and I'll help you. After that we'll see what happens, but there are no guarantees.'

He smiled, offering his hand to her again. She hesitated, but eased her hand forward and clutched his. For a fleeting moment their eyes met and she remembered the moment they had kissed. The warm cascade of dizzying emotions surged through her again, and for a moment she let them take over her body. Then she smothered them, burying them deep inside. She looked Aran in the eye.

'Let's try to get some sleep. We have a long journey ahead in the morning.'

5

Morning came, bringing with it calm, bright weather. The blizzard of the day before had left layers of fresh snow, adding even greater depth, and making the prospect of travelling even more of a challenge. They had taken watch in turns the night before, allowing the other to grab some much needed sleep. Aran wanted Gaia to sleep while he kept guard all night, but she refused. They would work as a team, each taking equal share. Gaia was not there to be carried or pampered, and could more than hold her own. She understood why he had offered though, so much more now than she had before.

Aran had hidden a rucksack in the cave before heading towards the house. It was well stocked with food and they ate a good breakfast of boiled eggs, cheese, and bread. As soon as they had eaten he packed away while Gaia prepared her things. There had been little conversation all morning; everything that needed to be said had been shared the night before, and despite their candour, emotions were still raw.

They pushed on all morning, making the best of the calm weather. The sun hung low in the clear blue sky, the light intensified as it bounced off the gleaming, white surface. Gaia's eyes burned with the brilliant sunshine, the pain eased by the beauty of their surroundings, unveiled in all its glory once more. The bland uniformity of the moorland was gone as they moved up the hills and through valleys. The landscape was dotted with neat hedgerows and ancient woodland of snow capped trees. They crossed fences and bulging streams, the clear water below topped with the grey lustre of ice. There were few signs of life, just a few animal footprints dotted here and there. Together, they walked alone in the icy, winter wilderness, the biting cold making Gaia feel alive again, and the euphoria of the majestic countryside lifting her spirits. She felt a sense of the freedom they had in their escape from the island. The journey, the drive and purpose all gave her a feeling of renewed vigour. The dull monotony of her existence in the village felt stale in comparison. It was lifeless and inert, rotting and dying.

She thought a lot about what Aran had said the night before. The anger of his betrayal was still there, as much as she fought with it. She thought of the leaders, Joe and Savas, feeling a pang of guilt towards them. When she and Aran had fled she had weakened the whole, exposing them both to death or capture. Neither deserved that. They were both following orders to take her to The Haven, and had treated her with decency and respect, which could not be said for all the leaders. The song Savas had sung flashed through her head, just fragments of the melody, the occasional words and lines, *'when the trumpets ring, the thrust of a poor man's arm will go, through the heart of the proudest king...'*

Words remained few throughout that first morning of their journey, with only the occasional instruction from Aran, reminding Gaia of the need to keep up the pace. After several hours of constant walking they reached a small copse of trees, some of which had been cut down leaving just a few scattered trunks. These formed a disjointed ring which invited them to rest. Aran approached the circle of stumps, removed his rucksack, and sat on one of them.

'We'll stop here for lunch. We've made good progress this morning. How are you feeling?' he said.

'Good. I'd forgotten just how beautiful it is out here, though it looks very different from when we left the island.'

Aran smiled.

'I know. It seems so long ago now. Sometimes it feels like I dreamt the whole thing.'

'Me too.'

He prepared a small fire while Gaia sorted through the rations of food. There was bread, butter, cheese and a few more eggs. Aran made a coffee like drink from some crushed dried leaves of a dandelion, while they both shared the bread and cheese. Gaia was starving and could have eaten just about anything. The bread was cold and stale, but tasted good washed down with the hot drink. Both ate like it was their last meal. The combination of the cold, fight, and the adrenalin of their escape had sapped Gaia's energy much faster than normal. She'd not slept well the night before and though she needed the rest, stopping had only let fatigue set in. Her eyes felt heavy, and on a couple of occasions she nodded off. Aran filled their cups with more of the dandelion brew and pulled out some surprise biscuits, smiling as he passed them to Gaia. She took one, studied it and took a bite.

'Where did you get these?' she asked.

'I've been hiding them for emergencies, and special occasions.'

'So which one is this?'

He laughed.

'I guess it's a bit of both.'

She shook her head, took another bite, then studied the biscuit.

'These taste familiar. Who made them?'

A broad grin stretched across Aran's face.

'Who do you think?' he replied.

She frowned.

'Was it Hannah?'

He smiled and nodded.

A strong feeling of sadness swept over Gaia as she thought of Hannah sitting in the armchair on their final evening.

'Did you speak with her before you left?' she said.

'I did,' he replied.

'How was she?'

'You know Hannah. She was calm and at peace with things. She's been prepared for the end for a while now. She's suffered a lot of pain and loss in her life. I think she was tired of hiding and pretending to be something she's not.'

Gaia felt choked and could feel the tears trickling from her eyes. Aran reached a hand out and wiped them. She recoiled and pushed his hand away, as he avoided her accusative look.

'Let's make something clear Aran. Don't go thinking everything is sorted between us.'

She paused.

'I'm here because you can help me save Freya. You owe me that at least.'

He looked up, staring at her and nodded.

'I understand. I just wanted to help. I know how you're feeling. I was fond of Hannah too.'

She crunched on the biscuit and stared at the ground. Emotions were wrestling within her, a mixture of sadness at Hannah, and remorse at her impulsive reaction to Aran's kindness. She wanted to say sorry, but couldn't bring herself to say it. Now was not the moment. She tried to shift her thoughts to other things and focus on the practical issues of the journey. The sweet taste of the biscuit was melting in her mouth softening the bitter taste of the dandelion coffee. She found the texture and taste soothing and comforting, just like she felt when she was with Hannah. She smiled at the thought.

'How far is it to The Haven?' Gaia asked.

Aran struggled to remove some biscuit from his teeth with his tongue.

'It's only a few hours away, well within reach before nightfall. We'll take shelter on the outskirts of the town. I know someone we can trust. He'll help us get inside.'

Gaia looked worried.

'Someone we can trust? Who?' she said.

'Don't worry. This guy is fine. He has a lot more reasons to hate The Community than any of us, and he has history with Kali and despises her more than anyone.'

She wasn't convinced, but knew there was little chance of them finding Freya without taking some risks. They needed any help they could get.

'What do you know of The Haven? People have spoken of it since I was a child, yet I know very little about the place,' Gaia said.

'Its old name was 'Murder Path' because the town was on route to the island. Pilgrims and worshippers of the old ways made special journeys to the island. It was a religious sanctuary and people would travel for miles to visit. Do you remember the old ruins? That was a place of worship for someone who had brought religion here. His name was Cuthbert. People would travel for miles to the island, but the land around here was wild, much like it is now. The road was full of thieves and bandits preying on priests and the wealthy pilgrims. Can you remember the gibbet where they came for us? Why do you think that was there? They would hang the bodies and severed heads of criminals from it as a warning. This is a place of beauty, but a wilderness of great danger too. It's always been that way.'

Gaia thought back to the time they stood in the rain by the gibbet, with the shadowy, masked figures moving towards them. She felt something in her hand, and looked down expecting to see the two girls by her side, but they were gone. A sharp pain shot through her, as the faces of the girls flashed into her head. Where were they now? How could they have survived? Aran broke the thought as he continued.

'After The Poison, when The Community began to emerge, they soon grew in strength and numbers and took charge of the town. It has a river and castle keep. They've built walls around it making it easy to defend and keep out the creatures. They renamed it The Haven, as they wanted it to be their main community and place of safety.'

Gaia's curiosity was roused and she continued with her questions.

'Who did they take it from? The Others?'

Aran nodded.

'Yes. It was a brutal battle by all accounts, and The Community showed no mercy. Women and children were slaughtered which is why the Others despise The Community so much. Don't let the name fool you either. It isn't what it seems or sounds like. You'll have heard many stories about it, and I've been told a good few more. Most of what you'll have been told is untrue. It's anything but a haven. It's not safe, especially after dark. The Community controls those that it wants, but there are those it has let go, leaving them to rot, fend for themselves, and die. The leaders don't care as long as they destroy each other and leave The Community alone. There are many on the margins in The Haven and you have to be careful who you trust. We just need to get in there, find Cal and Freya then get out.'

'Cal!'

'Yes, Cal!'

Gaia smiled.

'Sorry, it's just that's the first time you've said his name.'

Gaia played with her cup, swirling the last few drops of her drink in the bottom as she replied.

'He seems more real now he has a name.'

She sensed a change in Aran's mood and expression, and could see his eyes filling up. She leant forward.

'Don't worry. Maybe he's still alive.'

She looked into his eyes and the tenderness returned again. The same softness in their moments together on the escape from the island. She wished she could turn back time, back to before the torture, before everything changed.

'What about Kali?' She said.

He took a long while before answering.

'I'm sure she'll be there waiting for us.'

Gaia thought back to the time of her torture, and those final moments when Freya attacked Kali. Aran continued.

'She might still be weak though. It takes time to recover from those kind of injuries, even for someone like her. Now's the best time to make our move.'

Gaia saw the fear in Aran's face.

'She'll be angry and wanting revenge. Joe and Savas were taking me to The Haven for a reason, and they said Kali had instructed them. She seems keen to keep Freya and me alive for some reason. Hannah seemed to think she had plans for us.'

Aran frowned, his voice quiet and cracked as he responded.

'I don't know. You hear lots of rumours. People sometimes fill in the blanks. I don't pay much attention to it. You're alive and if that's the way she wants to keep it then all the better. It means there's more chance Freya will still be alive too.'

Gaia thought of Freya, her enemy now her sister. The girl she had wanted to kill, she was now risking everything for.

'Let's just get there and do what we have to do. We need to get moving and get to the house before sundown. There are many dangers around The Haven. The towns and villages draw the creatures at night,' Aran said.

'Dogs?' Gaia said.

'Yes. They're much worse. They know it's where the people are, and The Community keep them fed with…'

Aran paused, and Gaia replied.

'I know. Hannah told me.'

Aran continued.

'It's not just the dogs. There are other dangers on this road. There are lots of Others around here. The group that attacked last night come from a village not far from here. They're part of a large group, and they're well armed and organised. If they find us, we don't stand much chance on our own.'

He got to his feet.

'And there are the rats too, of course.'

Gaia grimaced, remembering their old enemy.

'How could I forget. I wish I hadn't asked now.'

Reaching down, he helped Gaia to her feet, and after packing up their things they set off. They moved to lower ground where the snow was thinner and walking became much easier. More of the fields were enclosed with fences and hedgerows presenting a different set of obstacles. The copses of ancient trees were replaced with manufactured woodland. Abandoned sheds and outbuildings appeared, as well as the odd isolated farmhouse and cottage. They avoided getting too close to the buildings for fear of encountering Others, many of whom had taken control of the buildings in this area. There was far more evidence of the life before The Poison, of the world that had been been built and lost. There was a fragmented order in the midst of chaos, of nature having been tamed. Gaia now had a sense of the isolation of The Community on the island and in the hills. The sites were chosen for a reason. The Community wanted to keep their people divided, especially the young. Isolation and fear were important parts of their nurturing. It kept the young submissive and easier to control. They would become what The Community wanted them to be.

Gaia pictured Yann - his smile, laid back air, and laconic walk. Images flashed through her head of their time together fleeing the island. She recalled something he said, possibly the first thing she had ever heard him say. He spoke of how it wasn't the world that was messed up, it was humanity. He was right. The world would survive long after The Community had gone. People thought the world was theirs to own, but they were wrong. They were the temporary guardians, nothing more. The

Community were faint embers in the ashes of a dead fire, gasping for air, hoping to burst into life again. This time of monsters was humanity's last desperate cry for survival. Even if the flames rose again, what next? Another cycle of destruction? The more Gaia was becoming aware of the world beyond the island, the more she was piecing together the jigsaw of the past. The more she saw, the more each and every piece began to fit. Her escape, this journey - each were part of Gaia's awakening.

The abandoned buildings, forgotten fields and roads were relics of another world - pieces of a gravestone - a reminder of mankind's greed, arrogance, and stupidity. She was waking from the fear and anger, and seeing the world beyond: a place of immeasurable beauty. The sights, sounds, and smells assaulted her senses, each an intrinsic part of an evolving whole, something rich in its infinite variety. The beauty had always been there, but she had been too absorbed in her own world to see it. All that had mattered was her survival, the struggle for freedom, but the struggle itself had become her prison.

She was beginning to understand why the old world had been doomed. People had been too wrapped up in their own worlds and communities. They had become indifferent and complacent. They looked, but didn't see. They took all they had for granted, and then it was too late. One world had gone, another emerged. Shards of broken glass being pieced together in an attempted new beginning, another chance to rebuild. Before beauty, there is survival, and this was The Community now. They had to find all they had lost, the beauty beyond and within. Yann had found it. He knew what the world could give, and that was his gift to Gaia. She was beginning to see where her future lay, a world beyond The Community, a place of her own making.

6

They reached the outskirts of The Haven just before sunset. Nearing the town they followed a narrow country road lined with a mixture of hedgerows, fences and dry stone walls. A number of deserted farmhouses were set back from the road, each offering ideal shelter for the night, but Aran pushed on. He knew where he wanted to go. They crossed a wooden stile straddling an old stone wall, then snaked along the edge of a field, their feet crunching through the snow, leaving deep fresh footprints as they went. There was no point covering their tracks, if they were followed their only hope was to run or fight. At the far end of the field they leapt the fence lining another narrow, more secluded road. Aran looked up and down the road.

'Where's this place you're taking us to?' Gaia asked.

'Don't worry. It isn't far now.'

They pressed on, avoiding walking the open roads and sticking to the fields and woods that lined them. The light was fading fast and both knew the importance of finding shelter before nightfall. The scattered fragments of civilisation were of little comfort, as the darkness was now ruled by the creatures.

As they approached the edge of the town they came to a side road which veered off to the right. It was lined with tall overhanging trees whose branches were now bare, but in the summer months they provided a natural tunnel of protection all along the road. Aran headed down the side road and Gaia followed. They came to a gate beyond which was a large detached house set back in a wide and open courtyard. It was strewn with all sorts of random junk - car parts, farming machinery, plastic containers, and wooden barrels. It was as though someone had emptied a garage of all its contents and not bothered to put them back. Each item was capped with snow, a number were submerged. The house was large, though nowhere near the grandeur or size of the one the night before. While not yet in total disrepair, it looked well past its best days, and there were few signs it was still lived in. The courtyard was surrounded by tall trees and Gaia could hear the sound of fast flowing water nearby. Other than that, there was an unsettling silence.

Dodging the assorted junk, Aran weaved his way towards a huge oak door, dominated by an imposing knocker in the shape of lion's head. The snow by the door had melted, but a number of footprints remained. The prints were deep and fresh.

Aran knocked and waited. He knocked again, but still no-one came. Gaia began to walk around in a circle kicking the snow with her feet, and stepping into her old footprints, compressing the snow even further. There was a noise in the courtyard, and she turned to see a spear pointing straight at her. Holding it was a tall, well-built man, looking dishevelled, but with a menacing expression. His hair was shoulder length embracing a long scruffy beard. She focused on the piercing, hazel brown eyes fixed upon her, as he stared back, never blinking. He spoke, his voice deep and gravelly.

'Who are you, and what do you want?'

Aran replied.

'We're from the village in the hills. We've escaped and need help to get into The Haven. I was told you were a friend and could help us.'

The man's face was hidden by the mass of hair. All Gaia could see to gauge his reaction were his eyes, still wide and glaring, filled with suspicion. The man studied them awhile then replied.

'Who told you I was here?'

'Hannah. She said you were an old friend and could be trusted,' Aran said.

'Hannah?'

'Yes.'

There was a long pause, as the man's eyes softened, and the grip on the spear seemed to slacken. The menace in his voice was now gone.

'How is she? It's been a long time,' he said.

Aran and Gaia exchanged looks and Aran lowered his head. The meaning of their silence hit the man, and the tension in his body seemed to melt, while the spear began to lower. His stare drifted towards the ground, his shoulders beginning to slump and his head dropping. Aran stepped forward and spoke, his voice soft and comforting.

'I'm sorry. She told me to give you this.'

Reaching into the pocket of his jacket, he passed something to the man. He held it in the palm of his hand, gazing at it. Gaia could see the object, a small piece of wood carved in the shape of an eye. The man seemed transfixed. Eventually, he put the eye in his pocket, and looked up.

'Wait here,' he said.

Walking back into the courtyard, he disappeared around the side of the house. They waited a few minutes in silence, then heard the bolts of the door before it opened and the man stepped outside. Gaia noticed his jeans were covered in dirt and stains, and he looked as though he had never washed. His voice now had a quiet, warmer tone, but with the same deep, rattle.

'I'm Ben. Come in.'

He beckoned them inside and closed the door, securing it with a number of heavy bolts.

'You can't take any risks around here. I don't get many visitors, but the ones I do are usually unwelcome.'

Aran removed his gloves and held out his hand.

'I'm Aran and this is Gaia. It's good to meet you Ben. Hannah told me a lot about you.'

Ben took Aran's hand, giving it firm shake. He nodded at Gaia, and she suspected there was a glimmer of a smile under the forest of facial hair.

'Hannah was special, too good for this world. We go back a long way,' Ben said.

He paused, his eyes glazing over, and mind drifting. Aran and Gaia watched and waited, until his thoughts returned. He shook his head.

'Sorry. Where were we? Yes, come through, let's get you warm. No doubt you're hungry.'

Gaia and Aran removed their boots, gloves and jackets and Ben led them through the hall into a large living room. He gestured to the sofa that lined the roaring fire, and Gaia sank into the soft leather cushions, stretching her stockinged feet as close to the flames as she could. Aran sat alongside, leaning forward and warming his hands.

'Food! Drink! I'll go and make some tea and see what I can find in the larder. Make yourselves at home,' Ben roared.

Aran smiled and nodded.

'Thank you Ben.'

Ben left the room, while Gaia and Aran remained slouched on the sofa, savouring the warmth and comfort of the fire. She felt her stomach rumble, while the heat of the flames thawed her frozen and aching bones. Her mind drifted and her gaze wandered around the room. It was dominated by the massive fireplace and ornate stone surround, the mantelpiece littered with photographs, mostly of a woman and two children. Gaia recognised Ben on one or two of the images. He was much younger, thinner and smarter in his dress, without the ragged beard and long hair. She noticed how handsome he looked, his face lit up with a sparkle in his eyes now gone. The room mirrored the courtyard: cluttered, dirty, and neglected. The pictures on the wall were crooked, with one missing revealing a small rectangular area, the paint much lighter than surrounding walls. A long wooden coffee table stood to the right of a tall, imposing leather armchair. The table was littered with glasses of all shapes and sizes, and a few bottles of which all but one were empty. A stale and musty smell mingled with the smoke from the fire which was beginning to catch the back of Gaia's throat.

Aran sat forward, warming his hands in the roaring flames. He stared into the fire, mesmerised, soaking up the heat as if it were the last he would ever feel. Neither spoke, both trying to savour the quiet comfort. Gaia looked on, feeling a tinge of sadness, wishing things could have been the way they were before. She recalled the time they had kissed on their escape from the island, the moments of tenderness. Anything had seemed possible then, their lives filled with hope. Bitterness began to smother the warmth as she remembered his betrayal.

She stared at him as he gazed at the dancing flames, his cheeks were pink as they caught the glow, his eyes lost. She wondered what he was thinking, if his thoughts were of her, and if they would ever be able to recapture what was lost. Could she ever forgive and trust him again? They sat in silence, together alone.

Ben returned with a tray packed with food. Laying it down on the table Gaia stared at the tea, milk, honey, biscuits and cakes. Warm and fresh, Gaia took a piece of carrot cake which melted in her mouth. It was so good she took a second piece, feeling sure it tasted even better than the first. They talked while they ate and drank, filling in Ben on the plight of the village, and the details of their journey. Ben commented on how foolish they had been to stay at the stately home, and how lucky they were to get out alive. He knew it well, and had visited many times when he was young, in the days before The Poison. It was the home of the Armstrong family, an engineer who had made a fortune through weapons of war. Gaia recalled the pictures on the walls, and the song Savas had sung. The words were even more poignant and ironic given what Ben had said. The conversation soon turned to the prospect of entering The Haven. Ben was concerned, and warned them of the danger they faced. However, he was willing to take the risk and help them, especially when they told him of Kali.

'The town is heavily guarded and surrounded by a wall. One of the first things The Community did was build it. The idea was to keep out their enemies, the Others and the creatures mainly, but also to keep everyone else in,' Ben said.

'It's still possible to get in without being noticed, isn't it?' Gaia asked.

Ben took a drink of tea and sat back in his chair.

'Yes. I know of a way. It's risky though, and you'd have to go at night.'

Gaia looked at Aran who frowned. He was leaning forward and studying each of Ben's words. He knew how dangerous attempting to enter The Haven would be, but was even more worried by what he had heard.

'Do we have to go at night?'

Ben nodded.

'It's the only way.'

There was a long pause. Gaia looked down at her cup, stirring the small fragments of biscuit floating on the surface. Aran continued.

'When can we go?'

Ben placed a biscuit in his mouth devouring it in one swift movement before replying.

'As soon as you like. The sooner the better.'

Ben finished off his tea and continued.

'I'm worried about those two leaders you mentioned. If they've made it out alive no doubt they'll have headed straight to The Haven, and warned them. If they did there's a good chance everyone will be on extra guard. I'll pay a visit tomorrow. I have some things I need to trade and it's market day. I'll see what I can find out and whether it's good to go. If things seem calm then we'll go tomorrow night.'

Gaia spluttered a response.

'Tomorrow?'

'The longer you leave it the more chance there is they'll find out you're missing. You may still have surprise on your side,' Ben said.

She looked at Aran who was nodding in agreement. She stared back at Ben, pausing for a moment before she spoke.

'Why are you doing this Ben? I mean why risk your life for us? We're total strangers. The Community tolerate you. They even let you trade with them. I don't see why you're risking that and everything else.'

Aran glared at Gaia.

'Gaia!'

Ben smiled as he responded.

'No Aran, please. She makes a good point. It's something I would want to know in your position. I mean, why trust me?'

He took a moment to think and compose himself before responding.

'The people on the outside owe The Community nothing. Most of us hate them, many are their enemies. Some fight them, but others like me co-operate with them, but only up to a point. I do it to survive. I'm not an army, and as you can see I live alone. If I tried to defeat them from the outside I'd lose and only make them stronger. It's smarter if I try to destroy them from within, that's if they don't destroy themselves first.'

Ben stood up and paced the room. Gaia and Aran's eyes were fixed on him as he moved. Approaching the fire, he looked at the photos on the mantelpiece, and leaning his head against it, he stared down into the flames.

'I have as good a reason to hate them as anyone, especially Kali. But, I choose my battles carefully, and there are far cleverer ways to fight. I chip away, and wait my time. One day it'll come. Who knows, maybe you're that time.'

Ben turned towards them, a wry grin etched on his face.

'Just so we're clear. I'll help you get inside, but I won't go in. You're on your own once you're in there.'

Aran spoke.

'We understand. Just show us how to get in. I've been told of people who can help once we get inside.'

Ben nodded and smiled.

'Good. Now drink up and I'll make us some supper.'

They ate some more and then retired to bed early. Ben offered them each a room, though Aran opted to sleep on one of the sofas in the living room. Exhausted from their trip, Gaia welcomed the comfortable bed, though her sleep was fitful and punctured by dark, vivid nightmares. In one she was standing in a large room lined with steel framed beds. The light was dim and the room was filled with the acrid odour of stale urine. It was so overpowering it burned the back of Gaia's throat. There were others alongside her, but she couldn't be sure who. She sensed their presence, but could not take her eyes from one of the beds. Blankets were strewn in a heap at its base, the sheets soiled and bloodied. On it lay a woman with long matted hair draped across her face. She was on her side, tucked into a ball like a foetus, trembling and muttering to herself. Gaia heard the sounds of crying and whimpering, as she edged forward towards where the woman lay. With each step the cries of pain got louder. Then another sound rose high above the rest. It was the cry of baby. Loud and piercing at first, then fading away as though it had evaporated. All that remained was darkness and silence, and the sharp, sickly stench.

She woke with a start, her head feeling heavy with the strange sensation of a stolen night. She opened her eyes, the first blast of light burning her tender eyes. It was another day, time to begin again. Perching on the bottom of the bed, she gazed out of the window as the sunlight crept over the horizon. At first she forgot where she was, but layer by layer the confusion lifted and memories of the days before returned. She pictured Aran, her mind racing and stomach churning with a cocktail of emotions. Every day was revealing something new, some hidden secret. She knew more of him now than ever, but still felt like she knew little. His face kept pushing to the forefront of her thoughts, and the more she tried to push it aside, the more it seemed to appear. All Gaia knew was she needed him, for now, at least until they found Freya.

Gaia had thought a lot about her sister since the capture and her recovery. Struggling to come to terms with all that this meant, she focused on the one thing she could influence and change. Freya had saved her life, with her loyalty beyond question. Whatever the future held, Gaia had a duty to save her, or at least try. This was her purpose now, along with survival. She only hoped it was not too late. Once she had found Freya they would seek their revenge, together.

Creeping downstairs, Gaia entered the living room where Aran was sat on the sofa drinking tea. New life had burst from the embers of the fire, fresh flames dancing up the chimney. Their heat had not yet filled the room, and as the new rays of morning light seeped through the windows, Gaia wrapped a blanket around her as she snuggled into an armchair. Aran's voice was a fragile early morning whisper.

'Did you sleep well?' he said.

'I've slept better. Where's Ben?'

'He's left already. He went at sunrise. He said he had a lot to do when he gets there and wants to get back early so we can prepare for later. Do you want some tea?'

Aran sat forward.

'No. I'm fine. I'll get some in a moment,' she replied

Aran placed his cup on the table, and there was a long, awkward silence. Gaia had much to say, but couldn't bring herself to speak. Aran was first to break the deadlock.

'I know a lot has happened between us, but I'm on your side. You have to trust me.'

Avoiding eye contact, she stared into the rising flames, then turned and looked straight at him.

'Is there anything else I need to know? Anything else you're hiding? Now's the time to tell me.'

He looked down at the carpet.

'This isn't just about you and me, Gaia. There are others I need to protect. I've told you all I can, all you need to know for now. Things will become clearer when they need to. That's the best I can do.'

Gaia sat up and scowled at Aran, unable to contain her simmering anger.

'This is the problem exactly, Aran. You try to assure me we're on the same side. You expect me to trust you, but you don't seem to trust me enough to tell me what the hell's going on.'

His head remained bowed as he replied.

'I know I'm asking a lot and I can see you have little reason to trust me, but I'm not setting out to hurt you. One day, you'll see this is all about protecting you.'

Gaia moved towards him.

'Let's be clear, Aran. The only reason I'm here is I need your help to save Freya. You're my best chance of doing that. Once we've found her, we go our separate ways.'

He began to fumble with his fingers, and there was a long, awkward pause before he replied.

'At least we're clear on that.'

Aran went into the kitchen while Gaia remained, gazing into the flames as they grew in strength. She approached the fire, feeling the heat against her cold skin and bones. She scanned the photos, her eyes stopping at one. Taking it down, Gaia focused on the three people in the picture. One was a much younger Ben, the shape of the face, the bone structure unmistakable. He stood alongside an attractive woman with a striking face. Such was her beauty and the radiance of her smile Gaia could not help but focus on her. By the woman's side was a young girl. It was difficult to tell her age, but she could be no more than five years old. Gaia studied the face of the girl, feeling there was something familiar about her - the shape of her lips, the sharp features, the serious expression. For now, the identity of the girl evaded Gaia, trapped in the dark shadows of her mind.

7

The moonlight shone on the icy water. It was cooler here than the hills and the river was free to breathe and flow as it made its way towards the chaos of the sea. They walked along its frozen banks, as Gaia looked up and down, listening for any sign of danger. Just ahead were Aran and Ben, the older man leading the way. They had left the house soon after sunset when the blanket of darkness first began to smother the golden light of the evening. The sky was now a deep and dark rich blue, bathed in the silvery white of the waxing moon. Their footsteps pressed the icy snow, no longer fresh, but still crisp under their heavy boots. A woollen hat and scarf protected Gaia's cheeks from the bitter chill of the night. They walked for a couple of miles, snaking along the same path that hugged the river. It was an ancient route once followed by lovers looking to be alone, and families on Sunday strolls. This was before The Community, when the family was the building block of social order, when kinship mattered. Few walked this path now, and none at this hour. Gaia's gloved hand pressed against the handle of the dagger by her side. She knew the risk they were taking, and the dangers that lay ahead.

Ben stopped, and the others waited behind.

'What is it?' Aran whispered.

'Did you see that?' Ben replied.

'What?'

Ben scanned the sky, then Gaia saw it. There was only a fleeting shadow, as something flashed across the moonlight. She had seen such shadows before.

'Night birds,' she said.

They waited, watching for any more signs of the creatures. The sky was clear, and the only sound was the gentle trickle of the flowing water. Gaia heard something else, faint at first, but soon getting louder. It was a familiar clicking sound, the eerie and ominous signal the Night birds were almost upon them. Suddenly, there was a swoosh and a sharp blast of icy air as something swept past their faces. It was so close Gaia could almost feel the wings as they rushed by. Ben set off running down the path.

'Follow me!' he cried.

Aran and Gaia sped after the old man as he sprinted ahead. Gaia could hear more clicking noises close behind, hurtling towards them through the air, followed by wave after wave of blasts of wind as the the creatures swooped and dived. She felt something grip her hair, followed by a sharp tug and a piercing pain in her head. The woollen hat was yanked free along with a clump of her long red hair. She stumbled, winded by the pain, and looking ahead saw another Night bird attacking Aran. The creature was still draped in the shadow of the night, but she could see the long, spindly legs, and sharp talons as they clawed at Aran's head. Huge wings flapped either side of a body covered in jet black fur, and canopies of black skin were spread across thin, skeletal arms. Ferocious jaws, and needle-like teeth protruded from its hideous face as it snapped at Aran.

Gaia slipped her machete from its sheath and with one swift action plunged the blade into the neck of the creature. There was a terrifying high pitched squeal as it fell to the ground, and without a moment's thought she crushed its skull with the heel of her boot. Meanwhile, Ben and Aran were fending off another attack; Ben thrusting his spear at the birds as they swept towards them. The clicking had been replaced by a series of shrill, intermittent shrieks, similar to the dying cry of Gaia's victim. The wave of attacks were intensifying and they each struggled to fend the creatures off. A string of heavy, accurate blows saw several of the birds fly off injured, while several more tumbled against the river bank to their deaths in the icy water. The squeals of the creatures and the flurry of noise from the fighting echoed around the valley. The attacks were relentless, but began to lessen, and one by one the remaining birds made a final assault and then flew off into the blackness of the night. All that remained were their silhouettes across the silvery moon.

Ben stood bent over, gasping for air, while Aran looked to Gaia.

'Are you hurt?' he asked.

She was panting, the icy air burning her lungs. The only pain she could feel was a sharp stabbing where the clump of hair and been ripped from her scalp.

'Take a look at my head, will you?'

She leant forward as Aran inspected her wound.

'There's a bit of blood, but it's not too bad. You'll be fine, but we'll get you patched up once we get in.'

Aran turned to Ben.

'Are you OK?'

Ben spat blood onto the clean, white snow.

'I've had worse,' he replied.

Standing upright Ben groaned as he struggled to stretch his aching body.

'I'm getting too old for this.'

Aran put his arm on Ben's shoulder.

'Are you sure you're OK?'

Ben looked at him and smiled.

'Don't worry there's a bit of life left in me yet. Come on we need to get moving. They could come back any minute.'

Gaia looked down at the bloodied corpses of the slain creatures.

'What are those things?'

Ben replied.

'They're bats, but a mutant strain created by The Poison. They usually keep their distance, but they must be desperate, as there isn't much for them to feed off in this weather. All the creatures are getting desperate. That's why we need to keep moving. We're at our most vulnerable out here in the dark. Get your things and let's go.'

They pushed on along the river bank for another mile, then Ben began to slow. Soon he stopped, took off his backpack, and leant against a tree.

'We're almost there.'

Gaia spoke, her voice agitated.

'Where exactly are we going? You still haven't told us how we're going to get in.'

Ben took a long drink of water before replying.

'There's an old tunnel just over there. The entrance is concealed. It's been there hundreds of years. It was used by monks to flee the town when they were under attack. There are hiding holes in the woods all around here. The tunnel leads under the wall and into the cellar of an old house on the edge of the wall.'

Gaia looked at Aran who was frowning.

'Is it guarded?' she asked.

Ben shook his head.

'The tunnel is fine. I've been using it for years. No-one on the inside seems to know about it, at least not as far as I'm aware. The entrance in the cellar is hidden inside a chimney, and it's well concealed. It's not the sort of thing you would find unless you knew it was there. There is a bit of a problem though.'

Aran and Gaia exchanged worried looks..

'What kind of problem?' Aran said.

Ben lifted himself upright again.

'The house is occupied and you'll need to find a way to get out without being seen.'

Gaia spat out her response, trying to keep quiet, but struggling to maintain a whisper.

'What? And you tell us this now.'

Ben held up his hand, shaking his head as he replied.

'I know what you're thinking, but seriously as long as you're careful it'll be safe. The cellar is never used and there are stairs that lead up to a passage at the back of the house. The house is huge and no-one goes into that part at this time of night. I've used it many times and never seen or heard a soul. But that's why we had to do this at night. The risks out here are nothing to when you get inside.'

There was a silence as Gaia and Aran each waited for the other to respond. Despite all her reservations, she knew this would be their best chance of getting inside. There were huge risks, but the alternatives were worse. They had to get in, find Aran's contacts, then work out a plan from there.

'We haven't got any better options. How long is the tunnel?' Gaia asked.

'It takes about ten minutes to reach the entrance to the cellar. Like I said, it's in a chimney, so you'll need to climb down from a ledge. Here - you'll need this.'

Ben handed Gaia a slim rubber object. She inspected it. There was a wide end with glass covering it, attached to a narrow stem.

'What is it?' she asked.

Ben looked bemused.

'Don't tell me you've never seen a torch?'

Gaia and Aran both shook their heads.

'No,' she replied.

Ben laughed.

'They do keep you sheltered on that island, don't they? It's just a light, powered by electric batteries. Press the button here to switch it on.'

Ben's expression changed as he looked at Aran.

'I want it back though. It's one of the few I have left that still work. Leave it with one of your contacts and tell them to get it back to me next time I'm inside.'

Aran nodded.

'There's something else I need to tell you,' Ben said.

'What?' Aran replied.

Ben looked at them both in turn before speaking. He paused, almost as though he was composing himself.

'It's about your brother and sister.'

He took a brief moment again before continuing.

'I spoke to some people when I was in there this morning. They're holding the girl in the old castle keep. She was taken there as soon as they arrived. The word is she's still alive in one of the cells, but...'

He stopped and looked at Gaia.

'They said she's in a bad way. There are lots of rumours about what goes on in the castle. I'm sure most of it is exaggerated, but you need to get to her as quickly as you can.'

Aran spoke.

'What about my brother, Cal? Did they have any news on him?'

Ben shook his head.

'I'm sorry, I couldn't get any information on your brother, but they won't be holding him in the keep.'

Aran became agitated.

'How can you be sure?' he asked.

Ben continued.

'I know it isn't what you want to hear, but they only hold girls there.'

Gaia look confused.

'Why?' she said.

'I don't know, exactly. Again there are lots of rumours as to what they do in there, and I don't think it would do any good me sharing speculation with you. All I know for sure is, they take young female prisoners to the castle, and they're never seen or heard from again. That's why you have to get in there and find her.'

Aran lowered his head, as Ben put his hand on the boy's shoulder. Leaning forward, Ben spoke, his voice was calm and reassuring.

'I'm sorry son. It doesn't mean your brother isn't still alive somewhere else. Maybe your contacts will know more.'

Gaia was touched by Ben's warmth, though something was still troubling her.

'What about Kali? Does anyone know where she is?'

Ben looked awkward, fumbled with his words as he replied.

'I don't know. I didn't ask about her.'

Aran lifted his head and stared at Ben. As he spoke his words were slow and placed, his voice soft, but with an edge that puzzled Gaia.

'I know you asked about her, Ben. Is she in the castle? We need to know what to expect.'

Ben lowered his hand from Aran's shoulder and moved away.

'Look I told you. I don't anything about Kali.'

Aran stared at Ben who was trying to avoid catching his eye. Gaia sensed the tension, the first time she had seen this between them. She watched Aran, waiting to see how he would respond, if he would push this any further. There was a long, awkward silence.

'Is there anything else we need to know before we go in?' Aran asked.

Ben nodded.

'One more thing. Neither of you have been to The Haven before, so I need to warn you, it won't be what you expect. Especially not the streets at night. Be careful. Whatever they told you on the island, forget it. The Haven is a dangerous place when it's dark.'

Gaia was puzzled.

'In what way?' she asked.

Ben's expression was dark, the words of his response chosen with care.

'The wall keeps the creatures out, but it isn't the animals you need to fear. Who needs to fear creatures when you have people?'

'What do we need to be looking for exactly?' Aran responded.

Ben twisted his face.

'You'll see when you get there. Just be on your guard on the streets at night. Keep your heads down, and try and stay out of sight. Get to wherever you need to as quickly as you can.'

Aran stared at Gaia who shrugged, as Ben spoke again.

'Take care. I'll be back in town to do some trading tomorrow, so if you're in any trouble and can get to me, I'll help if I can.'

Ben paused, his expression turning sombre.

'The Community fill your heads with all sorts in those training camps, but the world isn't as they make out. It's all bullshit. You need to find the truth for yourself. Don't accept their version. Once you see what it is they've created, you'll start to see that truth.'

There was a pause as they both reflected on his words. Ben continued.

'We need to get a move on. I have to make it back alone and the longer I'm out here the more chance I have of being found. This way.'

Ben flung the bag on his back and crept through some bushes lining the path. Aran and Gaia followed, as Ben kept crouched low. They climbed a fence and entered a field, hugging the hedge that surrounded it. At the far end of the field, next to a small copse of trees he paused, scanning the area, as the moonlight glistened off the white blanket of snow smothering the earth all around them. Only silence and the eerie grey darkness of the winter night filled the air. Ben slipped into the trees, as Aran looked at Gaia, nodded, and then followed. She waited, alone, gazing into the crystal night, at the emptiness and isolation. Taking a long, deep breath, she inhaled the icy air. For all its danger and uncertainty, Gaia preferred it out here in the country. In her world without freedom, this was the best she might hope to find. But for now, Freya and her freedom was all that mattered. She owed at least that much to her sister. There was a strong sense of duty, a debt to repay, but also something more. Gaia wasn't quite sure what it was yet, but her compulsion to save Freya was overwhelming. Something was driving her, telling her this was the right thing to do. She heard a loud whisper from within the trees.

'Come on Gaia,' Aran cried.

Creeping through the narrow gap in the trees, she left only silver light and silence behind. Her world was about to change; nothing would ever be the same again.

8

Ben and Aran stood over an open hatch, and Ben shone a torch into the darkness. Metal ladders led down into the shaft, the dim light from the torch revealing only the top of the entrance, and not how far they stretched below. Both men stared at Gaia as she approached, their faces etched with light and shadows.

'What kept you?' Aran said.

She gave him a cutting stare.

'There was something I needed to do.'

Ben interrupted the terse exchange.

'The ladders go down about ten metres. At the bottom there's only one way you can go. The tunnel's narrow and low so you'll have to crawl along it. I can get along there, so you'll be fine, but take your rucksacks off and push them.'

Gaia spoke, her voice agitated.

'Is it safe?'

Ben nodded.

'It's sturdy and been there for a few hundred years. There are no creatures down there, if that's what you mean. Neither of you are claustrophobic, are you?'

Gaia looked at Aran as she replied.

'I'm not.'

Aran avoided her eye contact.

'I should be OK.'

She frowned.

'What do you mean *should be*? Is there something you need to tell us?'

Aran caught her eye.

'It won't be a problem. Let's just get going.'

Gaia and Ben exchanged glances, and the old man looked worried, but was growing impatient, conscious he needed to head back home soon.

'Aran's right. You have to go,' Ben said.

Gaia removed the torch from the rucksack and slipped it through her belt. She dropped the bag down the shaft, and a muffled thud echoed as it hit the bottom. As she was about to enter the shaft Ben held out his hand.

'Take care, Gaia. I'm sure we'll be seeing each other again soon.'

She gripped Ben's hand and shook it, a soft smile on her face as she lowered herself down the ladders. Slipping into the darkness below, all she could see was the faint glow from Ben's torch above her. When she reached the bottom of the shaft she removed the torch from her belt. Pressing the button, the light streamed from it, dazzling her eyes. She pointed the torch up the shaft, watching as Aran climbed onto the ladders and began to descend. A loud bang echoed through the tunnel as Ben closed the hatch. Aran approached.

'Are you OK?' she said.

"Yes, I'm fine. Let's get through this as quickly as we can.'

Gaia reached out her hand and touched his arm.

'Stay close behind and try to focus. If you need anything just say and we'll take a breather.'

Aran nodded and smiled.

'Thanks Gaia.'

She turned and began to crawl along the tunnel. Movement was difficult, as the tunnel was much narrower than she thought. She wondered how Ben ever got along it, and whether he'd said this to reassure them. She was forced to hold the torch with one hand while nudging the rucksack as they slid forward. Aran shuffled along close behind her, a single beam of light stretching out ahead, revealing the narrow black silhouette of the tunnel. She bumped her head on the roof of the chamber several times, but she struggled on, metre by metre, her knees aching as they ground onto the stone floor..

After a few minutes of dragging herself towards their unseen destination she stopped. Adjusting her grip on the torch, she listened and realised there was no movement behind. All she could hear was the sound of heavy panting, Aran gasping for breath. The speed and urgency of his panting began to build, soon reaching a frenzied pace. She tried to turn around, but the tunnel was too tight to manoeuvre her body back the way she had come. Pausing for a moment, she whispered into the darkness, her voice only as loud as she dared.

'Are you alright, Aran?'

The panting continued, but he managed to splutter a few broken words between the flurry of desperate breathing.

'I...can't...seem...to...get...any...air...I'm suffocating!'

Gaia was growing more worried. She had never seen him like this before, and with each gasp of air and pleading cry she felt more certain she might lose him. Something told her to remain calm, take control, knowing it was her best chance of saving him.

'You're not suffocating, Aran. You just think you are. Stay calm and try to relax. You need to breathe slowly. Listen to my voice, Aran. Focus. You can do this,' she whispered.

The frantic panting continued, and Aran struggled to respond.

'There's…no…air, Gaia. I…can't…breath.'

'Aran listen to me. Focus on my words.'

Her head began to whirl, desperate to think of a way to calm him and concentrate his mind. Images flashed through her head, memories of their moments together, a string of fragmented pictures rolling into one steady blur of motion. One image kept recurring, appearing with more and more clarity in her head. She tried to ignore it, but the memory continued to wrestle and fight, forcing out the others, until it was the only one she could see. Surrendering to it, she clutched at the image in her mind and began to describe it, the words flowing from her mouth in a calm, reassuring whisper.

'Remember the time in the barn, Aran. We were lying together in each other's arms. We talked, and held each other, then we kissed. Can you remember that first kiss, Aran? Try and picture it in your mind, Aran. Focus on that moment. Picture us together. Think about how you felt. How special the moment was. Can you see it, Aran?

There was no response. She listened and heard the sound of Aran's breathing slowing. Soon it was back to a steady pace. Waiting a while longer, just to be sure, she whispered again.

'Don't worry, Aran. I'm here. You're safe. We're almost there now. Just follow me and everything will be alright. I'll get us out of here. Trust me. I promise.'

There was a long pause, then a cough and Aran's voice echoing from the shadows.

'I'm think I'm OK now. Keep moving.'

His voice wavered. Gaia waited a moment and began to edge forward again, her movement slower, all the while listening behind. She wanted to be sure he was near, and remained calm. They crept onward without further words. Bit by bit, edging closer to the end she still couldn't see despite her assurances to Aran. The torch beam kept swallowing the darkness, and with every metre, she kept straining her eyes ahead, hoping for a glimpse, desperate for the tunnel to end. After what seemed an age, the light caught a wall ahead. Her heart was racing now, a mixture of excitement and relief rushing through her. The end was just metres away, well within her reach. She whispered, her voice still gentle and comforting.

'We're almost there.'

She reached a hole in the floor of the tunnel, and shining the light into the darkness below, Gaia could see a short drop onto a stone floor. She struggled to pull her legs round, and had to press her head and neck hard against the tunnel roof. Managing to squeeze her legs into the hole, she lowered herself onto the floor. She shone the torchlight up the chimney towards Aran who passed the rucksacks to her, before edging his legs down. Shifting the beam of light into the cellar, they surveyed the dark, cold chamber. They were in the back of a huge fireplace, high enough to enter without lowering their heads. The cellar was long and narrow, the walls lined with row upon row of shelving stacked with bottles. There was a damp and dusty odour, and misty vapour seeped from their mouths as they exhaled. Gaia picked up her rucksack and whispered,

'Where do we need to go when we get out of here?'

'There's a clocktower on the main street. Once we see that I should be able to find the house. I have directions and a door number.'

Gaia frowned.

'OK. Let's get out of here.'

They made their way to the far end of the cellar, passing what seemed like endless lines of old bottles. Cobwebs clung to the shelves and draped the semi-circular arch of the ceiling. The cellar looked like it had been carved from the underground rock, and the stairs at the end were forged from the same heavy stone. The steps were steep and tricky, and they climbed using both hands and feet. At the top was an arched wooden door with a large iron latch. Gaia waited for Aran to reach her, then pressing her head against the door, she listened before lifting the lever. The latch groaned as she edged it upward, and there was a loud, unsettling creak as the door slid open. The sound echoed down the stairs and into the cavernous cellar. She looked back at Aran, his face locked in a nervous grimace.

Peering through the crack in the door, Gaia slipped through the opening and into a large passage. The beam scanned the floor ahead, as they both tiptoed forward. The walls were lined with wooden panelling and covered in pictures, lamps, and dusty ornaments, trophies from a long forgotten time. They passed several doors before reaching a high arched doorway at the end of the passage. Gaia pressed her ear close to the door, and gripped the handle, waiting, listening for any sound or movement. The silence brought with it an added edge of fear, mixed with the darkness and desperation to find a way out. She turned off the torch, eased the handle and teased open a crack in the door. As it widened she squeezed through, pressing her body against the wall on the other side. Aran followed, both listening and searching in the pitch black of the room.

The sound of voices came from above, the words muffled and indistinct, but there were several people, a mix of men and women. Gaia pointed the torch at her feet and switched it on. The full force of the beam pierced the wooden floor below, its glow spreading a circle of light around them. With this to guide them, they shuffled around the walls of the room until they found the only other door. Turning off the torch, they waited. The voices were accompanied by the pounding of footsteps which rose then faded as they moved across the room. Gaia heard the footsteps again, this time different, coming from beyond the door, faint at first but then building as they rattled down a wooden staircase.

She turned off the torch as they both remained hugging the wall, focusing on the direction of the door. They couldn't see anything, but listened for any sign of it opening. Gripping their weapons, they waited, poised and ready. The footsteps grew louder, reaching a crescendo as though they were about to burst through the door. They stopped, followed by a long silence, broken only by the continuing mumble of the voices above. Gaia tightened the grip on her dagger, slowing her breathing. She could feel Aran alongside, his arm pressed against hers. The footsteps began again, loud at first, but soon drifting away and fading until they disappeared leaving only the muffled sounds overhead.

Aran leant into Gaia, pressing his lips close to her ear.

'Let's wait. Give it a few minutes. Hopefully, they'll go back upstairs,' he whispered.

They stayed close together in the darkness, still against the wall, silent, willing the dragging seconds to roll by. The rattle of footsteps and voices from above only made things worse, a constant reminder of their need to get out. The minutes passed, neither of them sure how many, each convinced it was enough, but not willing to take the chance. Aran began to fidget.

'Come on. We can't wait here all night,' Gaia said.

There was a pause, as Aran mulled over his response.

'You're right. Let's go.'

Aran eased past Gaia, opened the door, and crept outside. They entered a hallway which was lit by a few wall lamps, casting a hazy orange glow. The walls were the same dark wood panels, each smothered in portraits of the forgotten dead. The faces gazed down, the eyes following as they moved around the room. The lips were trapped in the same knowing, half smile. They edged towards an entrance at the far side with a grand door decorated in tall stained glass windows. Aran tried the handle, but it was locked. Looking at Gaia, he frowned. She turned, scanning the porch area for any sign of a key. On the wall in the corner she noticed a series of hooks, with a number of keys hanging from each. Tiptoeing towards them, she grabbed each of the keys and returned, passing them to Aran.

He was just about to put the first key in the lock when there was a noise from outside. Through the frosted glass panels a silhouette was moving towards them. They fell back against the wall, weapons at the ready, listening to the footsteps coming up the path.

There was a click in the lock and the door opened. A man stepped into the porch, and as he turned to close the door, he stopped and stared at the floor. There was a long pause before he looked up, and turned to face them, his eyes glaring, a look of shock and horror on his face. Without hesitation Gaia whipped her dagger from its sheath and lunged forward. Placing her hand over his mouth, and twisting his head to one side, she slit his throat with one swift action. It was all over in a split second, before the victim had time to make any movement or sound. She held the weight of his body, still covering his mouth as she lowered him to the floor. His eyes were locked in startled agony, the final realisation of what had happened as his life slipped away. She looked into his deep blue eyes waiting until she was sure they were lifeless, then looked up at Aran.

'We need to hide the body and clear away the blood,' she said.

Grabbing the dead man's legs and arms, they carried the corpse back into the hallway. Scanning the room, Gaia spotted a hidden door in the opposite corner. It was concealed by the same wooden panels, but the gaps around its edge revealed its presence. Led by Gaia, they shuffled towards it with the body. Behind the door was a cupboard, scattered with various mops, buckets and brushes. Gesturing to Aran with the flick of her head they dumped the body inside, and wiped up the blood. Returning to the main door, they left, locking the door. Gaia paused looking at the key.

'What should I do with this?' she asked.

Aran thought for a moment.

'We may need it if we have to use the tunnel again. Give it here.'

Gaia handed him the key which he concealed under a plant pot by the porch. They made their way through a large yard at the rear, and round the side of the house. Both kept low, slipping out of a side gate and into a dark cobbled stone alley. Aran paused, looking up and down the street, unsure of which direction to take. He looked into the night sky, focusing on the moon as a guide, before they headed off through the twisting silent streets and deserted alleys.

Aran stopped, the sound of voices and laughter ahead. He peered round the corner, then pulling his head back, he turned to Gaia a look of disgust on his face. Creeping forward she could see a few metres away there were a pile of rubbish sacks. On them lay a woman, her dress lifted around her waist. She was smothered by a large man, his body pumping and writhing against her. Both were groaning, with the woman letting out the occasional high pitched squeal. Her eyes were closed, a blank expression on her face.

Gaia pulled her head back and stared at Aran. She was well aware of what he was thinking, begging with his eyes for her not to do it. Pausing for a moment and taking a silent breath, she grimaced before stepping out from behind the wall and marching towards the couple, dagger by her side. As she approached, the woman opened her eyes, and with a look of alarm let out a loud scream. Before the cries could carry too far into the night, Gaia struck the woman in the face. She then grabbed her liaison by the hair and pressed the knife against his throat.

'Make a sound and you're dead,' she said.

She waited, hands held firm, ensuring each was silent before removing the dagger, and returning it to her belt. Aran stood at her shoulder, gazing down at the unconscious woman.

'Gag her and tie her up,' Gaia said.

'Are you sure? We can't take any risks. If they're found we're as good as dead.'

Aran shook his head, still looking at the body, draped on the plastic sacks at their feet.

'They're just two kids messing around. They're harming no one,' Gaia replied.

Gagging and binding them both, they dragged them into a nearby yard. In the corner was an old outhouse. Gaia tried the door.

'It's open. Let's put them in here,' she said.

Placing the boy and girl inside, they tied them together, hands behind their backs, wrapped them in a piece of tarpaulin. Aran handed her a bag left by the girl. She opened it, and pulled out some crumpled notes. There was something else. Gripping it between her fingers, she passed Aran the thin plastic object with a needle on the end.

'What's this?' she asked.

Aran frowned.

'You heard what Ben said about this place, especially at night. You need to prepared for things you've never seen before. Let's just do what we came for and get out.'

Gaia threw the handbag to the ground, and some of the notes fell out. The young girl was now conscious and struggling to get free. Gaia shone her torch into the girl's face. She was maybe a few year's older, but still only a girl. Then she noticed the eyes.

'Look,' she said, gesturing to Aran.

He crouched down and studied the girl's face. Her mouth was open, stuffed with the cloth and bound with rope. There was an expression of terror on her pale, pretty features, and specks of blood peppering her cheeks.

'Look at the eyes,' Gaia said.

Aran looked closer, and noticed they were brown not blue.

'She's an outsider, one of the Others,' Gaia said.

Gaia switched off the torch and returned it to her belt.

'Why are the Others roaming the streets at night?'

He looked up at her.

'I don't know. Maybe no-one knows she's here,' he replied.

'Or maybe they're just looking away, pretending this sort of thing isn't happening.'

She looked at the girl and back at Aran.

'Doesn't it anger you?' she said.

'What?'

'The way they treat your people.'

He jumped to his feet.

'What do you mean *my* people?'

Seeing Aran's anger, she paused a moment before answering.

'I didn't mean it like that. I meant you're not one of The Community either.'

Leaning towards Gaia, she could see he was incensed, his face bristling with ire.

'Is that how you think of me? Not one of *us*, but one of *them*.'

'No, of course not. It's just…them or us. I'm not sure of anything at the moment. Everything I've known and been told seems to be a lie. It just came out wrong.'

His eyes were filled with emotion, while Gaia's were tinged with shame. He waited, mulling over what she'd said, realising he'd over-reacted.

'Let's just forget about it,' he said.

Gaia reached out, placing her arm on his shoulder.

'Let's just get going,' she said.

They did one final check on the boy and girl, making sure they couldn't get free or raise the alarm, then set off again. Following the alleys for a couple more streets, they remained wary and alert, ducking into doorways and hiding in the shadows of the walls and hedgerows. Gaia led now, and Aran followed. They kept up a good pace, but would pause and take cover at the slightest sound. As they approached the end of a dark, narrow alley they heard music, voices and laughter. With their backs up against the wall, Gaia crept closer to the entrance of the lane, with Aran just behind. Reaching the end of the alley, she crouched on her hands and knees and crawled behind a couple of dustbins in the next lane. Aran followed and tucked in alongside.

Midway down the lane, on the other side of the street a group of men and women had spilled out into the road. Light from the windows of an adjacent house spread over them. Music mixed with the babble of loud animated conversation was coming from inside the house. The group on the street were rowdy, a number shouting and arguing with one another. A couple were dancing in the middle of the road, both unsteady on their feet. One of the men was trying to force a woman to kiss him, but she resisted, pushing him away, laughing and shrieking all the while. Another man and woman had broken away from the main group. Leaning against the wall of a neighbouring house, the man was wrapping a belt around the arm of the woman. Rolling her sleeves up, he placed a syringe against her forearm, and watched as the woman plunged her head back and slipped into a delirious smile. As the woman's arm fell by her side, the man plunged his face into her neck, kissing her as though he might never kiss again. All the while the woman was rolling her head from side to side, locked in a fleeting momentary rapture.

Gaia looked past the group to the farthest end of the lane where the street opened up and widened. Every now and then someone would cross the entrance, paying little or no attention to the commotion. The woman who had been resisting the forceful advances had now succumbed and both were locked in a ravenous embrace, more animal than amorous. The others carried on with their loud, bawdy, bickering. The couple shuffled towards the wall, and as the woman leant against it, the man hitched up her skirt and pressed against her. Gaia and Aran watched as the liaison unfolded without warmth or shame. Aran edged closer to her.

'Let's find another street,' he whispered.

Gaia nodded.

'OK. We can head back and see if there's another route. Wait!'

Staring back down the lane, she noticed the couple had broken off their encounter, and had begun to stumble towards them. Neither was paying much attention to anything around them, both too preoccupied with the other. They seemed in a hurry to get somewhere, and the man was dragging the woman by the arm, as she struggled to keep up. Gaia gestured to Aran with a flick of her head, then turned and began to crawl back towards the side alley. He was tucked in just behind her, and as they reached the entrance Gaia heard a loud voice from behind her at the bottom of the street.

'What do you think you're up to?'

She turned to see the man running towards them, hand outstretched and pointing. The woman was standing in the street behind, staring at Gaia and Aran as they crouched on all fours. As the man ran towards them the woman turned and screamed back at the rest of the group.

'We've got a couple of perverts watching us here.'

Leaping to their feet, Gaia and Aran sprinted down the alley into a side street. Behind them was the sound of excited screaming and hollering as the mob had begun their pursuit. They both kept running, darting in and out of lanes, changing direction all the time, until the noise of their chasers began to fade. Turning a corner, they saw an old, stone church basked in the moonlight. It was surrounded by an enclosed graveyard, peppered with the bare skeletons of trees, draped in smatterings of snow. They leapt over the wall and weaved their way between the gravestones. Aran was close behind Gaia, and their pursuers could no longer be heard. She spotted a small, ornate stone structure with iron gates, the entrance to some sort of tomb. One of the gates was hanging from its hinges allowing enough of a gap to squeeze through. She stopped and gestured Aran towards the gates.

'Over there.'

They made their way to the entrance and squeezed through the opening, slipping into the shadows within. Crouching low in the corner of the cold chamber, they waited, catching their breath, trying to control it and dampen the sound in the cavernous stone vault. Gaia's eyes were focused on the crooked iron gates, the mist of the silvery moon draping the doorway as she watched and listened. At one point she thought there was a distant scream. After a long wait in silence Aran spoke, his voice little more than a whisper, the words echoing in the tomb.

'It looks as though we lost them. We need to find the clocktower and the house.'

'I hope your contacts are reliable. I take it they're expecting us,' she said.

Aran was silent as he lowered his head, and Gaia sighed.

9

Crawling towards the iron gates, Gaia leant against the wall by the opening and gestured back to Aran.

'Here. Look at this.'

Aran shuffled towards her, and as he approached she pointed through the gates.

'Do you see the gap between those two rows of houses? Look through it. What can you see?'

He scanned the houses beyond the graveyard wall, then he saw it. Bathed in artificial light, he could just make out a clock face perched on the crest of a stone tower. Gaia whispered again.

'It's not far, so the house must be around here somewhere. We'll head towards it, but stay in the back streets as much as we can. There are more people around than I thought. There doesn't seem to be any kind of curfew like on the island and the hills.'

Aran nodded.

'It's like Ben said, The Haven is different. We need to expect anything. Nothing is ever as it seems with The Community.'

Gaia looked at Aran, but his attention was focused on the scene beyond the tomb. The phrase 'nothing is ever as it seems' was a familiar one. She had heard it said before, and each time it reminded her of the message she had found in the bottle on the island. Perhaps it was nothing, but there was a formality to the phrase which aroused her suspicions. It was not a phrase she would expect, at least not from Aran.

'Who told you that?' she asked.

Aran looked confused.

'What do you mean?'

'Who said 'Nothing is ever as it seems'?'

He shrugged and shook his head.

'I don't know. It's just something people say.'

Gaia was not willing to be brushed aside.

'But those words, they're very specific and distinct. Who said them to you?'

Aran sighed as he began to seem agitated.

'No-one said those exact words, at least not that I can remember. It's just a phrase. People use it all the time. Why does it matter?'

Gaia thought back to her conversations with Hannah, and recalled her final words - Trust no one. Nothing is ever as it seems. At the time the words struck her as odd, and of echoing the message in the bottle. She was convinced Kali had planted the bottle, and it was all part of the plan to persuade her to escape with Aran. Now Hannah and Aran had used the same phrase. She felt sure there wouldn't be any answers now, and they had other things to worry about.

'Maybe you're right. Let's get going.'

They left the shelter of the tomb and the graveyard, creeping through the dark alleys in the direction of the tower. Every now and then they would catch a glimpse of the clock face as they zipped past openings in the houses and entrances to the lanes. The back streets were empty, but on occasion they would see someone crossing the far end of a street. They slipped in and out of the shadows of walls and gateways, silent and unseen, like ghosts. With each passing alley and fleeting glimpse the clocktower loomed ever larger until they reached the final street running parallel to the one on which the tower stood. Gaia waited by the entrance of a narrow alleyway with Aran tucked in close behind. At the far end was an opening which led into the main square.

Gaia stuffed her hair into her woollen hat, ensuring it was concealed, then pulled the hood of the jacket over her head. She gestured to Aran who shook his head. Being less conspicuous in his colouring, he left his hood down. She spoke.

'We're going to have to go into the square. It's the quickest way to find the street with your contact's house.'

They headed down the alleyway and stepped out into the wide square. Dominating the centre was the clocktower which was met by four roads, forming a cross as they stretched off in opposite directions. Crude gas lamps lined the streets, casting a strange, unsettling glow on the snow coated roads and shop fronts. There were a couple of people, each with heads bowed, shuffling across the iced white pavements. Neither seemed keen to dawdle or hang around, and there was no acknowledgement as they passed each other. Avoiding all eye contact, the silent strangers scurried to their destinations, each making sharp turns and disappearing into the shadows of the side alleys.

Entering the square, they adopted the same direct, purposeful, but indifferent approach. Crossing the icy road, they paused at the foot of the clocktower, hugging the protection of its shadows. The thick sandstone walls, capped with medieval turrets stretched above them. Aran scanned the streets lining the roads to the tower while a bitter breeze whistled past and snapped at their cheeks. He saw what he was looking for, and nudging Gaia's arm led her towards a side street about a couple of hundred yards from the tower. As they approached she looked at the grounds of the building next door. Next to the tall, metal gates of the courtyard was a faded, rusting sign. She could just make out one of the words, 'School.' Below were some other words which were clearer, but written in a strange foreign language. They read: 'Sic Luceat Lux Vestra.'

'It means, 'Let your light shine.' It's in Latin. It's one of the old languages. There were lots of things on the island written in it, especially in the ruins of the Abbey. It was the language of the old religion,' Aran said.

Gaia studied the words on the sign and then looked beyond into the courtyard. The gates were bound shut with a padlock and thick metal chain. Within the clean, blanket of snow the courtyard was overgrown, cluttered and abandoned. There was an eerie, ominous silence across the school. Like the words, the place was now a relic of the former world, no longer needed, as there were no children here. They had been sent to the hills and countryside, to abandoned stately homes and remote islands. The Haven was the place some would come to, some who were chosen, those that had Become.

Aran led them into the lane beyond the archway, past doorways, some numbered and stopped outside one. Scanning the lane, he stepped forward and raised his fist to the door. He looked back at Gaia and frowned before knocking. They waited for what seemed a long time, before he rapped his knuckles against the door again. Gaia caught something in the corner of her eye, and looking up she saw the curtains move in one of the upstairs windows. Moments later the sound of a bolt opening came from the other side of the door, then a series of scrapes and clicks as more bolts were opened and locks turned. A narrow crack appeared and they heard a voice from within. It was deep and threatening.

'Who are you?' he said.

Aran raised his hand, making a strange ovular shape while replying to the shadow beyond the door.

'Hannah sent me. She said you could help us.'

There was a long silence. Gaia peered through the gap in the door, but could see nothing but darkness. The voice was stern and with an edge she did not like.

'You have to leave. It's too dangerous here at the moment. Whatever you came for, go before you're found. You aren't safe. None of us are safe.'

Aran and Gaia exchanged nervous looks, then Aran stepped closer to the door and whispered.

'Please. I was told you could help, that you were one of us.'

There was an uncomfortable pause before the voice replied.

'There is no us any more. Things are dangerous. We've all been told to lie low and not take any risks. Sorry, but you're on your own. Now go!'

Before the man could slam the door shut Aran wedged his foot in the crack. Leaning forward even more he spoke again, this time the desperation was clear in his voice.

'We've come a long way to get here. I know it isn't safe and we don't want to put you in any more danger. But all we need are a few answers.'

The shadow remained silent, but Aran continued.

'We've come to find a young man and woman, Cal and Freya. We think they might be being held captive here. The girl hasn't been here long, but the boy could have been here for months now. We need to get to them soon before it's too late.'

The voice spoke from the darkness.

'I know of the girl. She's being held in the castle. But the boy. I've not heard any mention of him, and I've been here long enough to know.'

Aran's head and shoulders dropped, as he stared at the ground. Shuffling backwards he removed his foot from the gap in the door. Gaia edged closer and placed her arm on his shoulder, as she looked towards the door and spoke.

'The girl. Is her name Freya?'

'Yes, Freya. There have been rumours of her for some time now. She was brought here weeks ago from the hills. The word is she was brought here for some purpose, but no-one knows what exactly.'

'Is she alive?' Gaia replied.

'I don't know. All we hear are fragments. Look that's all I can tell you.'

'What about Kali? Do you know where she is?'

The door slammed shut, and they both stepped back. She looked across at Aran, and incensed and seething, she began hammering on the door. Leaning her face against the wood she berated the stranger beyond in the loudest voice she could risk.

'Open the door. All we want are a few more answers.'

Gaia continued to thump her fist against the door, but still there was no response. Aran looked on, shaking his head, waiting for her to calm down.

'It's no use Gaia. He's not going to open it. Let's just go.'

She gave him a menacing look.

'Where exactly are we going to go? You said you had contacts who would help us. Some help they've turned out to be. Come on what's the plan?' she snarled.

He replied, his voice simmering with anger. Coupled with the uncertainty about his brother, Gaia's cold, insensitive attitude was the final straw.

'Will you just leave it!'

He paused, as Gaia lowered her head.

'We'll find somewhere to hide for the night, then we'll work things out from there,' he continued.

There was a pause before Gaia looked up.

'I'm sorry,' she said.

Aran turned and trudged back through the snow towards the entrance to the street. Gaia waited a moment, staring back at the door. She looked up at the window, feeling sure the curtains had moved again. Aran stood in the road, signalling for Gaia to follow. She shuffled through the snow towards him, as he peered back and forth along one of the roads leading to the clocktower. It was the smallest of the four roads, and the streets either side were deserted. She realised he had no idea what to do now. He wanted to lead, find a way forward, make things right, but there was no plan B. He had been relying on those contacts, but they both knew no-one could be trusted.

Gaia stared at the railings of the abandoned school, and with one final scan of the street pulled herself up onto the wall.

'Come on,' she said.

'What are you doing?' Aran replied.

Gaia looked down at him.

'You said we need somewhere to hide for the night. Do you have a better idea?'

She leapt over the railings, and landed with a thud in the snow of the courtyard. Peering back through the railings she smiled at Aran.

'Get a move on. You can't stay out there all night. Hurry before someone comes and sees us.'

Aran threw his rucksack over the iron fence and followed, with Gaia making her way through the courtyard towards the main building. Windows were smashed and the stonework was covered in a collage of colourful graffiti. After trying a couple of locked doors, Gaia led Aran to the rear of the building. They approached a porch, noticing one of the doors was ajar. It stank with the acrid smell of urine which burned the back of Gaia's throat. Easing the door open, she pushed through the gap, turned on the torch and shone the beam down the corridor. Chairs, paper, plastic bottles and an assortment of other rubbish were strewn everywhere. Either side of the corridor were a line of doors and windows. Some doors were open, and the majority of windows were broken leaving only fragments of jagged glass spread across the floor.

They made their way down the corridor moving in random zig-zags, dodging the rubbish along the way. Reaching the end, they paused by a pair of double doors. Gaia opened one and peered inside. The light from the torch flashed across the room, catching objects on the floor, shadows flickering and appearing to move. It was a large hall with a raised stage at one end. Wooden beams lined the sides, and a row of climbing apparatus covered the wall at the back. She eased into the room, shining the torchlight from side to side, over the dark heaps which were scattered everywhere. Lifeless bundles littered the floor, all packed close together. Edging closer to the mounds, she crouched to inspect one.

Gripping the machete by her side, she stretched her other hand forward and pulled back the ragged, filthy blankets. She could see a head, that of a boy, not much older than them. His face and hair were haggard and filthy, his features skeletal and drawn. Open mouthed, he lay with his eyes closed, and it was difficult to tell if he was alive or dead. Alongside him was an assortment of objects - a spoon, some cotton wool, foil, and needles, each soaked in dark crimson blood. She looked back at Aran who was staring down at the lifeless creature, his face intense with concentration. He was watching and listening, searching for breathing, any signs of movement or life.

Without warning, the boy's eyes opened, a look of shock on his face. For a moment he was confused as though awakening from a nightmare, unsure of what is real and imagination. This soon dissolved into a lost smile, as his dry, cracked lips moved.

'Help me, please,' he whispered.

Gaia looked at Aran then the boy. Crouching down beside the boy, she leant forward and spoke.

'What is it? What do you want?'

The boy coughed before forcing a reply. His blue eyes were dull and listless, devoid of all sparkle and life.

'Can you take away the pain?'

His eyes pleaded with Gaia, before the vacant expression and smile returned, and his eyelids flickered before closing once more. Seeming to drift off to sleep again, they watched and waited, staring down at his limp body as he lay. She felt Aran's hand touch her shoulder as he spoke.

'Come on. Just leave him.'

She remained crouched alongside the boy weighing up what she had to do. His words echoed through her head, the desperation in his voice and eyes. She looked at his face and hair, and could smell the stale stench of vomit mixed with sweat. The boy's breathing was slow and shallow, as though he was clinging to the last moments of life. Gaia reached forward and pressing her hand against the boy's mouth, she put the whole of her weight and strength against his body. The boy began flailing, struggling to force a scream and wrestle free. His eyes were open and wide with panic, as he continued to writhe beneath her. Looking on, Aran spoke, his voice quiet, still, but filled with a pleading panic.

'Gaia. No. Leave him. Don't!.'

Still pressing down on the boy, she looked up at Aran.

'Help me.'

'No Gaia. Please!'

Her face turned into a scowl as she thrust a threatening look at Aran.

'I have to. He's dying anyway. Now help me.'

Aran leant down and grabbed the boy's arms. Once she was sure he had control, Gaia reached over and took a cushion from by the boy's side. The boy looked on, continuing to struggle, and realising what she was about to do, his body gained a new surge of frenzied power, his eyes raging with fear. Aran pushed down harder on his frantic torso, as Gaia placed the cushion on the boy's face. Pressing hard, she waited until the thrashing eased and then stopped. Removing the cushion, she gazed into the boy's eyes. The horror of earlier had dissolved into the peaceful serenity of death, with all its comfort and release.

Exchanging looks, they were each filled with a mixture of emotions, shame and regret. Aran was angry, but understood why Gaia had done it. She looked down at the boy one more time, then turned to Aran and whispered.

'We did the right thing. He's free now. We need to go.'

She closed the boy's eyelids, his face still and lifeless. They heard the rustling of other bodies fidgeting in the room, and realised this was just one boy, in a sea of squalor. Aran stood about to make his way towards the entrance, and Gaia reached out and grabbed his hand.

'What about the others? We can't just leave them like this?'

Aran crouched beside her.

'What do you want to do? You can't kill them all.'

He spat out his words. Gaia looked away, and listened as the slumbering corpses coughed and groaned. She cast the glow of the torch across the room, lighting the shadowy faces. They were all girls and boys probably a similar age to them. However, these were not the chosen, they would not Become. These were the abandoned and forgotten, used for whatever purposes The Community had, then left to die.

'We can't just go. Look at them. What sort of a life is this?' Gaia asked.

Aran stared around the room.

'I know, but we have two choices: we either take them with us or we kill them. I don't think you want either of those, do you?'

She lowered her head. The truth of his words stung. She had saved one, but there was no hope of saving the others. They were lost, and would need to find their own way out of this. Gaia nodded.

'You're right.'

They tiptoed towards the entrance, stepping between the bodies. Reaching the doors, Gaia turned and swept the torchlight across the room once more. The sea of living dead lay still and silent once more. Closing the door to the hall they moved back along the corridor, and slipped into one of the side rooms. Gaia shone the torch around the room checking they were alone. The room had been ransacked and was littered with overturned desks, chairs, ripped paper and books. Shelves had been ripped down, and fragments of posters clung to the walls. She scanned the room again, tracking the beam of the torch. She paused at something, a map. Drawing closer, she could see the shapes laid out, each in a different colour or shade, with names etched in bold - India, Pakistan, China, Russia, France, the U.S.A. There were hundreds of names, most unfamiliar, a few she recognised from her younger days. Aran crept alongside her, staring at the wall and studying the map, his face awash with awe and wonder.

'Where are we?' Gaia asked.

Aran pressed a finger against a tiny island in the upper half of the map. It looked odd, misshapen, nestled close to a much larger mass of land, only separated by a narrow stretch of water. Gaia realised she had spent her whole life desperate to escape an island, only to find she was now trapped on another much larger one. She leant in close to read the words.

'The United Kingdom,' she said.

Gaia laughed.

'What's so funny?'

'I don't know. It just sounds strange to me.'

'It's one of the old names, but there were others. Great Britain was another.'

Gaia sighed, shaking her head in disbelief. Aran looked on puzzled.

'What?' he said.

'United Kingdom. Great Britain. It all sounds so pompous and grand. They had everything and threw it all away. They had the chance to make things better - look what they left us with. They were meant to give us the future and this is what we got.'

There was a long silence, each of them continuing to gaze at the places on the map.

'It's strange looking at the world like this,' Gaia said.

Aran frowned.

'How do you mean?'

'Look at how dull it is. There's no beauty. It makes everything seem like nothing, just lines drawn on a page. Is this how they taught young people to see the world? No wonder no-one cared. To love something, you have to experience it.'

Gaia smiled as an image flashed into her head. Aran caught the smile, and guessed who she was thinking of.

'Yann would have agreed with you,' Aran whispered.

For a moment their eyes met. Silent, they both stared, each knowing what the other was thinking. Gaia broke her eyes away and turned to look at the map again. The reflection from the torch shimmering across the shiny surface, catching the coloured patchwork of places, the myriad of shapes and mysterious names.

'Do you think there are others out there?' she said.

'I'm sure of it. The leaders claim we're the only ones who survived The Poison, that the rest of the world was wiped out, but I don't believe it. Somewhere there'll be another island or isolated community that managed to escape. There has to be.'

Gaia nodded as she replied.

'We can't be all that's left.'

She spoke again, her voice so quiet it was almost as though she was speaking to herself.

'One day we'll find others.'

She tried to picture what was happening in some of those far off places, and if people were still alive. She remembered being told the world was small, but even on this picture it seemed vast and beyond reach. There was so much to know and discover, but the only world she had known had been just a few square miles. She felt the same rush of emotion she used to have with her moments alone on the beach, the same longing to escape and explore. The world was inviting her now, as the mainland had done from the island. Maybe this was how it was meant to be? Maybe life was an endless urge to discover? Perhaps that's what gave it meaning and purpose. She lifted her arm and pointed to a small area on the map. It was also an island, north of their own and coloured dark blue.

'There!'

Aran peered at the tiny emboldened letters.

'What?'

'That's where I'm going to go and live,' she said.

Aran grinned.

'Iceland. It doesn't sound very warm.'

'I don't care. I want to get away from here. The Community. Everything. I'm going to start a new life, discover new things, find new people, and build a new world.'

'And how are you going to get there?' Aran asked.

Gaia looked at him and shrugged her shoulders.

'I've no idea, but I'll figure it out.'

He thought for a moment, smiling to himself.

'Maybe I'll come with you.'

Their eyes met for a moment, and there was that connection again, the one they had in the barn. It was the briefest of feelings, but it was enough, and they both felt it. Gaia felt a rush of blood to her cheeks and averting his stare she gazed at her feet.

'Sorry. It was only a joke,' he said.

Gaia looked up and smiled.

'Who knows? Maybe we can all go.'

They both looked at the map again, each lost in their own thoughts.

'Don't you want to just run away from all of this?' Gaia sighed.

Incredulous, Aran stared back at her.

'Of course I do! I've been running all my life.'

He paused, turning away and lowering his eyes, his words choked for a moment.

'But we know it'll never happen,' he said.

Gaia shook her head, a puzzled frown on her face.

'Why not?' she asked.

'There are things I need to do here first. I can't just run away.'

She scowled, shaking her head in disbelief.

'There's no way I'm spending my life here. They told us this was the place we'd thrive once we had Become. The Haven they call it. That's all they ever talked about on the island. But look at it. It's a cess pit. They told us they were building something new, something we'd be part of, and lead, but this is their answer? This is their idea of the new world?'

Their eyes met, their expressions saying everything.

'There has to be something better than this,' she said.

Aran gazed back at Gaia.

'What if there isn't? What if this is all there is? What if this is the future?' he replied.

There was an uncomfortable pause, a suffocating silence, before Gaia replied.

'Then we'll find something better, and if we don't find it, we'll build it.'

She moved away from the wall, picked up one of the overturned chairs and sat. Aran looked on, thinking of her words. Shining the torch into the far corner of the room, Gaia began to play with the beam, flashing it across the ceiling.

'What are we going to do now?' she said.

He picked up another chair and sat opposite, leaning forward, staring at his hands and playing with his fingers. After some thought he answered.

'We've got two choices. Either we try to find the castle now, or we sit it out till morning and see if we can find Ben. He might be able to help us.'

Gaia frowned.

'What do you think?' he asked.

She took a long time before responding.

'I think we should try to find them tonight. The longer we wait, the more likely we are to get found.

At the moment surprise is our best chance. I'm worried about those two leaders who were bringing you here. If they got out alive they might have returned and they'll be expecting us. Even then we stand a better chance at night.'

He hesitated a moment, thinking it through.

'It isn't going to be easy with just the two of us. I thought we might have some more help,' he said.

'Perhaps they won't be expecting us and we'll still have surprise on our side. We just have to hope for that.'

'And if they are?' he replied.

Gaia sighed.

'Either way the place will be guarded, and they'll be well trained. We need to use our heads, survey the castle, work out the best way to get inside. There's got to be a way to get in without raising the alarm. Once we're in, we pick them off one by one. If we move quickly, we'll be in and out before they can raise the alarm.'

Aran pondered Gaia's words, weighing up the options again. He knew there was little point, as their choices were limited. They had come this far and had to see it through, whatever the outcome. The glow of the torch cast white light and dark shadows across their faces. He looked at Gaia and spoke.

'Let's do it. We can't turn back now.'

Gaia was just about to reply when there was a clatter in the corridor. Turning off the torch they both crouched low behind a desk. Watching through the broken panes of glass into the darkness, they heard a shuffling sound, and the occasional thud. A silhouette came into view as it edged past the window. The head was stooped and the back arched as the figure crept forward. Shuffling towards the exit, the shadow was lost in a drugged haze. They watched and waited, Gaia's hand pressed against the handle of her dagger, concentrating on the dark figure, listening to the slow, near silent movement of her own breathing.

The shadow slipped out of sight, and there was another thump. It was the sound of something being knocked over, followed by footsteps moving nearer. Both remained kneeling on the floor, tucked in behind the desk. After a brief moment that seemed much longer, another black silhouette moved past the shattered windows of the room. This figure was taller, more upright, the steps swifter and with greater purpose. They waited until the shadow was gone and all sounds had ended, then crept along the floor to the door. Weaving through the desks, chairs and debris, Gaia paused and peered round the door, scanning both ways. Once she was sure there was no-one else, she signalled to Aran and they both slipped from the room.

Leaving the school by the same door they had entered, they headed further into the school grounds away from the main gates and road. Gaia led them down a gentle slope until they reached a perimeter wall topped with metal railings. Aran helped Gaia mount the wall, and once on top, she reached down and pulled him up. They both jumped into the deep snow on the other side and scrambled for the shelter of some trees nearby. Once they were sure they were alone she spoke, her voice just above a whisper.

'The river's just down there. We'll follow it and see if we can find the castle. It can't be that hard to spot.'

As she spoke they both looked out beyond the trees, surveying the area for any sign of people approaching. The night was cold, crisp and the same eerie silence echoed around them. The reflection of the moon's light on the white snow gave off a strange light, unsettling, but also magical. The houses that lined the river looked empty and dead to the world. There were no lights from any windows, no sounds, only shadows.

'We're going to be more exposed down there. It'll be easy to see us,' Aran said.

'We'll stick to higher ground, follow the edges of the streets and use any trees we can for cover. We're more likely to be seen if we stay inside the town. I don't want to stray back into those alleys if we can avoid it,' Gaia replied.

They left the cover of the trees and hugged a wall running parallel to the river. The only sound of the night was their breathing and the crunch of their footsteps in the snow. There were a few scattered footprints already, but they were no longer fresh, the makers long since gone. The river was calm and iced over, the moonlight glistening on its still, glassy surface. The opposite bank was lined with trees stretching far back up the hill. The street they followed curved in a wide arc, then ended by an area of open land, peppered with a smattering of trees. The land sloped down towards the water, and at the base was a narrow footbridge. Across the water, just visible beyond the brow of a mound of earth were the turrets of the keep. Gaia crouched low with Aran tucked in beside her. Crawling behind one of the trees, they peered down below, their eyes focused on something on the other side of the river; the last thing they wanted to see.

10

On the bridge were the group that chased them earlier, five of them. The amorous couple were still playing flirtatious games, while two of the young men leant on railings and stared down into the water. Alongside them was a girl, sitting with her legs dangling from the side of the bridge, her head back looking up at the sky. The couple were laughing, wrestling, and stumbling as the man continued to press his shunned advances. The others were silent, lost in a world of their own. Gaia and Aran exchanged worried looks.

'What do you think?' Aran whispered.

Gaia raised her eyebrows.

'We need to get over there to reach the castle. There could be another way, but this would be quickest if it wasn't for them.'

She looked back down at the bridge. None of the group seemed in any hurry to move soon.

'We could wait to see if they leave. They can't stay here all night,' Aran said.

Gaia replied, all the while her eyes still fixed on the group.

'We can't waste any more time. We need to get into the castle, free them, and get away. We have to give ourselves a good head start before daybreak.'

There was an awkward silence, neither wanting to say what they were both thinking.

'You take the couple, and I'll deal with the other three,' Gaia said.

Aran nodded, and they both jumped to their feet and strolled down the slope towards the bridge. There was no attempt to creep up, or disguise their presence. They had no time, nor interest in the element of surprise. They knew it would not be needed. As they neared, the amorous woman spotted them. Pushing the man away she gasped and shouted, pointing at them as they approached.

'Look! It's them.'

Her partner turned to face Gaia and Aran as the others saw them advancing, got to their feet and tucked in behind him. They edged forward while Gaia stopped and stared at them each in turn, Aran standing alongside her. They all watched and waited, hands by their sides. It was one of the lovers who spoke first, the man now shunned.

'Look who we have here then. Our little peeping Toms are back again,' he said.

Gaia replied, her voice calm.

'We don't want any trouble, we just need to get across the bridge. Move out the way and we won't harm you.'

The man laughed, glancing back at his companions and gesturing. They looked on, smiling and laughing, as he replied in a mocking tone.

'What? Across there? I'm not sure we can allow that. You see this is our bridge and we're very choosy about who we let cross. What do you think? Should we let them cross?'

He turned to the others, and his partner replied.

'No. They'll have to swim.'

'Or slide, on their bellies,' one of the other men said.

Laughter broke out from the group, while Gaia and Aran looked ahead, remaining calm, and showing no emotion or expression. Gaia waited for the group to settle and then replied in the same measured tone.

'We won't be swimming or sliding. We will walk, with your permission, or without it. Now move out of the way, go home and forget you ever met us. Believe me, it's the best thing for all of you.'

The mood of the group shifted, turning from mocking laughter to menace. Pulling something from his pocket, the man edged forward lifting his arm. It was a knife, the blade pointing towards Gaia as he approached. Edging forward he spoke, his voice growing louder, and filled with anger and venom.

'Did you hear that? They think they're going to get past us. Now we're not going to let that happen, are we?'

He paused as he drew nearer, then shuffled forward, his arm still raised with the blade poised.

'You heard her. Swim!' he said.

Aran stepped towards him, while Gaia began to move towards the others. Their eyes remained on their targets, one by one they knew who they would eliminate. All the while they were wary of the others, ready for any sudden movements. Their programming and training would take over, both knowing instinctively each incisive blow before they came. It was all over in seconds. Just as the group were about to move, Gaia slipped out her dagger and with a few swift, precise sweeping motions bodies lay slumped at her feet. She looked across at Aran who was standing over the twitching corpses of the man and woman.

Warm, crimson blood seeped across the crisp white snow, as the victims were drained of the final remnants of life. One of the bodies continued to twitch at Gaia's feet as she stared down at their faces.

They were only young, though the ravages of their short anarchic lives had taken its toll.

'Why did it have to be this way? Why didn't they just walk away?' Gaia asked.

Looking down at the corpses, Aran sighed.

'Maybe in some ways it's for the best. What kind of a life do they have? These are the ones The Community never speak of, the underworld of The Haven. The leaders tolerate and ignore them, because they're the cause of it.'

He paused and knelt by one of them.

'They're no different to us, except they've been discarded because they failed to make the grade. The Community has no use for them, so the leaders let them rot and carve out their own deaths.'

'Could they be from the island?' Gaia said.

'Yes. That or one of the other training camps scattered around. This is what happens if you don't become good enough for The Community. They promise us all a future, but it's only really for the chosen few. And then there are the special ones like us.'

Gaia frowned.

'The ones they chose to become leaders?' Gaia said.

'Yes. Though with Freya and you I'm sure Kali has something different in mind.'

Gaia looked puzzled.

'Like what?' she asked.

'That's something we need to find out.'

They both looked at the corpses, and Gaia scanned their faces for any sign of familiarity. Maybe they had met before, or their paths had crossed on the island. Perhaps they had been on a mission together, or in the same team assigned to defend against the onslaught of the rats. Maybe one of them had saved her life.

'What should we do with the bodies?' Gaia said.

'We'll hide them in the river, under the ice. No-one will look for them, and they won't be missed. If they are found, we should be long gone by then.'

'Let's hope you're right.'

Lifting the bodies, they dumped them by the edge of the water in the shadow of the bridge. Aran smashed a hole in the thick ice and together they pushed the corpses into the freezing water below. One by one they were caught by the current and dragged downstream, submerged beneath the river's frozen blanket. There was no ceremony, only a few silent words from Gaia, tinged with sadness, regret, and the knowledge that, but for some mysterious accident of birth, this could have been either of them.

After covering the blood stains in clean, crisp snow, they made their way across the bridge into the cover of trees. Meandering through the heavy undergrowth they headed towards the hill, beyond which stood the target of the old castle keep. Stopping on the brow of the hill, crouched low in bushes, they surveyed the area. It was a perfect vantage point to plan their break in to the castle.

No longer a discarded ruin, the keep was tall and imposing, rebuilt much later from fresh sandstone that replaced the original heavy stone walls. The golden surface of the stone had become soiled with dirt over the decades. Smoke from years of wood fires that warmed The Community buildings had stained the walls further. The main entrance to the keep was dominated by a huge, ornate wooden gate, adorned with rows of black metal studs, and held in place with thick iron hinges. There was a side door, perhaps a good chance of gaining entry, but first they would have to scale the imposing walls surrounding the castle grounds without being seen.

They scanned the courtyard for any sign of guards, but there were none. They waited and watched for several minutes, but not a soul appeared, nor was there any sign of movement. As Gaia scanned the surroundings, she noticed how the silence engulfed them, amplified in the cold, crisp winter air. It was an ominous and unsettling calm, a stillness that masked the twisted and sinister world below. She could taste the bitter smoke from the home fires smouldering through the night. It stung her eyes, and small tears trickled down her frozen cheeks. Aran looked across and spoke, his voice quiet and tender.

'Are you OK?'

She wiped the tears from her face.

'It's just the cold and this smoke,' she replied.

Aran scanned the night sky.

'We're not used to it on the island. The air's rotten here,' he said.

'Everything is rotten here.'

An image of the island flashed into Gaia's head, coupled with a strange feeling of loss. She had felt like this often since they had escaped. Having spent most of her young life longing to flee, she found herself missing it now. While she had felt trapped on the island, the chaos and madness of the world beyond its secluded shores scared her even more. She had found a kind of freedom, but at least on the island she had structure and order, and she knew her enemies. She no longer knew who to trust anymore, and it seemed everyone and everything was a threat.

Life was relentless and exhausting, a constant struggle to keep moving and evade capture. There was no escape now. She was trapped again, just in a different way. She had fled to find a different community, her freedom, and somewhere she could be herself. This was not what she had imagined or hoped it to be. She felt so alone. She knew she needed to find Freya. Only then could they decide what the future held and where they had to go.

She felt Aran take hold of her hand, and heard his soft gentle voice as he spoke.

'Don't worry. We'll find them.'

Gaia smiled as their eyes met.

'I was just thinking about the island,' she said.

'What about it?' Aran replied.

'Do you miss it?' she asked.

There was a moment of silence as Aran gathered his thoughts.

'It's not something I think about a lot. Though there are times when I wish we could stop running. Things seemed a little easier there,' he said.

'Me too. I just wish this could all be over. Do you think they'll ever stop chasing us and just let us go?'

Aran pondered the question for a while, knowing what he felt, but cautious how to frame his reply. They both knew the answer they wanted, and the truth neither cared to admit.

'Only when Kali's dead.'

Gaia mulled over the words. He was right. Somehow Kali was the key to all of this. While she was still alive they could never be free. It all sounded so simple. Just a few words. A long silence followed with both continuing to scan the castle grounds. Gaia surveyed the keep and its tall, seemingly impenetrable walls. Were Freya and Kali in there?

Hannah had once said to Gaia that life was all about moments, that you had to find the opportunities to create them, and when you did you had to make the most of them. She had said that when she looked back on her life she would know if it had been successful because it should be filled with those kind of moments. Gaia sensed an opportunity now, the time to seize a defining moment. The next few hours could make or break their lives, and their futures beyond that.

'How are we going to get in?' she whispered.

Aran pointed to the perimeter wall.

'We could climb the wall over there in the corner. There's a side door we could try.'

She shook her head in disbelief.

'They're not going to just let us in,' she replied.

They both studied the walls, silent and towering, knowing the options were few. The windows were narrow and beyond reach. The walls themselves were too high to scale by hand alone. Apart from the main entrance, there was only the one side door they could see. The door looked heavy and sturdy, made from ancient wood, and was probably several inches thick. Aran sat shaking his head, deep in thought.

'Maybe there's another entrance round the back,' he said.

'Even if there is, what use will it be? It'll be locked, bolted and no doubt guarded. There's no way we can break those doors down. They're fortified and too strong.'

Aran let out a huge sigh, as she continued.

'There's no point us giving in now. There has to be a way in. Freya's in there. I know she is, and we have to get in somehow, but we have to move fast. It'll be sunrise in a few hours.'

Aran's face lit up, a grin sweeping across his face. He smiled at Gaia who looked on puzzled.

'What is it?' she said.

'Follow me.'

Staying low, Aran made his was back down the hill and towards the river where a narrow path hugged the water's edge. They followed it until they reached a dense wall of bushes. The path snaked off back towards the town along the edge of the old castle walls. Aran paused before peeling back the branches and making his way into the thick vegetation. Gaia followed close behind, pushing the low hanging branches out of her way, until the bushes began to thin and the going eased. He stayed close to the riverbank, scanning the area, as though he was searching for something. Suddenly he stopped and tilted his head as though he was listening for something. Gaia waited in silence, the movement of her chest and pounding heart the only sound she could hear. Then she heard the faintest of noises somewhere in the bushes beyond. It was a slight trickling sound of running water. They began to move towards it, and with each step the sound grew louder and more distinctive. Soon they reached a small opening where they stopped. Turning, Aran smiled at Gaia.

'Here it is. Our doorway to the keep.'

He stepped to one side and with a sweep of his arm gestured at Gaia to look behind. An iron grate was set back into a wall, with water flowing from a tunnel beyond it, forming a small stream that trickled towards the river. Steam belched from the opening and Gaia could feel occasional blasts of its warmth. She approached the grate, removed her gloves and touched the water.

'It's warm!'

Aran smiled.

'It's the drainage system for the castle. The tunnel leads inside.'

She inspected the grate which was bolted to the wall. It was old, rusting, and fixed solid.

'We'll need to get this off first though,' she said.

Aran took his axe and struck one of the bolts, snapping it clean off. He looked at Gaia.

'They've probably been here hundreds of years. They won't take long to get off.'

Together they removed each of the bolts one by one, striking them several times before they shattered under their heavy blows. The grate creaked and groaned until Aran smashed his axe against the final bolt, and the iron structure crashed to the ground. Gaia stared into the blackness of the narrow tunnel, with the flowing water echoing throughout.

'How long do you think it is?' She said.

'The main part of the castle is just beyond the walls back there. I don't know, a few hundred yards.'

Gaia frowned.

'Will you be alright?'

He looked into the darkness then up at Gaia, giving her a reassuring nod.

'Don't worry,' he replied.

Gaia reached out and took Aran's hand. He looked down, gazing at his hand wrapped in hers. Both were gloved, preventing them from feeling the warmth of each other's touch. She spoke.

'You go first this time. If you start to feel anything, just stop. Remember I'm right behind you.'

He raised his head and smiled.

'Thanks.'

For a moment Gaia's heart softened and a flood of emotion raced through her, feelings she had been burying since the village. The anger and bitterness at his betrayal were smothered by longing and desire. She felt a pang of regret, wanting it to be as it had been, as though the ordeal of her torture had been a dream, and Aran had never been there. She imagined they were two different people, and it had happened to others not them. In a way she knew they were. The past was only images in her head, fragments of discarded pictures, echoes of a reality lost, only a certain kind of truth. It was the present that mattered. Now. The actions and decisions she made would shape her future, and at this moment Gaia couldn't imagine a future without him. Her thoughts were surrounded in a mist, her feelings overwhelming all senses. She eased her head towards him and placed her lips close to his ear. She spoke in the softest of whispers, her warm breath caressing his skin.

'If we don't make it through this I want you to know that I do care. Despite everything that's happened.'

Aran's voice was choked, as he struggled to find his words.

'Please Gaia, you have to know that if I could have done it any other way I would. I never wanted to hurt you.'

She felt his lips against her cheek, and turning her head their lips touched, his warm breath merging with hers as they kissed. Eyes closed, all she could see was a rainbow of colours floating in the darkness of her mind. Her heart was racing, a giddy tingle of excitement rushing throughout her body. She could taste him as their lips moved, and she never wanted the moment to end. Aran eased his lips away and pressed his forehead against hers. Placing his hand on the back of her head, he stroked her hair as he spoke.

'I didn't want something to happen without you knowing how I feel.'

Their warm, sweet breath swirled together in the cold night air. Gaia's eyes remained closed, her mind still fixed upon the lingering joy of the kiss, feeling the warmth of his head pressed against hers.

'Let's just get through this first,' she said.

They kissed again, then wrapped their arms around each other. For the briefest of moments they remained, neither wanting to move, each knowing the next few hours could be their last together. Gaia broke the silence, releasing her grip and ushering Aran into the darkness.

'We have to go,' she said.

He paused a moment, staring into her eyes. Leaning forward, he pecked her on the lips before climbing into the tunnel. Crouched low, only just able to stand, he began shuffling into the black emptiness. Gaia looked back, scanning the moonlit trees around her, taking one final look at the outside world she was only beginning to know. She was discovering its truth: a sinister, unforgiving world where you had to fight for any fragments of joy. A world where all they had was each other. She knew this could be her last taste of night, of cold air - the foul, bitter, smoke stained air. She looked at the moon, wondering if it was the last time she would see its glow. She turned and clambered into the tunnel, stooped with her back arched low, Aran just up ahead.

Soon the entrance was gone, and the cavernous echo of the stone walls enveloped them. The only sound was the sloshing of their boots through the steady stream of water. She could feel the warm current seeping through the leather, her socks soaked and squelching with every step. They pressed ahead through the black chamber, keen to preserve the batteries of the torchlight, but with the intensity of the darkness burning their eyes. The loss of sight helped their other senses spring to life, and Gaia could taste the damp, putrid air, and smell the rotting mould from centuries of slow decay. The echo of the water seemed to grow, their feet pounding out a regular rhythm as they marched on. Their steps were as one, each matching the other with the same monotonous beat.

She listened for Aran's breathing, trying to catch any hint of panic. There was nothing, only footsteps and the flow of the stream. Gaia had a growing ache in her back, the muscles straining to maintain her crouch. Her calves and thighs were burning, and as she weakened, her head began to bump and scrape against the tunnel roof. Pressing her hand against the wall, she tried to compensate, hoping this would ease the intermittent blows. Sensing her increasing discomfort Aran stopped, his whispered tones echoing throughout the darkness that surrounded them.

'Are you OK?' he asked.

'I'm fine. Do you think there's much further to go?'

His hand clutched hers.

'I don't think so. Stay close,' he replied.

The footsteps began to play out their rhythm again as Aran set off down the tunnel, with Gaia still tucked in close behind. They moved another few hundred steps, and Aran paused again. This time there were no words, Gaia sensing the tension in his body heighten. He took another step, then another, each one slow and cautious. She couldn't see past him, but knew there must be something ahead. She tried to peer beyond, hoping to catch a glimpse of what he could see, but the tunnel was too narrow and filled by Aran's frame. Gaia could feel her heart racing more and more with every step. She tried to slow her breathing, placing each foot forward with greater measure and care. Aran slowed, shuffling almost to a stop. Then Gaia saw it. They were just flashes at first; fragments of light flickering on water ahead. They both stopped and stared above.

Thin shafts of yellow light poked through a grate in the ceiling, as they focused on the opening, both listening for any sounds. Aran crept forward, trying to be as quiet as he could, pausing at the base of the grate. Edging his face towards the gaps, he peered into a corridor above, looking for any signs of life or movement. He looked back at Gaia and nodded. She moved towards him, while Aran reached up and placed his hands through the gaps, gripping the iron. His face strained as he pressed against the metal, the whole force of his body pushing against it. Seeing there was no movement, Gaia lifted her arms and pushed. She could feel the pressure of its resistance, year upon year of neglect welding the iron structure to the floor. She looked at Aran's face which was turning an ever deepening red as they both pushed with every ounce of their strength. He stopped and gasped for air, looking at Gaia in dismay, and shaking his head, They pushed again but to no avail, with not even the smallest sign of the stubborn structure budging.

Aran had a look of despair, while Gaia was agitated, her mind a whirl of activity. She was rifling through ideas flashing through her mind, desperate to find a solution, knowing there must be a way to free the grate. She was determined not to let this defeat her. They had come this far, and were so close now. This was their best chance to get into the castle, their only chance. Time was slipping away, and the fresh light of dawn would arrive outside soon. This was when the castle would come to life again. There was no turning back now; they had to remove this cover somehow.

Then something came to her, and the faintest of grins crept across her lips. Taking her knife, she began gorging the tip of the blade where the grate and ceiling joined. She pressed hard, tracing a circular motion around the edge. Over and over she repeated it as Aran looked on. Fragments of dirt mixed with paintwork and metal fell to the floor, sometimes catching their faces and lips. She spluttered and spat the tiny pieces out as she continued, trying to stay as quiet as she could. She kept scraping in the same circular motion for a few minutes more, then stopped.

Replacing her knife, she gestured to Aran to push against the grate together again. There was little movement at first, but then they felt something, the merest hint that it was giving way. They began to press much harder, sensing the century old bonds were starting to break. More and more dirt was falling from the area where the grate and ceiling joined. Then came a creaking sound as the heavy structure began to move and rise. It was Aran's side that gave way first, breaking free and lifting into the corridor above. Gaia's side soon followed, with the whole structure coming away with a jolt. Together they held the iron grate above their heads, taking the full force of its weight, easing it onto the floor of the corridor. They paused and stared at the opening above. Gaia's heart pounded in her chest, a mixture of excitement and apprehension. They had done it; reached their journey's end. Memories of the last few days flashed through her head, the twists and turns, the struggle to get this far. They were so close now, but she knew this was just another beginning; there was still a long way to go. She felt the thrill of hope, of finding Freya, and maybe even Cal. Then the image of Kali's face appeared in her mind, and thoughts of Gaia's torture back in the village. The face had a knowing smile, as though she was mocking Gaia, beckoning her to come. Gaia felt a cold shiver run through her body, and tried to concentrate on the glimmer of light above, smothering the dark thoughts.

Aran lifted his head through the narrow opening, looking both ways along the long empty corridor, and at heavy wooden doors either side. The doors were all closed, and bathed in shadow, no hint of what lay behind them. Blazing torches mounted the ancient stone walls casting a warm yellow light into the passage. The only sound was the crackle and fizz of the flames. Aran lifted himself through the opening and reaching down helped Gaia up. They replaced the grate and brushed the stray dirt into the hole, ensuring there was no trace to alert anyone. Climbing to their feet, they listened and surveyed the corridor in each direction. Other than the crackle of the flames from the torches it was quiet, with shadows dancing in the faint flickering light. Aran tip-toed towards the end of the passage and the base of a flight of steep stone steps leading up to the floor above.

Gaia followed, pausing by one of the doors. She listened, sure she heard a sound from within. Leaning her head towards the door, she pressed her ear close to the gnarled oak frame. There was a shuffling sound - faint, muffled - but distinct. By her head, in the centre of the door was a closed shutter with a small handle attached. She slid it open and peered inside. The room was bathed in darkness, and she could see nothing beyond the veil of pitch black. She heard the sound of something moving again, this time clearer, as though fabric was being rubbed together. Then she heard something else: a whimper, high pitched, perhaps a woman's voice. Rummaging through her rucksack, she took out the torch, shining the bright beam through the small square opening and into the room.

The narrow beam of light crept across the room revealing several pieces of tattered furniture - an old wardrobe, a desk and chair, a chest of drawers. On the floor in the centre of the room was a patterned rug with discarded clothes strewn upon it. To the left of the rug, tucked against the wall was a wooden bed. As the light swallowed up the shadows, Gaia saw a body covered in blankets lying on the bed. She paused, leaving the light upon the body, watching and waiting for any sign of movement. Suddenly, it stirred and rolled over. Gaia switched off the torch and listened into the darkness, but her breathing was the only sound. Turning to look down the corridor she could see Aran looking on, his face puzzled and questioning. There was a long pause, and only when she was sure the room was silent again, she turned on the torch. The pure white beam pierced the darkness and bathed the bed in a shaft of light revealing the face of a young girl. She was asleep, her brow furrowed, and a troubled expression on her face. Her long hair was swept back and draped across the pillow. Gaia's heart stopped. For a moment she thought it was Freya. Perhaps it was her mind playing tricks, or just that she wanted it to be her so much, but it was a different girl, a similar age, but not her sister.

Something struck Gaia as she gazed at the sleeping girl, something odd about the scene. She moved the beam around the room again. On the desk were books, a writing pad, a candle, and a picture on the far wall. It was a strange image of some long forgotten woman lying in a river surrounded by flowers, her expression tranquil, at peace. There was a cushion on the chair, and a dress strewn across the back. The room looked comfortable, lived in. This was no cell, or at least not how she would have expected a prisoner to be kept.

Gaia reached down and gripped the door handle. Turning it, there was a click and it slid open with a groan. She looked across at Aran, both sharing confused looks. She lifted the torch and shone the light on the girl's face again. The girl moved, stretching her legs out from under the blanket. Gaia held her breath, watching and waiting, making sure she would be ready if she awoke. The girl settled again, and Gaia tiptoed into the room, lowering the torch beam. She slipped round the edge of the room, running her fingers over the desk. On it was a notebook which she opened, looking down at the writing on the page. At the top of the page, written in bold letters was, *'Day 84'*. Gaia read the neat handwriting:

'He came again today and didn't even speak, just got dressed and left. I could still taste his foul breath and stale sweat hours after he had gone. She came later, told me The Community was proud of me, and that some day I would be rewarded. She gave me a gift, told me to wait until she had gone before I opened it. Then she left, and I was alone again.'

Gaia stopped reading and closed the notebook. By the side of it on the table was a small parcel still wrapped in brown paper with a single piece of white string in a crude bow. There was a shuffling on the bed as the girl stirred in her sleep. She began to groan and mumble some words. Gaia switched off the torch, and slowing her breath until it had almost stopped she stood as still as possible, waiting for the girl to settle. Once there was silence again, she made her way towards the door. Slipping outside, and closing the door, she moved along the corridor to where Aran stood at the foot of the stairs. Leaning over she whispered in his ear,

'Something's not right. There's a girl sleeping in there. The room looks normal and the door isn't locked. She's not a prisoner.'

'Maybe she's a leader?' Aran replied.

Gaia shook her head.

'She's too young. She can't have been that much older than us. There was a notebook on her desk. I read some of it.'

She paused.

'What is it?' he asked.

'There's something pretty fucked up going on in here.'

Aran could see the look of concern on Gaia's face.

'What did it say?'

Gaia shook her head.

'Not now...Later. We need to find Freya and get her out of here.'

'I don't understand why they leave the doors unlocked,' Aran said.

'There's no way out. The place is probably too heavily guarded to escape. They're helpless here.'

'Why take the risk? It doesn't make sense,' he replied.

They both exchanged puzzled looks.

'What did the notebook say exactly? Tell me.' he said, his voice reflecting his frustration. Gaia looked away as she spoke.

'Never mind. Let's just find what we came for and get out as soon as we can.'

Realising he would get no further answers from her now, Aran crept up the staircase, with Gaia following close behind. The steps were steep, so much so they had to use their hands to steady themselves as they made their way to the floor above. The staircase led to another corridor, identical to the one below. Moving along the passage, they slid the shutters in the doors of several rooms and looked inside. The rooms were the same, each had a girl in it, alone and asleep in a bed. None of the doors were locked, and there was no sign of any guards. The corridor was silent and deserted, but for the fizz of the flickering flames that lined the walls.

Climbing up another staircase the scene they encountered was different. These steps led to a large hall with dark wooden floorboards and a high ceiling lined with heavy oak beams. The walls were bare stone and a huge open fireplace dominated the room. Dying embers smouldered in its heart, flaring with occasional flashes of bright orange as they caught their last gasps of oxygen. Wooden benches formed a horseshoe around the ashen hearth, and the same seating hugged each wall, creating a perimeter that stretched all around the room. Cushions were strewn across the floor, reminding Gaia of the island and the daily ritual gatherings. An image flashed into her mind, the last time she sat there, her number was being called out, and she was taking the stage for the reading. Like so much of the island it seemed like a distant dream to her now, fragile and ever fading. It was as though she was looking in on the life of someone else.

At the far end of the hall an open doorway led into another corridor. They tiptoed towards it, and as they approached footsteps came from the passage outside. Darting to the corner of the room, they both crouched beneath a bench, pressing themselves low against the wall. Their eyes were fixed upon the entrance, while Gaia focused on her breathing, slowing the motion of her chest, allowing the air from her lungs to brush past her lips. She watched and waited as the footsteps grew louder, echoing in the cavernous hall as they neared the door.

The dark silhouette of a figure entered the hall and marched across it to the opposite doorway. Tall and stocky, they walked with a clear purpose paying no attention to their surroundings. In one hand they carried a flaming torch, and Gaia noticed their boots as they rattled across the wooden floorboards. They were the familiar boots of a leader. Waiting a moment after they had left, they both climbed to their feet and approached the doorway again. Their steps were ever more cautious as they edged towards it, and all the while Gaia kept looking back at the opposite door. Slipping outside, they tiptoed along another long corridor, their backs pressed against the walls opposite another row of closed doors. Aran led the way, but about halfway along the passage Gaia grabbed his arm and leant in close.

'Shouldn't we be checking the rooms? What if Freya is in one of them?' she asked.

Aran frowned. Reaching forward he grasped the handle of one of the doors and turned it. The heavy oak door creaked open. Gaia twisted her face as Aran eased it shut and let go of the handle. Glaring at her, he spoke, his voice louder and unsettling given the unnerving echo in the corridor.

'None of the doors are locked. Would they be mad enough to keep Freya in an unlocked room?'

Aran waited for the response he didn't need. She raised her eyebrows and sighed.

'So what are we going to do? We can't just wander the corridors,' she asked.

'These look like living quarters. There must be somewhere they keep the prisoners, somewhere away from the main corridors. We know it isn't lower down, so I suspect it's somewhere higher up. We need to keep looking.'

Footsteps echoed from the top of the staircase at the far end of the corridor. Gaia turned and ran back along the passage into the hall. Leaning against the wall by the door, she waited until Aran was tucked in close behind. She removed the machete from her belt, holding it poised in her hand ready to strike. The footsteps continued along the corridor, beating out a steady rhythm, growing louder with every step until they were almost upon them.

A shadow entered the room and in an instant Gaia pounced. Grabbing the figure by the hair from behind, she pressed the machete against their throat, forcing them down onto their knees. As she held them, Aran moved in front and stared down at their captive. It was a woman dressed in leader's clothes, her face looked shocked and twisted in pain, her eyes and expression spitting disdain at Aran. He reached down and removed a knife from the sheath in her belt. Looking at the knife, he rolled it in his hand as he spoke.

'We're looking for a girl. Her name is Freya. She's being held here and you're going to take us to her.'

The woman spat out her reply.

'I don't know what you're talking about. There are no prisoners here.'

Gaia yanked at her hair, and she winced as Aran leant closer.

'You're lying. Take us to her or my friend here will be very upset. She isn't someone you want to be around when she's upset.'

The woman pursed her lips, twisting her mouth in a mocking grin.

'This place is swarming with leaders. You'll never get out of here alive,' she said.

Aran crouched down in front of her, struggling to contain his growing anger. He lifted the knife and pressed the point of the blade against the woman's cheek. Pushing just hard enough to break the skin, a small drop of blood began to ooze from her cheek. Beads of sweat peppered her brow as her eyes flared with fear. Aran scowled at her as he spoke, his voice a menacing whisper.

'Take us to her, or I promise you won't be getting out of here alive.'

There was a long silence, punctured only by the nervous panting of the leader. Aran and the woman's eyes remained fixed on each other. His enflamed with anger and suspicion, hers flickering with fear and contempt. She searched his expression, looking for any sign of weakness, then stopped struggling and began to soften as she realised co-operation was her only choice. She knew they would probably kill her whatever she did, so her best chance of survival was to stay alive for as long as possible. They may be discovered, or an opportunity to attack or escape might come.

'I know the girl. She's the one who came with Kali from the village,' the leader said.

Aran nodded as Gaia loosened her grip, the anger turning to growing excitement at the mention of Freya's name and the hope she may still be alive. The leader continued, her voice filled with a mocking tone of pleasure now, her face almost bursting into a smile.

'I'll take you to her, but you won't like what you find.'

11

They made their way out of the same door through which the leader had entered, up a long flight of spiral stairs, and along another corridor. Aran held the leader close in front, hands bound behind her back, strapped together with her own leather belt. She led the way, without any struggle or fuss. Her steps were determined and direct, too loud for Gaia's comfort. Halfway along the corridor Gaia tugged on Aran's arm and brought them all to a halt. Leaning towards the leader's ear, Gaia whispered.

'Quit the marching boots.'

The leader sneered at Gaia.

'Make one wrong move or sound and I'll slit your throat before you can utter another word. Do you understand?' Gaia said.

The leader looked though she wanted to spit in Gaia's face. Through a grin of disdain she replied.

'I know who you are, and I understand.'

Gaia smiled, a touch confused by the response.

'Then you'll know I'm serious,' Gaia replied

They continued to the end of the corridor where the leader stopped. To the left was a staircase leading to the floor above, and to the right was a short passage leading to another door. The leader nodded towards it.

'She's in there,' she said.

Gaia looked at Aran then back at the leader.

'Are you sure? You've been warned.'

'You asked me to take you to her and that's where she is,' the leader replied.

Gaia and Aran exchanged nervous looks. Her heart was pounding and her throat had tightened. It was as though all the air had been sucked from the corridor and she was struggling to capture any that still remained. She paused, trying to slow her breathing, and steady herself. Small beads of cold sweat began to form on her forehead and then trickled down the side of her face. She could feel her whole body being overwhelmed by an icy grip. Leaning back against the wall, her head began to spin. For a moment, there was a sense of all consciousness slipping away. She fought it with all her will. Closing her eyes, she tried to focus on a positive thought, something comforting, anything to distract her mind from the spiral into darkness. An image flashed into her head of when she was a small child. She was in a garden, a sea of colour, the sun was blazing, and she could feel the heat from its rays against her bare skin. There were lots of voices and laughter, several people were there, and another child was running around her in circles, giggling all the while. Gaia focused on the child's face which was somehow familiar. As she gazed at the child, skipping and dancing around her someone approached from behind and lifted Gaia from the ground. Lifting her into their arms they spoke, and though she couldn't make out the words she recognised the voice. It was distinctive, one she would recognise anywhere.

The image dissolved, and as the haze lifted from her mind, Gaia noticed both Aran and the leader staring at her with looks a mixture of puzzled and concerned.

'Are you OK, Gaia?' Aran asked.

'It's nothing. Something just came over me. Let me catch my breath for a moment.'

Gaia took a few slow, deep breaths, with the voice from the image still echoing in her head. Having gathered her composure, she made her way along the short passage towards the door. Aran and the leader waited by the foot of the stairs. Aran still with a firm grip on the belt binding the arms of the leader together. There was a dagger in his other hand, poised should she make any sudden movement. They both watched Gaia; the leader with anger and frustration while Aran was filled with nervous anticipation.

Reaching the door, Gaia paused and stared down at the handle. Her hands were moist with sweat as she gripped it, easing the cold metal downward until she could move it no further. She tugged on the door, but there was no movement. She gave it another pull, this time firmer, but still the door refused to budge. Gaia looked back down the passage, and noticed the faintest grin on the face of the leader. She made her way back towards the staircase, all the while staring at their captive. As she reached them she pressed her face close to the leaders and spoke, spitting out her whispered words.

'It's locked, but you knew that anyway, didn't you?'

The leader replied with a look of contempt.

'What did you expect? We're not going to let someone like her come and go as she pleases.'

Gaia fought to control herself.

'Give me the key,' she said.

'I don't have it.'

Aran pressed the blade of his dagger against the throat of the leader.

'So where is it?' he demanded.

The leader fell silent, seething with a burning hatred for them. After a long pause the leader answered.

'You're going to kill me anyway so why should I tell you where it is.'

Aran and Gaia exchanged looks.

'Tell us where the key is and we won't harm you,' Aran said.

'You're lying. Do you think I'm stupid?'

Gaia looked at Aran again.

'You have our word. Just give us the key or tell us where it is,' Gaia said.

The leader thought for a moment before responding.

'How do I know I can trust you?'

Gaia smiled.

'You don't, but what choice do you have? Either way you could die. We need the key and if you don't have it then we'll find it with or without your help.'

The leader let out a mocking laugh.

'You don't know what you're talking about. Do you think they're just going to hand it over.'

Gaia was simmering with growing anger and frustration now.

'If they won't give it to us then we'll have to take it, Either way we'll get it. We're not leaving here without her,' Gaia said.

'There's one key for the room and only one person is allowed to keep it.'

The words hit Gaia like a stone, as she realised what the leader was saying. She could feel the eyes of both the leader and Aran upon her, waiting for her to respond. *One key. One person.* She played with the words in her head, trying to deny the truth. Gaia knew who it was. There could be only one person who would hold the key.

'So where is she?' Gaia asked.

A smug grin crept across the leader's face. Each word was like a knife being twisted into Gaia for her pleasure and revenge.

'I don't know.'

Gaia raised her machete, pressing it against the leader's throat as she spoke.

'Think hard. You have a minute to tell me.'

The leader leant back, feeling Aran still gripping her arms behind her, and with the cold steel of Gaia's blade pressed up against her neck she replied,

'I've given you what you want. I've taken you to the girl and told you where the key is. That was the deal.'

The anger was reaching boiling point inside Gaia, and she was fighting her every urge to kill the leader now. Aran could see her close to snapping and spoke.

'She's told us all she knows, Gaia. What more can she do?'

Gaia continued to wrestle with the red mist inside her. She knew Aran was right. The leader could give them no more, and even if she did know where Kali was, they would still have to find her and take the key. That would never be an easy task for just the two of them. The anger began to dissolve turning into a growing frustration as she realised how close they were, but how impossible the task still seemed. Lowering the machete she stared at Aran, a look of resignation on her face.

'Wait here. There's something I need to do,' she said.

Gaia moved back along the passage, and pressing her head against the thick, wooden door, she lifted her fist and gave it a gentle knock. She paused, listening all the while for any sounds of movement. She knocked again and then spoke, her voice little more than a whisper.

'Freya. It's me, Gaia.'

There was a long pause, followed by another knock from Gaia.

'Can you hear me, Freya? It's Gaia and Aran. We've come for you. We're going to get you out of here.'

Gaia listened and was sure she had heard something. There was a creak, then the muffled patter of footsteps. She listened and waited and then heard a soft, fragile voice.

'Gaia? Is it really you?'

The sound of the voice, however frail still washed over Gaia like a sea of relief. She felt sick with excitement, as she struggled to put together her words.

'Yes! Freya it's me. It's so good to hear your voice again. We weren't sure if you were alive or not. Are you OK?'

There was a silence while Gaia waited for Freya to respond. No words came, only silence.

'Are you OK, Freya? What is it?'

There was another long, uncomfortable pause before Freya responded, her voice sounding lost and and even more broken.

'Just go Gaia. Leave me here. It's not safe. If she finds you, she'll do to you what she's done to me. Please just go. Save yourself.'

Gaia felt the sting of Freya's words, and the total dejection in her sister's voice. This was not the Freya she knew; the bold, defiant girl who had been so clinical and without fear during their escape from the island.

'What has she done to you?'

Freya replied, this time her words were pleading, pained with despair.

'Please Gaia. Do as I ask. There's nothing you can do for me here now. It's over.'

Gaia pressed her body against the door, desperate to reach through and hold and comfort her sister. Gaia was struggling to hide her growing emotion.

'I'm not going anywhere without you. Do you hear me? Whatever she's done to you she'll pay for it. We're going to find the key and get you out of here.'

Freya's voice cut through the door again, piercing Gaia with every word.

'Please Gaia. No!'

Gaia waited and listened, straining to hear every sound from beyond the door. She could hear something, a sound she'd not heard for a long time, and one she never thought she would hear from Freya. It was the sound of sobbing. Not the gentle crying of loss and suffering, but the desperate, uncontrollable tears of someone who had lost all purpose and hope. Whatever Kali had done, she had shattered something inside her sister.

Gaia listened to her sister crying, and felt the emotion building inside her. It was emotion she had seldom felt, feelings such as these had been equated with weakness on the island. They were something berated and beaten out of you from an early age. You felt for no-one but The Community. They controlled your feelings and fears, owned your thoughts and emotions. The Community was everything, and you were simply a part of that greater whole.

Forbidden tears began to fill Gaia's eyes too. She reached up and wiped them clear, concealing the warm, wet water which felt soft and delicate to the touch. Looking down at her fingers, she watched as the tender fragments of liquid evaporated from her skin. Gaia leant in close to the door, and pressing her face against the wood she whispered.

'Stay strong, Freya. I promise you we'll be back. Don't worry - I won't let her hurt you again.'

Wiping her eyes once more, Gaia turned and made her way back towards Aran and the leader. As she reached them she struck the leader hard across the face. The woman winced as her head turned with the force of the blow. Steadying herself, she looked up and a trickle of blood flowed from the side of her mouth. She spat, red and bloodied at their feet.

'You fucking savages. Now I'll ask you again. Where's Kali?' Gaia demanded.

She smashed the leader in the face again, her clenched fist crunching against the cheekbone as the leader let out a whimpering cry. Aran looked on, still gripping the leader's hands tight as she mumbled another reply, her lips bloodied and swollen.

'I told you. I don't know, but she's not here. Kali doesn't stay here at night. She arrives each morning first thing. There are only a few of us keeping watch, but believe me we have nothing to do with the experiments. That's all down to Kali and the doctors.'

Gaia looked at Aran, a puzzled expression on his face, then back at the leader.

'What do you mean? What kind of experiments?'

The leader spluttered out a swift reply, wary of receiving another blow.

'I don't know. It's all Kali's doing. She's running everything now since she returned. She has a special interest in the girls, but I'm not sure what. They keep everything very secretive. But if you want the key, you'll have to wait for Kali arriving in the morning.'

Gaia thought about the leaders words, trying to find another answer.

'We'll wait here until morning. At least we'll have the element of surprise,' Aran said.

Gaia thought for a moment and looked down at the leader.

'How many of you are here now?' Gaia asked.

'Four of us,' the leader replied.

'Where are the others?'

The leader paused for a moment, and Gaia sensed her reluctance to answer.

'Just tell me where they are,' Gaia said.

'Upstairs. Two floors above. They're sleeping. I'm on watch, but I'm meant to wake one of the others soon to take over from me.'

Gaia continued pressing the leader, hoping she might slip and provide some answers.

'How many people does Kali usually arrive with in the morning?'

'No-one. Kali gets here first, the others come later, an hour or so after Kali has arrived.'

'So she always comes alone?' Gaia asked.

'Mostly. Once she arrived with someone else, but that's the only time since I've been on guard here.'

Gaia looked at Aran.

'What do you think?'

Aran frowned.

'We sort the guards out first, then we stay here and wait for Kali. The two of us should be able to overpower her if we plan it carefully. I don't see we have any other choice, do you?'

Gaia nodded.

'You're right. There's no way we'll be able to break down those doors. They're too solid. That's what we'll do.'

Gaia stared at the leader.

'Are there keys for any other doors?'

The leader stuttered again with her answer.

'Don't try anything funny. Just tell me or the deal's off,' Gaia said.

The leader lowered her head and whispered a reply.

'We have a key for the guard's room upstairs.'

'Where is it?'

'It's in the room. One of the others has it.'

Gaia looked at Aran.

'You stay here with her. I'll go and see what I can find. Make sure she doesn't get away.'

Aran tugged on the leader's arms as he replied.

'She's going nowhere. Don't do anything stupid.'

Gaia forced a half smile, resigned to whatever was coming next.

'Don't worry. I won't.'

Gaia crept up the staircase onto the floor above, followed the corridor to the next flight of stairs and waited. She listened for a moment then edged her way up stair by stair. The narrow chamber and cold, stone walls seemed to amplify and echo her breathing along with every step. When she had almost reached the top she crouched low and leaning forward peered around the wall into the passageway. Other than the torches, the corridor was silent and deserted. Climbing to her feet Gaia removed her machete and tiptoed from room to room. Sliding back the small slat on each of the doors she peered inside. Furnished in the same style and layout, there were no girls sleeping in these rooms, only empty beds.

Reaching the far end of the corridor, she came to the final room. As she was about to open the slat she heard a dry, throaty cough from inside. She paused a moment, slowing her breathing and leaning closer to the door. Gripping the machete tighter, she placed the other hand on the handle. Pressing down, she felt a click and the door crept open. Gaia eased the door further ajar, just enough so she could squeeze through the narrow gap, and leaving a thin shaft of light so she could see. She could just make out the layout of the room. It was larger than the others, big enough to cram in four beds, a table and wardrobe and nothing else. Three of the beds were occupied, the other with crumpled sheets strewn across it.

Gaia waited, all the while with her weapon poised. Apart from the occasional cough and some fidgeting there was no sign of the leaders waking. She approached the table where several dirty cups and plates lay, but there were no keys. Tiptoeing along the base of the beds, she scanned the floors alongside, but there was nothing but discarded clothes and boots. One of the leaders groaned and rolled over to face her. Staring at his eyes, she paused until she was sure he wouldn't wake. Her heart raced, and she could feel adrenalin pumping through her. The skin of her hands felt stuck to the handle of the blade, glued with the sweat from her palms. Her mind began to race through the options. What if she couldn't find the key? It had to be here somewhere, and the only place she hadn't searched was the wardrobe or the pockets of the leader's clothes.

Lowering herself to her knees, she lay on the floor and slid down the narrow gap between two of the beds. She grabbed the leg of a pair of trousers and pulled them towards her. Rifling through the pockets there was still no sign of what she came for. Moving round to the other beds, she continued to gather up garments and search them. She found nothing but a handkerchief and some pieces of paper. There was another cough and shuffle from one of the beds. Gaia lay pressed against the floor. They coughed again, then another, each one becoming louder and more intense. There was a groan from another bed, then a voice.

'Will you get that sorted.'

'Stop moaning and go back to sleep,' another voice replied.

There was a pause, filled only by the low rattle of someone's breathing.

'Isn't it your turn for watch now? Hasn't Cassie been back?'

'Not yet, but she shouldn't be long.'

The conversation ended, and the two men lay silent while Gaia waited, listening and considering her next move. The minutes began to seem like hours as she kept low, still hugging the stone floor. The cold from the slabs was seeping through her clothes, while the hard unforgiving surface seemed to be crushing her bones. She tried to control her breathing, but it was getting more difficult with every passing minute. Time was running out, and she would have to make a move soon. She was reaching the point where she could stand the discomfort from the hard floor no longer, and began to slide towards the door. Reaching it, she sat up and shuffled round to check the beds. The men were silent, and appeared to be lost in a deep sleep again. The coughing had stopped since their brief exchange. Gaia climbed to her feet, pulled the door ajar and slipped from the room, turning to edge the door closed behind her.

She leant back against the wall facing the door, her head pointed to the ceiling with her eyes closed. She felt a mixture of anger and frustration, as the narrowing choices played out in her head. Her attempt to retrieve the key had failed, and now they would need to consider other options. Their captive would be expected to return to the others soon, and failure to do so would alert them something was wrong. It would then be four leaders against the two of them. This was possible, but risky given the leader's superior strength and training. These leaders were guards, and probably chosen for their skills. She had to find another way.

Gaia made her way back down the stairs to Aran and the leader. He was standing over the leader who was now on her knees with her head leant against and facing the wall. Aran looked up, acknowledging Gaia as she approached.

'Did you get it?' Aran asked.

Gaia shook her head and frowned.

'No. I found the room and searched everywhere inside, but there was no sign of any key.'

Gaia grabbed the leader by the hair and pressed her face hard into the stone. Gaia snarled at her.

'I've had enough of your games. Now tell me, is there a key or was that all just a ploy?'

The leader struggled to speak as her cheek and lips were crushed against the wall.

'There is one. it's usually on the table.'

Gaia replied, spitting out venom with every word.

'You're lying. I looked on the table, and searched their clothes. There is no key.'

The leader continued, a growing desperation in her voice.

'What about the wardrobe? Did you try that? Maybe it was in a coat pocket in there.'

Gaia thought for a moment, and eased her grip. There was a pause, before Aran broke the silence.

'Did you check the wardrobe?'

Gaia shook her head.

'I couldn't. I didn't get a chance to. Two of them woke and started talking. I had to lie low on the floor. I was lucky they didn't notice me or the door slightly open. After that I couldn't take any more risks, so I just got out of there.'

'Maybe she's right. What if it's in the wardrobe?' Aran replied.

Gaia frowned.

'If it is, we aren't going to get it the easy way. There are three of them like she said, and they're expecting her back soon. We need to act quickly.'

She looked across at Aran, trying to tell him her thoughts without words. Aran returned the look, a bemused look on his face. He spoke, mouthing the words without saying them.

'What is it?'

Gaia looked down at the leader and grimaced. Aran shook his head and again mouthed a response.

'No, Gaia. We promised.'

Gaia gripped her machete in one hand and pulled back the head of the leader with the other. She pressed the blade against her neck and spoke.

'You could be lying or you could be telling us the truth. I've no way of knowing that now. We can't take any more risks though. I'm sorry, I know we had a deal, but this is the only way.'

The leader began to struggle, trying to break free of Gaia's grip, her voice pleading with desperation.

'Wait! Please! I can get you the key. I know where it is.'

Gaia tugged hard on the leader's hair.

'You're lying. You've had enough time to tell us. I've had enough of your games.'

The leader continued, now almost in tears as Gaia was poised to act.

'Please. I'm not lying. If I tell you will you let me go?'

Gaia pressed her face close to the leader, her anger plain to see.

'Just fucking tell me!' she insisted.

'It's in my pocket. The key's in my coat pocket.'

Easing her hold on the leader, she looked at Aran who began to search the pockets. Aran stopped and pulled out his hand. Between his finger and thumb was a black, iron key. At first Gaia felt a burst of relief, but this was soon replaced with anger when she realised the leader's betrayal.

'You see. I told you it was there,' the leader said.

Gaia yanked at the woman's hair.

'Why didn't you tell us at the very start. You lied and let me risk my life going to find it.'

'But...'

With one swift sweeping motion Gaia slid the blade of the machete across the leader's throat. Blood oozed from the wound as she looked up at Gaia with a confused, pitiful expression. Gaia gripped her hair until she felt the body become limp, then let go allowing it to fall to the floor. The body lay in a contorted heap, amid a growing a pool of dark crimson blood. They both stared down at the corpse, and Gaia placed the machete back in its sheath. Aran placed his hand against his brow and shook his head. Gaia spoke.

'What choice did I have? She lied, stringing us along in the hope the others would wake and find us.'

'Maybe you're right,' he replied.

They both looked at the leader in silence, while Aran put his hand on Gaia's shoulder.

'Is it ever going to end?' he said.

Gaia moved away, turning her back on both Aran and the leader's corpse.

'It'll end when The Community is over. When we're free. They made this, with their rules: it's their world, not ours. We're only doing what we must to survive. This is what they've always told us to do. Kill or be killed. Isn't that what Kali always said?' she said.

'But we're becoming like them,' Aran replied, waiting a moment to compose himself before he continued.

'At least, we're no better than them. I thought we escaped the island so we could become something better, so we could change.'

Gaia remained with her back to Aran, as she pondered his words, each one puncturing the cold, hard shell The Community had built around her. They did need to change, become better: just not now. This moment was about survival, at all costs; the revenge and justice would come later. She would make sure Kali paid for what she'd done. Once this was over, they could build again, but only then could they look to create something better. Without survival all that would be lost. The future was theirs, but only if they took it.

Aran sensed Gaia's tension, almost reading her thoughts. He stepped forward he placed his hand on her shoulder.

'Let's just get through this first,' he said.

He then moved round in front of her, leant over and kissed her cheek. Gaia didn't look up, her thoughts still elsewhere, her eyes a vacant stare.

'What do we do now?' he asked.

Gaia looked at him.

'We have the key now. We'll lock the guards in the room and wait. But we need a plan. How are we going to deal with Kali?'

12

There were voices on the other side of the door, followed by hammering and yanking of the handle.

'Cassie? Are you there, Cassie? What's going on? Open the door?'

Someone began to kick the door, over and over along with repeated, frantic pulling on the door handle.

'Cassie. What the fuck's going on.'

The kicking and banging was relentless now. Gaia and Aran stood back against the wall and waited. Both had weapons in their hands, waiting in case the guards, now turned prisoners had another key, or somehow managed to break out. After a few minutes of the hammering and protests Gaia spoke.

'They're going nowhere. There's no way they'll get out of there. Looks like that's one thing she didn't lie about - there's only one key.'

Aran seemed more cautious, still poised and with an anxious expression.

'Let's wait a few more minutes,' he said.

Gaia tugged at his arm.

'Come on. Leave them. There's things we need to do.'

They made their way back down several flights and into the large open plan room where they'd first encountered the leader. Gaia sat on one of the benches surrounding the fireplace, and Aran sat alongside. Both were locked in thought, reflecting on the events of the night, and considering their moves in the next few hours. Aran was the first to break the silence.

'What are we going to do now?'

Gaia leant forward, her arms resting on her legs, chin nestled in the palm of her hands.

'We've got to get Freya out somehow, but we can't take on Kali alone,' she said.

'We'll have surprise on our side,' Aran replied.

Raising her eyebrows, Gaia looked at him in disbelief.

'It'll give us a second or two at most. This is Kali we're talking about. We know her, what she's capable of. If we don't kill her in the first couple of seconds, we'll have no chance.'

Aran got to his feet and paced back and forward as he spoke.

'There are two of us, and only one of her.'

Gaia watched him as he walked.

'Are you serious? Do you honestly think that matters?'

Aran stopped pacing and turned to face Gaia.

'What other choice do we have? We've come all this way and found Freya. If we want to get her out of here, we have to get that key.'

The room fell silent again, as they both returned to their thoughts. Gaia could see no way out. She couldn't abandon Freya, but she knew any confrontation with Kali was likely to end in defeat. Kali had trained them, and was the best of all the leaders by far. She excelled at armed conflict, and used weapons with precision and ease. Any minor weaknesses, of which there were few, she more than made up for in her calm, focused concentration, and ability to channel her anger into strength. They had both fought Kali many times in training and despite developing great skill as a result, there was always the sense she was toying with them. Kali knew she was stronger, better, fitter and she knew their every flaw.

In her mind she knew she was superior and that would give her a vital edge. Gaia and Aran knew it too, so they would need to strike a fatal blow in the narrowest window of surprise, the flicker of that first moment when they caught her off guard. It would be the briefest of moments, and Kali's instincts and training would trigger in an instant. Then it would be over. The risk was too great, and meant almost certain death, but without the key, Freya's chances were over too. They had come so far and were so close, there had to be another way.

Gaia got to her feet and moved towards the staircase.

'Where are you going?' Aran asked.

'To see Freya, maybe she knows something that will help. We have to find another way. Taking on Kali is suicide. We've got until dawn to come up with something and get out of here.'

Gaia climbed the staircase, and could hear Aran following close behind. She made her way along and up the remaining corridors and stairs until she reached the edge of the passage leading to Freya's cell. Stepping over the leader's body, she approached the door to the room. After a brief, anxious pause she knocked on the door.

'Freya, it's me again,' she said.

There was a long, unsettling silence before Freya replied.

'I thought I told you to go.'

'That's not going to happen. We're not leaving without you. If you want us all to get out of here alive we need your help.'

'I told you. Leave while you still can. Forget about me.'

Gaia pressed her head against the door, sensing Aran just beyond her shoulder.

'We're not going anywhere. So either you help us in any way you can or we'll all die. Kali will be arriving soon and we need to try and find a way of getting you out of here before she gets here. Think, Freya. Think! You have to help us!' Gaia pleaded.

They waited, listening beyond the door, hoping that Freya had some fragment of information that might help. After an agonising pause Freya spoke, her voice quieter than before.

'I rarely saw the guards, only when they were with Kali, but there was one night when I thought I heard someone in my room, then I heard the door close and a key turn. It woke me, but when I got to the door it was locked. I waited by the door and was sure I heard footsteps in the hall. It could have been a dream though. The next morning I wasn't sure if it had happened or not. But if it happened, it was too late for Kali. It had to be someone else, maybe one of the guards.'

Freya paused for a moment then continued.

'I'm not sure what's real and what's just in my head anymore.'

Her voice tailed off with the final few words.

Gaia listened to Freya, mulling over her words, then something hit her; a realisation, a glimmer of hope. It may be nothing, but it was a chance. She turned to Aran unable to contain the excitement in her voice.

'Give me the key to the guard's room,' Gaia demanded.

Aran looked puzzled as he fumbled in his pockets for the key. He passed it to Gaia who placed it in the lock. She stopped, taking a breath before turning it.

There was a click as the key moved full circle in the lock. Clutching at the handle, Gaia pressed it downwards and felt the door open. She glanced back at Aran, whose wide-eyed expression needed no words. Gaia smiled.

'There's only one key for all the rooms,' she said.

Pushing the door open, Gaia stared into the room. The glow of the torches in the corridor lit the entrance, but the rest of the room was bathed in darkness and silence. She watched and waited, then saw bare feet and legs enter into the light. They paused for a moment before stepping forward. Freya stood just back from the doorway, her face staring ahead, bathed in the warm glow. She was expressionless, her hair lank and draped across her shoulders. Gaia hesitated, looking for an invitation, but unable to contain her joy and relief any longer she lunged forward, wrapping her arms around her sister, hugging her close. Freya stood still, allowing Gaia to continue, but showing no response. Gaia eased her grip and stood back.

'It's so good to see you again,' Gaia said.

Freya lowered her eyes, mumbling her reply.

'You shouldn't have come.'

Gaia placed her hand on Freya's shoulder.

'There's no way I was going to leave you here alone. You saved my life. I owe you.'

The two sisters stood together for a moment, Gaia waiting for Freya to respond, wary not to push her sister too hard. Freya's head remained bowed, her voice still quiet.

'She's still alive though, and if she finds you here she'll do to you what she's done to me,' Freya replied.

Gaia frowned, leaning forward so her head was closer to her sister's.

'What do you mean?' she asked.

Freya lifted her head, and Gaia could see tears in her eyes. There was something different about her, something broken and lost. The fire of old had gone. As she replied, her voice sounded cracked and fragile.

'We're all here for a reason, Gaia. It's all part of The Community's plan. Kali wants us more than anyone, but if she can't break us, she'll start again.'

Gaia looked back at Aran, who was looking on, his expression a mixture of confusion and concern.

'I don't understand,' Gaia said.

Freya shook her head, looking beyond her sister into the darkness beyond as she replied.

'Not now. It doesn't matter. We have no choice now. We have to get out of here before she comes.'

Freya paused for a moment, looking straight into Gaia's eyes.

'I warn you. She'll come after us and she won't stop until she find us. We both have something she wants.'

Gaia eased her head forward and kissed her sister on the cheek, then looking across at Aran, she whispered into Freya's ear.

'We have each other now. No-one's going to harm us.'

They waited while Freya got dressed. As they were about to leave she paused by the doorway and took one last look. Gaia put her arm around her.

'Come on. It's time to go,' she said.

Aran led them back down the staircases and corridors to the lower floor, pausing by the metal grate that took them into the tunnel below.

Removing the grate, they lowered themselves into the sewer in turn. Once they were all below Aran slid the grate back in place and they made their way back through the water towards the entrance. Freya remained silent, Gaia pausing on occasion to check and reassure her sister, Soon a faint greyish glow emerged in the distance as they drew closer to the entrance of the tunnel, but Gaia knew this was not the end. Once they were beyond the castle they would need to work out a plan to escape the walls of The Haven. In a few hours it would be dawn and Kali would return to the castle. As soon as she realised Freya was gone she would raise the alarm. The next few hours would be critical, and their only chance of survival was to get as far away as possible.

As they left the tunnel, Freya stopped and looked up at the moon. She began to take deep breaths, as if they were her first, or the last she would ever take. Gaia and Aran exchanged worried looks.

'It must feel strange being outside again after being locked in that room,' Gaia said.

'She told me I'd never see the sky again, and that when she was done with me I'd die in there.'

Aran stepped forward and took Freya by the arm, placing his hand on her chin he moved her face to look at him, and looked into her eyes.

'You've proven her wrong. You're out and free again. Now let's get as far away from here as we can.'

Staring straight at him, Freya shuddered.

'We'll never be free,' she said.

Aran pulled her head into his chest.

'We know someone who can help us,' he said.

Her head still pressed against Aran, Freya whispered a reply.

'She'll follow us wherever we go, and she won't stop.'

Aran stroked her hair as he hugged her.

'I know, but if she finds us we'll be sure we're ready,' he replied.

Aran turned to Gaia who looked concerned.

'What now?' she asked.

'We'll head back to the house and the tunnel. It's our best chance of getting out without being seen. We need to get back to Ben's. He'll help us get away.'

Gaia frowned.

'Are you sure the tunnel is the best way out? What if they've discovered the body?' Gaia said.

'It's our best option at the moment. Do you have any better suggestions?' Aran replied.

Gaia paused a moment, shaking her head.

'Let's move,' he said.

They slipped through the bushes and back along the path by the river towards the winding streets and alleys of the town. Aran led the way, sticking close to the walls and shadows, pausing at every corner, ducking in and out of gateways. If he sensed any danger, or heard any kind of noise he would usher them to the safety of the shadows, and they would wait until he was sure it was clear to continue. They saw no-one though, and managed to weave their way back to the house with relative ease. Approaching the lane where the house stood, Aran paused a moment, peering around the corner into the street. He held up his hand, then directed Gaia and Freya to follow him. They crept into the yard and tiptoed towards the door. Aran looked under the pot where he had concealed the key earlier. With a grin on his face, he held it up.

They entered the house, locking the door behind them and slipped across the hallway. Gaia stared at the door, beyond which they had hidden the dead body earlier. The house was quiet, the voices and footsteps had gone. It was late, and most likely everyone was sleeping. They made their way to the rear of the house and down the flight of stone steps that led to the cellar. As they approached the fireplace concealing the entrance to the tunnel, Aran paused.

'Are you going to be OK in there?' Gaia said.

'Let me go first this time.'

Gaia reached out and took hold of his hand. Freya looked at her, and Gaia pulled away her hand.

'There's a tunnel inside this chimney. It leads under the walls to the outside. It's a tight squeeze. How are you with confined spaces?' Gaia asked.

'I've just spent weeks locked in a prison cell. I'm sure I can cope with a few minutes in there. It sounds as though not everyone can though.'

Freya looked at Aran as he caught her eye.

'It's not that bad. I just get the odd panic attack. I wasn't too bad on the way in,' he said.

Gaia frowned and shook her head, catching what she was sure was the faintest of smiles on Freya's face.

'Was that a smile I saw, Freya?' Gaia said.

A huge grin crept across her sister's face.

'It's good to see you again. Both of you,' Freya replied, as some of the shadows seemed to disappear.

'Thank you,' she continued.

Gaia and Aran looked at each other, a look of silent acknowledgement on their faces.

'We couldn't leave you, and they were bringing me here anyway. Kali seems to have plans for me. It was Aran who saved me,' Gaia said.

Freya's expression changed, with a grave look on her face.

'She does have plans for you. The same as she has for me. You're lucky Aran got to you first.'

Sensing the change in Freya's mood, Gaia reached out her arm and began to stroke her sister's cheek. Freya lowered her eyes.

'We don't need to talk about it now, Freya,' Gaia said.

Freya lowered her head.

'There's something I need to tell you both before we go any further. It might change everything,' Freya replied, her voice returning to the fragile whisper from earlier.

There was a long silence as they each stared at one another, waiting for Freya to continue.

'What is it?' Gaia asked.

Freya looked at Gaia and Aran, as though she was having doubts now, struggling to think of what to say. Then lowering her gaze to the floor she whispered.

'I don't know, maybe I should leave it.'

Gaia stepped forward, and leant towards her sister, their faces only a few inches apart.

'What is it, Freya? You can tell us,' Gaia asked.

Freya lifted her head and looked straight into her sister's eyes. There was a pleading, a sorrow and weakness Gaia had never seen before. It was as though the shield of coldness she had wrapped herself in for so long was now gone. Her dry, cracked lips parted and she spoke.

'I'm pregnant.'

13

Freya was the last to leave the tunnel. Climbing the final rungs of the cold metal ladder, she stepped into the open night air and tasted another moment of freedom. The moon still cast its intense silvery glow across the cloudless sky. All around remained silent, but for the occasional rustle in the undergrowth, or the sway of branches caressed by a passing breeze. Gaia and Aran watched as Freya stood by the opening to the shaft, both still reeling from the shock of her announcement, struggling to make sense of it. None of them had spoken much since. Keen to leave the house without being found, they left made their way through the tunnel in silence. Gaia had been concerned about Aran, but her sister's revelation had focused his mind elsewhere and he made it to the entrance without any panic or alarm.

Aran closed the hatch to the tunnel.

'What now?' Freya asked.

'We'll head to Ben's house. He showed us this tunnel and helped us get in. He lives a few miles up river from here,' Gaia replied.

'Do you trust him?' Freya said.

Gaia thought for a moment. Trust. A word she had heard so often, and been warned about many times. *'Trust no-one. All is not what it seems.'*

'As much as we can. Aran was given him as a contact, and he seems a good man.'

Gaia looked at Aran who was standing alongside them. Aran spoke.

'Ben has history with The Community, despises them for good reason. But he's a smart guy, and uses them for what he needs, trades with them. He has a lot of contacts inside The Haven. He has been feeding us information for some time now.'

'Who is *us*?' Freya replied.

Gaia and Aran exchanged awkward looks.

'You'd better tell her,' Gaia said.

Aran waited a moment, composing himself, feeling the menacing gaze of both his companions as he spoke.

'There are some of us working on the inside of The Community. We've managed to infiltrate them and become part of them without raising any suspicion so far. We're growing in numbers and spread across many of their sites. When the time is right the plan is to overthrow the leaders. Kali is our main target. She's the key to all of this.'

Freya looked at Gaia and then back at Aran, a fierce scowl on her face.

'Do you believe him? Sorry, Aran, but the last time we were together you were looking on while Kali tortured Gaia close to death. I don't recall you doing much to intervene. Wasn't it you who set us all up?'

Aran lowered his head, and Gaia frowned. Both sisters waited for a response, but it was Gaia who answered.

'Believe me, I still have my doubts, Freya. But Aran helped me escape the leaders. We had an agreement we'd work together to find you and his brother. He's kept his side of the bargain so far.'

'A brother?' Freya replied looking at Aran.

'Yes,' he answered.

'His name is Cal. He escaped the island and was captured by Kali. She told me he was being held as a prisoner at The Haven and unless I co-operated with her she'd kill him. I didn't have a lot of choice, but to help her.'

Freya shook her head.

'You still had a choice,' she said.

Aran had a look of desperation on his face.

'Have you seen or heard of him?' he said.

Freya paused a moment.

'I never saw him, but Kali did speak of a boy who had escaped the island like us.' Freya replied.

'Did she say anything else? Think, Freya. It's important.'

Freya nodded.

'She said he'd been sent back to the island.'

Aran lowered his eyes, his shoulders sinking as her words hit him. Gaia moved towards him, placing a hand on his shoulder.

'Isn't that good news? At least he isn't dead,' she said.

Freya moved beside Aran and her sister.

'Gaia's right,' she said.

'Kali could have had him killed, or thrown out onto the streets to rot like the rest of them.'

Aran's head remained bowed, his mind lost in thought. Gaia gripped his shoulder with her hand.

'There's still hope, Aran. If she wanted him dead, it would have happened by now. At least there's still a chance he's alive and you know where he is,' she said.

'Kali must have a reason to keep him alive,' Freya said.

'If you're not one of the chosen, you're discarded and left to die. And the chosen…'

Freya's voice faded.

'What happens with them?' Gaia asked.

Freya took a deep breath before replying.

'The girls are kept in the rooms and visited in the evenings by selected leaders. Kali decides who goes where. It's all based on rewards and favours. It's one of the ways she holds power over the rest of them, but she wraps it all up in their commitment to the greater good.'

Clearing her throat, she closed her eyes as images flashed through her head. She focused her mind, trying to expel the memories of her recent past.

'It's all about keeping The Community going and growing numbers.'

She waited another moment before continuing.

'Kali tells the girls they are doing something special, giving back to The Community, ensuring it will survive and prosper. But we were slaves, trapped against our will, waiting to be raped and abused night after night.'

There was another moment of silence, her voice sounding fragile as the memories churned up the painful memories and the words mixed with emotion.

'They would arrive in the evening, sometimes the same leader, sometimes different. Some of the girls found favour with particular ones who saw them as their own. Others liked to move around and try someone new.'

Small beads of sweat had begun to form on Freya's brow as she recalled her experiences. Her voice had become more agitated.

'I had one who visited me more and more, until he was the only one I ever saw. He never told me his name, but I'd know him anywhere. I won't forget him.'

Freya paused, while Gaia and Aran looked on in silence, neither sure how to respond.

'It didn't matter who it was, the purpose was the same - to get us pregnant. Every morning someone would come for a sample and take it away for tests. If the visits stopped you knew why. Mine stopped two weeks ago, and Kali came a couple of days later to congratulate me. She was ecstatic. I've never seen her that way. She told me what a great moment it was, how I should be honoured, and how special my baby would be. That's when she mentioned you, Gaia. Said she had plans for us both and our children. That we were the key to everything.'

There was another moment of silence, Freya's eyes still focused on the ground, trying to avoid the look of concern from her sister and Aran. Gaia was trapped between horror, anger, and pain. She could feel the fury building inside her, and all she could see was the face of one person - Kali. Freya cleared her throat and continued.

'The castle is nothing more than a factory for The Community. The babies are taken from their mothers and cared for somewhere else, before they are sent out to the sites for nurturing and becoming. This is probably where we came from. All of us on the island will have started life there. Our mothers were probably some pitiful young creature lying in one of those rooms, waiting for a nameless stranger to come and take her. This is the truth behind the lies of The Community. This is their future.'

Freya stopped, raising her head and puffing clouds of vapour into the icy air. Her eyes were full, glistening with tears catching the light of the moon. Gaia stepped forward and wrapped her arms around her, clutching her close, rubbing a hand up and down her back as she hugged her. She held her sister for several minutes, as though she never wanted to let her go again. Gaia whispered in Freya's ear.

'I'm sorry, Freya. So, so sorry.'

Gaia's voice was cracked as she struggled to contain her emotions.

'I won't let her harm you again. I promise,' she said.

Bathed in moonlight, the sister's remained together in each other's arms, as Aran looked on. Choked with sorrow and anger, they thought about all they had been through both together and alone - what was, and what might have been. Reunited again, they savoured the relief of knowing things could have been so different.

Aran led them along the path by the river, heading back towards Ben's house. The night was deathly still and silent, with no sign of the Night Birds, or any other of the creatures that roamed this other world. The group moved in silence, heads bowed, trying to stay alert to danger, but each pondering Freya's words. There was a burning in Gaia's chest, sick with anger and desire to avenge her sister's suffering. Kali's face kept appearing in her thoughts, each time contemplating the different ways she would torture her before watching her die. One of the images kept returning. It was of Kali standing on a cliff edge, looking down at the precipice below, then back at Gaia as she edged closer. Gaia could see the panic in Kali's eyes as she neared, her machete poised and ready to strike. There was nowhere left for her to run, as she panted, beads of sweat dripping from her forehead. At the final moment, just before Gaia was about to attack, Kali turned and hurled herself into the abyss. Lurching forward, Gaia shouted something as she stared below, but all she saw was a canopy of trees, sprinkled with flecks of white snow. Then she heard the sound, a familiar noise she hadn't heard for some time, a sound that had haunted her for many years; the frenzied squeal of rats somewhere below the trees. The image was clear and vivid, as though it were playing in real time in her mind. Just when other thoughts flashed into her head, this scene would return as they moved on through the night.

Freya walked between Gaia and Aran, wrapped in a thick coat they had taken from the castle, Still she shivered though, as she battled with the bitter cold. Gaia stayed close behind, not wanting to let her sister from her sight. The glow of the moon was fading, creeping towards the horizon way beyond the trees. As they pressed ahead, Gaia knew dawn would be upon them soon. This was the time Kali would enter the castle, find the slain and imprisoned leaders, and realise Freya had gone. She would know who had taken her, and would act without hesitation, unleashing all the force she needed to hunt them down. Once she found them she would show no mercy.

Time was running out, and they needed to get to Ben's house soon if they were to make good their escape. Gaia didn't know where they would be going, but knew it would have to be somewhere remote and far from The Haven. Few places would be safe. Even on the run they would never be free from her, having to look over their shoulders at all times. Gaia knew it wasn't just a question of revenge, they would need to confront Kali and destroy her if they were ever to be free again.

They reached a bend in the river and saw the narrow path that led up to Ben's house. Aran pressed on leading them through an archway of overhanging trees and along a fenced pathway that approached the rear entrance to the garden. As they neared the gate he slowed, gesturing Gaia and Freya to stay back while he edged closer. He turned and whispered.

'Stay here, while I check it's safe.'

Opening the gate he crept towards the house, crouching low behind the wall, and disappearing out of sight around the corner. Gaia and Freya waited in silence, exchanging looks and the occasional half smile. The minutes dragged and Gaia could see Freya was becoming agitated. More and more time elapsed without any sign of Aran, and Gaia was also finding it difficult to disguise her concern.

'Where is he?' Freya whispered.

Gaia shook her head.

'I've no idea,' she replied.

'Should we go and see what's going on?' Freya said.

'No. We'll wait a bit longer.'

Moments later Aran came running from beyond the side of the house. From the expression on his face Gaia could see something was wrong. Reaching the gate, he leant over panting, and pausing a moment to catch his breath.

'What's wrong?' Gaia said.

'It's Ben! He's hurt. I found him collapsed in the passage way. He's bleeding badly,' Aran replied.

He turned and began to sprint back towards the house, Gaia and Freya following close behind. At the entrance to the front door Gaia noticed a trail of blood leading from the courtyard. The door was open and as they entered Ben was sprawled across the floor of the entrance hall. Clutching his side, his eyes were closed and face ashen white, a look of agony etched across it. Freya moved to his side first, crouching down and looking at the wound. She leant her head in close, listening, then looked up at the others.

'He's still breathing, but only just. We'll need to treat the wound and stop the bleeding. It looks like a stab wound.'

Ben opened his eyes. At first there was a look of panic on his face, then pursing his lips he tried to speak.

'Get some water,' Freya cried.

Aran ran into the kitchen and returned with a glass, passing it to Freya who lowered it to Ben's lips. He sipped at the water, with most of it dribbling down the side of his face and onto the floor. Freya paused for a moment, lifting the glass away as she leant in close and moved her ear towards his lips. Ben whispered something, and closed his eyes. Freya got to her feet.

'What did he say?' Gaia asked.

'He said, 'they're coming,' Freya replied.

They stared at each other in turn, each sharing the same grave expressions, looking to one another for words and answers. Gaia broke the silence.

'We need to get a move on, What should we do?'

'We'll head to the hills,' Aran answered.

'There's a place I know, a sanctuary. There's food and weapons there and it's sheltered. It'll give us a bit of time to work out what to do next.'

'And what about Ben? We can't just leave him here,' Gaia said.

'We'll take him with us,' he replied.

Gaia and Freya exchanged puzzled looks.

'He can't go anywhere in this condition. He can't move and we can't carry him,' Freya said.

'We'll take his Land Rover. It's in the courtyard. I can drive it,' he said.

'But he needs treatment soon or he'll die,' Freya said.

Aran paused, looking down at Ben. He lowered his voice to a whisper.

'If we stay here, we'll all die. If we take him with us, we can stop as soon as we think it's safe and treat him then.'

Freya shook her head.

'He won't last that long,' she said.

'Do you have a better idea?' Aran replied, his agitation clear.

'You're welcome to stay here with him, but whether we stay or go his chances aren't good, so at least this way we can save ourselves. It's what Ben would want us to do.'

Aran stared at the others, waiting for a response.

'He's right, Freya,' Gaia said.

Freya paused a moment and then nodded.

'Right, let's get our things together and go.'

Gaia ran upstairs to the bedroom and gathered the few possessions she had left behind. Running back downstairs, Aran had returned with a couple of small rucksacks, while Freya remained crouched on the floor beside Ben. She looked up as Gaia approached.

'Help me lift him,' Freya said.

Aran carried the bags outside while Gaia and Freya lifted Ben to his feet. He whimpered with pain as they lifted him, each of the sisters having to take the strain of his body on their shoulders. They shuffled towards the door, out into the courtyard, and towards the vehicle. Aran threw the bags into the back of the vehicle and helped the others as they laid Ben onto one of the rear seats. Freya climbed in alongside, crouching by him, holding his hand and comforting him. Aran and Gaia made their way around the front of the vehicle, Aran sitting in the driver's seat, with Gaia alongside. Staring down at the steering wheel, he shouted back to Freya.

'Where are the keys?'

Gaia sighed.

'You've really got this planned, haven't you?' she said.

Freya searched through Ben's pockets as he let out a wince and a groan. She waited, then continued to pick through each one.

'I can't find them,' she said.

'Shit!' Aran replied, banging the steering wheel.

'Wait here,' he said, climbing out of the Land Rover and heading back towards the house.

Gaia looked back at Freya and Ben. His breathing had become more laboured and he seemed to be slipping in and out of consciousness. Freya was talking to him, meaningless small talk, the kind of reassuring chatter that might keep him focused and awake. Gaia spoke.

'What do you think his chances are?'

Freya looked up at her and shook her head. They waited, and Gaia watched the entrance for Aran's return. Once again time seemed to slow, all the while Gaia cursing to herself under her breath. Eventually, he appeared, running across the courtyard and jumping into the driver's seat holding up a set of keys. He placed one in the ignition, pausing before turning it in the barrel, and grinding the starter motor over and over until the engine fired up. There was a roar and clatter as vibrations shuddered through the vehicle. He waited while the engine rumbled, listening until it reached a steady repetitive humming sound. Gaia looked on.

'Have you ever driven before?' she asked.

'A couple of times on the island.'

'Can you remember what to do?'

'Vaguely. Enough to get us out of here.'

Fumbling with the pedals at his feet, Gaia watched, making no attempt to disguise her anxiety. He crunched the Land Rover into gear, easing one foot onto one pedal, and the other off another. The vehicle jerked into motion and then began to creep forward. There was another jolt, which hurled Gaia against the dashboard. She glowered at Aran who twisted his face as the Land Rover spluttered forward.

'Are you sure you can drive this thing?' Gaia asked.

Aran barked out his reply, still juggling his concentration between the three pedals at his feet and the road ahead.

'Do you want to take over? I'm sure you could do much better.'

Gaia didn't respond, instead gazing at Aran's feet as they danced across the three metal levers beneath them.

'Be quiet and let me get on with it,' Aran said.

They lurched out of the courtyard and along a narrow side road leading to the main road ahead. The vehicle jerked and bumped as Aran tried to control the rickety, old machine. Gaia was struck by how alien the experience felt, locked in this metal box, surrounded by the noise of the engine, and the sickly smell of fumes. It was as though everything outside was just a series of passing images, like she was lost in a dream. The world was there, but somehow she no longer felt a part of it.

'Will this get us all the way to the hills?' Gaia asked.

'No,' Aran replied, his concentration still fixed on wrestling with the vehicle.

'The main roads might be passable, but as soon as we get near higher ground we'll have to abandon this and go on foot. The snow's too thick. It's why the leaders never use vehicles at this time of year, and why you had to walk from the village.'

Picking up pace and confidence, they were soon racing down the meandering, tree and hedge-lined roads. Aran had managed to put the lights of the vehicle on, and the bright beams stretched out in front of them, cutting through the silvery grey snow as the hedgerows flashed past. He drove with chaotic care, his urgency and nervousness on a par with his incompetence. A number of times he misjudged the angle of bends, and the back of the Land Rover slid away, and slowing, he would have to scramble to turn the wheel and gain control once more. Gaia's heart was pounding, the adrenalin of the escape and fear of an imminent crash both rushing through her veins. She had no idea where they were heading, and wasn't convinced Aran did either. However, she had no real choice and anywhere far away from The Haven and Kali would do for now.

Scanning the stretch of road ahead, Gaia searched for signs of danger, any movement, light, anything untoward. The first light of dawn was appearing, and the darkness was being seduced by a soft golden hue spreading across the sky. The roads ahead were still dark, the trees soaking up those first few beams of light and casting deep shadows ahead. They hurtled onward, alone in the wintery wilderness, still wrapped in the strange isolation of the machine, feeling protected and vulnerable at the same time. Gaia was wary and worried the noise and lights from the vehicle would be a magnet for any creatures still lurking in the night. Most hunted under the veil of darkness, but the long winter brought a desperation for food which saw more taking risks. Gaia knew they could never assume safety.

A sharp turn appeared and misjudging the angle of the bend, Aran panicked and they veered off the side of the road, hitting the embankment with a thud. The vehicle stalled and the engine died. There was a tense silence, and exchange of looks, broken only by the sound of the deep breathing of relief. Aran turned over the ignition, and it groaned but refused to spark into life. He repeated the action over and over, but still there was no sign of it starting. Ben lay in the back, fevered and delirious, but muttering words to Freya. His brow was covered in beads of cold sweat, and his head swayed from side to side as though he were trying to shake the fever from him. Leaning forward, Freya nestled her face close to his cheek as he grimaced with pain and tried to force out more fragments of words. His voice was strained and little more than a whisper.

'Tell him to wait, or he'll flood the engine,' he gasped.

Freya relayed the instructions to Aran, who waited, clinging to the key and counting in his head before trying again. Still the old, stubborn machine remained still and lifeless. There was another pause, and Aran tried again. As the tension mounted, Gaia looked out of the side window up and down the road. In the distance behind them, through the trees at the brow of the hill she noticed the flicker of lights. They were the briefest flashes bursting through the tiny gaps in the branches, but they were moving towards them, growing larger and brighter, and approaching at speed.

'They're coming. We need to get going now!' Gaia shouted.

Aran turned the ignition again, and the engine heaved and shrieked. Gaia and the others held their breath, willing it to start. All of a sudden there was a splutter and cough and the vehicle rattled into life and began to rumble again. Aran looked across at Gaia, his face filled with a mixture of panic and relief. Slipping the stick into gear, they pulled forward again, off the embankment and back onto the unbroken snow of the road. Building up speed, they snaked along the steady incline of the road weaving its way towards the hills. The engine screamed as it dragged them upwards, Aran pressing his foot hard against the pedal all the time. Eventually they reached the summit, and turning left slid down onto another main road, picking up pace again all the time. Meanwhile, Gaia kept scanning the road behind, looking for the lights, struggling to find them. For the briefest of moments she told herself they had gone, and they had lost them. Then she saw them again, emerging from a turn at the bottom of the hill, now flashing larger than ever.

'They're getting closer. We need to get a move on,' Gaia said.

Aran pressed his foot onto the pedal, trying to squeeze out more speed from the aged engine. Bit by bit, they felt the pace increase, and it now felt as though they were gliding down the hill, sliding across the snow like a giant iron sleigh. Aran was doing his best, but the more the speed increased the less control he had. They soon reached a worrying pace, with the Land Rover veering left and right across the road. Gaia pressed her arm against the dashboard, locking it to protect herself from the constant bumps and shakes. They were racing forward, the headlights offering false comfort and fake guidance through the dim light of dawn. Gaia's gaze switched back and forth between the danger ahead and the growing threat behind. Any sudden obstacle or change of direction could bring disaster. They both knew this all too well, and it was evident by the look of panic and intense concentration on Aran's face. Focusing on the winding road ahead, Aran pressed on, suppressing any panic, looking defiant and trying to focus on the power and movement of the Land Rover.

Meanwhile, in the back Freya cradled and comforted Ben, trying to shield him from the frequent bumps of the journey. She was still whispering words of comfort and distraction, now with an extra edge and urgency to her voice. Attentive and caring, she had tended to his wounds in a delicate manner, reassuring him despite the mounting tension and fear of the others. Gaia kept looking back through the rear window, seeing the lights of their pursuers more and more. They were still some distance behind, and no longer appeared to be gaining, but she was under no illusions about the threat. They had been seen and were being hunted and she felt certain they were from The Haven.

Aran remained focused on the road ahead, clutching the steering wheel, trying to anticipate and react to any shift and slide, maintaining the quickest speed he dared to go. He kept asking Gaia for updates, keen to know about the vehicle behind. He had no doubt they would be skilled drivers in a faster vehicle, and they would know the winding lanes surrounding The Haven well. These advantages would be difficult to overcome, and he knew they needed to lose them somehow, hoping a mistake would lead to an accident.

'Are they catching us?' he asked, unable to disguise his mounting panic.

'I don't think so. Not anymore,' Gaia replied.

'Shit! We have other problems now,' Aran cried.

Gaia turned and looked ahead to see a line of vehicles, and what looked like a barrier blocking the far end of the road. Several figures stood either side of the blockade, with a few more stood on the roofs of the vehicles. Aran slowed the Land Rover to a near stop, the engine clattering as it turned over and crept forward.

'What do we do now?' Gaia asked.

Ben stirred again, mumbling something, trying to muster what little energy he had to raise his voice. Freya placed her ear to his lips again and he whispered something. Freya sat up and called to the others.

'He says we should try to break through the hedge and drive across the field.'

Aran pulled the vehicle to a dead halt.

'He's joking right?' he said.

Gaia reached out and gripped Aran's hand on the wheel.

'Just do it, Aran. We haven't got time to argue and we won't get through that lot.'

Looking back, she saw the headlights of the vehicle following them as it came around the corner. It was almost upon them now, and was now no more than a few hundred metres away.

'Hurry up. They've almost caught us,' Gaia cried.

Aran pushed the pedal flat onto the floor, and the wheels began to screech and spin. There was a sudden jolt and they shot forward, hurtling towards the barricade, looming ever nearer as they sped through the snow. Gaia's arm was locked against the dashboard again, a mounting panic running through her as the barrier drew closer. Just as it seemed they were certain to crash into the blockade, Aran jerked the wheel to the right, and the Land Rover skidded across the road. After the briefest of pauses, he smashed his foot on the pedal again and they shot across a mound of earth and crashed through the hedge. Gaia flopped forward like a rag doll, her neck jerking backwards, banging her head against the headrest. All of a sudden, the Land Rover stuttered and slowed, the engine spluttering and threatening to stall. Aran crunched the stick into gear, and they pulled away and began to slide across the field. The vehicle rolled forward, skidding much less in this thicker virgin snow. Gaia kept looking back and could see the hunters were still in pursuit. They too had avoided the barrier, entered the field and were once again drawing closer. Gaia spoke, trying to mask the panic she felt.

'They're still following, but I don't think they're catching us.'

Aran continued to plough through the thick blanket of snow ahead, wrestling with the steering wheel, struggling to keep control. He blurted a reply, his voice shuddering with the jolts of the Land Rover.

'I'm trying my best with this thing, but I've no idea where this field will take us. We can't out-run them. How far are they now?'

Gaia could see they were continuing to gain, and were closer now than at any point.

'They're still some distance. Just keep looking ahead and drive.'

The cat and mouse continued across the wide open field of snow. Gaia could see the pursuers were edging closer all the time, but continued to feed lies of reassurance to Aran. The last thing she wanted was panic, and she could see he was fighting just to keep them moving at any kind of pace. Once he knew the hunters were upon them, he could lose concentration and control. Then it would be over. She told herself they just had to keep moving, then they stood a chance, though this was dwindling all the time. The Land Rover was old, the engine temperamental, and it felt as though it could break into pieces at any moment. Gaia felt threatened and unsafe within this machine. She was helpless; her destiny in hands of fate and others, and would have much preferred to be on foot and undercover of the trees.

A wooden gate appeared, and without any time to react Aran burst through it. The sound of the gate smashing against the front of the vehicle was deafening, and the shudder throughout rocked them all. Ben let out a cry in agony as he bounced into the air. Freya placed her hands on his cheek, pressing her body against his to prevent the shock and pain from any further jolts. Managing to maintain some control now, Aran slid the vehicle onto another winding road. They surged forward, still with the hunters following and gaining on them all the time.

Suddenly, something shot out from the hedges by the side of road and flashed past Gaia's eyes. A split second later there was a huge thud against the side of the Land Rover, and they slid sideways as Aran fought to keep it under control. Gaia screamed and Freya lurched forward crashing into Ben who also let out a startled cry.

'What was that?' Freya shouted.

The Land Rover had stopped again, though the engine was still running. Gaia looked out of the passenger window, staring all around, but could see nothing. Then Aran hollered in horror.

'What the hell!'

Instinct took over, and plunging his foot hard onto the pedal, they screeched forward, arching the steering wheel to a sharp right. They skidded across the road, as more darting shadows flashed past the windows. As the Land Rover steadied and began to move along the road again, Gaia caught a glimpse of something in the side mirror. The other vehicle was close behind, and would be upon them in a matter of seconds. Scouring the road for signs of anything else, she peered deep into the shadows, the silhouettes of the creatures still flashing in her mind. There was nothing but the white wilderness, dense tree lined roads, and the approaching lights of their pursuers. They were almost upon them now, and in a matter of seconds could pull alongside.

Then it appeared without warning, a huge, black silhouette hurtling from behind a hedgerow. Its mouth was open, the white daggers in its jaws poised, back arched and ready to pounce. Gaia let out a scream.

'Stop!' she cried.

Aran slammed his foot on the brakes, the Land Rover sliding to a standstill. They both turned and looked through the rear window, while Freya jumped up onto one of the seats. Looking on, they watched as the scene behind unfolded. The hunter's vehicle had jerked to the left and skidded across the field, careering towards the hedge and tipping onto its side. The front wheel was spinning, the headlights still blazing powerful beams ahead. Caught in the shaft of light stood the huge silhouette of a black dog, swinging its head back, and opening its mouth to reveal its razor sharp teeth and large slavering jaws. The beast let out a terrifying howl, then pounced onto the side of the upturned vehicle. Battering its head against the doors, blow after blow, the creature hammered and ripped at the metal frame. There were more flashes in the light, as shadows began to dart from all directions, and a steady stream of rabid beasts lunged from beyond the hedges. Each one encircled the metal tomb of their victims, before smashing their bodies and heads against the stricken vehicle in a frenzied attempt to get to the people inside.

Aran looked at Gaia in alarm.

'We need to get out of here, before they come after us.'

Gaia nodded, as Aran jumped round in his seat and tried to move the Land Rover forward. They could hear the screeching sound of the wheels, trapped and spinning in the snow, mingled with the howling and frenzied commotion of the attack behind. The tyres were struggling to get any grip, stuck in a deep patch of snow, and squealing in desperation as Aran tried to break them free. Gaia and Freya continued to watch, as the beasts continued their onslaught on the hunters. They had broken through both the side and rear doors now, and their triumphant howls were now mixed with the desperate screams of the victims. One of them was dragged into the road, gripped in the jaws of a dog, before being swamped by a pack of the creatures who tore them apart.

Still Aran struggled at the wheel, pumping the pedals and listening to the screeches. Then Gaia noticed one of the beasts pause, raise its head, and look back at them. They had heard the sound of the screaming engine and tyres above the melee of their own attack. The few seconds of hesitation by the beast, seemed to pause time, and Gaia had the strange sensation she was watching in slow motion. She could feel its growing realisation, and watched in horror as the dog began to move their way. Glaring in panic at Aran, she cried out as he was yanking at the gear stick and stamping on the pedals.

'They're coming, get us out of here quick!'

'I'm trying!' he shrieked.

'High gear!'

It was the voice of Ben crying from the back. Aran looked at Gaia, his eyes burning with panic, before switching the gear stick and turning over the engine again. There was a thud against the side of the passenger window, then another, the Land Rover rocking back and forth with successive waves of attacks from the beast. Gaia looked in horror as foaming red saliva sprayed against the window. More creatures had followed the first and now several were smashing themselves against the vehicle, trying to break in and reach them. She caught sight of the jaws of one of the dogs, its head swinging from side to side. The creature was in a frenzy, hammering the side window with a string of fierce blows, its frantic growls and snarls merged in a cacophony of terror. All the while, the engine continued to scream and groan as Aran continued his desperate attempt to drag the vehicle free.

There was another series of thuds against the rear doors as more dogs set upon them. Such was the power and ferocity of the beasts, the Land Rover began to lurch more and more with each wave of assault. Gaia looked at Freya who had her arm over Ben, her instinct to shield and protect him from the onslaught. Aran was still trying to gain any kind of grip and movement in the snow while the vehicle rocked and swayed. Gaia was sure it would tip at any moment, and knew if it happened, everything would be over. Their only hope was to get the wheels moving. There were too many dogs to fight, and they would soon be overpowered if they left the vehicle. Unless Aran could get them moving, it was only a matter of time before the dogs broke through and reached them.

There was a sudden jerk of the vehicle, different to the hammering, and the Land Rover began to move and slide. The engine screeched, and the back end slid from side to side as they edged forward. As the wheels of the vehicle took hold, they began to pull away and the pounding of the dogs eased. They sped across the remainder of the field and through another gate, and were soon weaving back down the road. Gaia looked across at Aran who was focused on the road ahead, his face almost paralysed with shock and relief. She looked out of the rear window to see three large creatures still in pursuit. At first they appeared to be gaining, but the Land Rover was picking up pace all the time and soon began to pull away. The creatures began to fade into the distance, the carnage left behind, dissolving in the dim light of the burgeoning dawn.

Gaia still caught occasional flashes of light from the headlights of the other vehicle, but the lights grew smaller, the flashes less frequent. Eventually, they disappeared. No one spoke as they raced along the narrow country roads, their silence broken only by the rumble of the engine and thuds of bumps in the road. Gaia and Aran were gathering their thoughts, trying to regain some composure, while Freya concentrated on nursing Ben, whispering and reassuring him, on her own personal mission to ensure he survived. Each was left to fill their own emptiness, pondering what might have been, knowing how close they had come. Aran was lost in thought, intense with concentration, his eyes fixed on the road, while his mind remained elsewhere.

'Have they gone?' he said.

'I think we've lost them,' Gaia replied.

Freya looked up and shuffled away from Ben, lifting herself onto one of the seats that lined each side of the rear. Leaning her head forward, she rested it on Gaia's seat, just by the shoulder of her sister.

'I thought they had us,' she said.

Still anxious, Aran gazed in the rear view mirror, checking to see the road behind.

'We'll keep going for a while. We need to put some distance between us and The Haven. There'll be more leaders to follow and I've no doubt Kali will be with them. We can be sure of it,' Aran said.

'What if she was in the one behind?' Freya asked.

'If she was, she's dead. There's no way anyone could survive that attack,' Gaia replied.

Aran shook his head.

'Let's not get our hopes up. Kali's more likely to still be at The Haven. I don't think they'll have known Freya had escaped when they went after Ben. They probably went looking for us, but I doubt they knew we had broken in.'

Gaia looked puzzled.

'How can you be so sure?' she said.

'I can't. I'm just saying we shouldn't jump to any conclusions. The last thing we want is us convincing ourselves Kali is dead.'

Gaia sensed the irritation in Aran's voice, the tension from their ordeal now spilling over.

'You're right. We should never assume Kali's dead,' she replied.

There was a pause before Freya spoke.

'They will know what's happened now though, and we need to keep running as far away as we can.'

Gaia felt the warm breath of her sister against her cheek as she turned to look down at Ben. His face was ashen white, eyes closed, wrapped in sleep. There was a faint movement from his chest, signs he was still clinging to life. Freya caught Gaia's gaze, and gave her sister a gentle smile. Gaia noticed her sister's eyes, and for the first time realised how similar they were to her own. On the island she had only ever seen hatred and suspicion in them, her expressions so often cold and clinical. That had gone now, replaced by a tenderness and warmth, matched by the care she had shown Ben.

'How is he?' Gaia asked.

'He seems settled for now, but we need to get him somewhere soon. We have to treat the wounds,' Freya said.

As she spoke the words, her face painted a contrasting picture. She looked at Gaia as she uttered the reassurances, frowning and shaking her head, making sure Ben had no chance of capturing the true meaning behind her words. Gaia caught her sister's knowing look, and leant over whispering to Aran.

'It looks bad. We need to find some place safe and soon.'

Aran slowed the Land Rover easing it to a halt. He turned and stared down at Ben.

'What are we going to do when we reach the forest?' Gaia said.

Freya looked at Aran.

'You're the one with all the plans,' she said.

Aran thought for a while.

'We have to keep going until we get there. If we stop anywhere on the way, they're bound to find us. We're driving through fresh snow that's never been touched. We may as well lay a trail of signs telling them where we are.'

They all exchanged worried looks, before Aran continued.

'I'll drive as far as we can then we'll set off on foot. They'll send others after us and they'll be in vehicles and faster ones than this. We can't afford to waste much more time. Once we get to the forest I know the way to the cave from there.'

'Is it far? We won't be able to carry him,' Freya said.

'It's quite far, but we'll make a stretcher from branches. There's rope in the back we can use. Don't worry, we won't abandon him.'

Gaia looked at Freya who shrugged.

'I don't think any of us has any better ideas,' Gaia said.

She looked down at Ben and back at Freya.

'What are his chances?' she whispered.

Freya checked if Ben was asleep, then frowned, shook her head, leant forward towards them and whispered.

'He'll be lucky if he regains consciousness. He's lost an awful lot of blood. The wound needs cleaning and stitching. I've tried to stop the flow as best I can, but it isn't looking good.'

Gaia watched: shallow and slow, his breathing seeming even weaker now. She had seen this before, the same look and colouring. These were the moments before death, when the body began to shut down and the soul gave up. It was the time of letting go, when life slipped away. She had seen very few turn things around from this point. Some clawed their way back to the living in one last defiant fight, but they succumbed eventually. Ben was older, weaker and unlikely to survive. It was only a matter of time. A pang of sorrow shot through her, feelings of emptiness and remorse. This was something she had not felt often, emotions she had been taught to no longer feel. She had been desensitised to death. It was an outcome not a loss. She gazed at his face as he lay helpless, still clinging to the fragments of life he had left. It was then she realised how little she knew about him. Here was a man who had sacrificed his life for them - strangers - people he owed nothing. They had brought him nothing but danger, and he had asked for nothing in return. They owed him so much.

'Does he have anyone else?' Gaia asked.

'No,' Aran replied.

'I noticed some photos at his house. He must have had a wife and child at some point,' Gaia said.

'Yes, his wife was murdered by his daughter,' Aran replied.

Gaia and Freya both looked at Aran.

'Murdered!' Freya cried.

'Yes. I told you Ben had more reason than most to hate The Community,' he said, pausing for a moment before continuing.

'They took his daughter from him when she was young, took her to one of the centres to be trained as a leader. Years later she returned to The Haven. Ben's wife found out and approached her, telling her who she was and begging her to return. But she'd turned by then. She'd been brainwashed into thinking The Community's way and been told her parents had abandoned her. She was about to be put forward to become a leader.'

Gaia watched Aran, noticing an increasing edginess as he spoke.

'There was a lot of bitterness at what there daughter thought was her rejection from her parents and she was desperate to impress those she now considered her own. The daughter told her mother she was a traitor and that she was betraying The Community by trying to encourage her to leave.'

Aran paused, as he negotiated a tricky bend in the road.

'The daughter showed no mercy, and reported her mother. She was tried and sentenced to death for treason. The daughter offered to perform the execution.'

Aran cleared his throat, before continuing.

'She slit her mother's throat in the town square in front of the crowd. It was a very public showing of her allegiance to her new world. They forced Ben to attend and watch. He was told it should be seen as a warning. Ben never got over it.'

Gaia gasped in horror.

'How could anyone do that to their mother?' she said, though part of her understood. It was a dreadful act and the ultimate betrayal by the daughter, but this was how The Community worked. It was how they made you think and was how they had been programmed too. This was the way of The Community, turning man against brother, daughter against mother, until the whole idea of family existed no more. To them, no bond was greater than The Community. They were all that mattered. Sensing her thoughts, Aran spoke.

'We know as well as anyone, Gaia. The young have all their independent thoughts stripped away from them. We're brainwashed to become their puppets and to serve. The daughter was committed more than most. Find the right mind and condition it and they can turn anyone. Ben vowed to avenge his wife's death, but he wasn't stupid. He played by their rules, but there were those that knew what he was planning in secret. That was one of the reasons we knew he could be trusted.'

There was a silence as Aran thought for a moment, pondering what he was about to say next.

'Did you look at the photos in the house closely?' he said.

Gaia shook her head.

'Not that closely. What was there to see?' she replied.

Aran waited, studying the faces of both Gaia and Freya, wondering if the realisation would come.

'If you'd looked closer, and knew what you were looking for, you might have noticed something about his daughter,' he said.

Gaia and Freya exchanged puzzled looks.

'What about her?' Gaia asked.

'You know who she is,' he replied.

By now it was beginning to sink in for Freya, but Gaia was taking longer. Perhaps part of her knew, but the other was in denial. She looked at Aran with the same puzzled expression. Then he said the word, uttered the name.

'Kali.'

No-one replied. They didn't have to. Gaia was horrified, vexed with herself for not realising sooner. She knew Kali and what she was capable of, but never thought even she could plunge to depths so low. It took a special kind of deranged evil to murder a parent, even in a world where family ties had been destroyed. She understood Ben's desire for vengeance, as she felt the same desire to avenge Kali's torture of herself. Even more she wanted Kali to pay for the abuse of her sister. Her instinct told her she wanted Kali to pay for her cruelty even more now. Something else gnawed away at Gaia though, a deep feeling of shame at how she was thinking. This was the problem with the new world. Revenge and hatred were the only emotions people knew anymore, even when it was born of love. The Community had stripped away their decency and compassion in the quest for order and control. Gaia had asked herself many questions as she had recovered in the village. Some she asked many times. Without feeling, without love was their any purpose to life other than survival? What was life without living?

Revving the engine, Aran broke the uncomfortable silence.

'We need to go,' he said.

They set off towards the hills again, the sun peering above the treetops, the sky clear and blue. Only the faintest image of the moon remained, a ghost moon. Soon they reached a crossroads, turning left onto a myriad of winding country roads snaking towards the forest in the hills. Aran drove on into the morning for miles. He was cautious and steady, avoiding a few near misses with collapsed trees. At one point they passed the carcass of a dog, lain on an embankment by the side of the road. It was uncovered by snow and could only have been dead a matter of hours, probably perishing in the night. It's throat had been ripped out, either by another dog or something larger, a predator. None of them spoke of what it might have been, not wanting to contemplate thoughts of anything more menacing than the dogs.

They drove further than any of them had expected, passing row upon row of monotonous fields, hedgerows of white, and a sprinkling of abandoned buildings. They crossed bridges built of ancient stone, forged and shaped with metal from the time before The Poison. There were signs by the roadside with mysterious names of once populated villages, now deserted or claimed with pockets of the Others. This was the old order, the structure of days gone by, the time when pleasure was purpose, when things were traded, and people sold their skills to survive. The Poison had reset society, forced a new focus upon those who had chosen to ignore the inevitable march to destruction for years. The signs were there, but no-one read them. The Community's life was built on this fear, teaching them that what humanity had lost, the world had gained. Nature always found a way to survive, but people forgot that. They believed they were greater, and more powerful. They had conquered nature with their machines, transforming it into wondrous things with imagination, skill, and creativity. They became driven by profit and greed, and lost control. They were told that only the strongest survive. It was the evolutionary law, and not even humanity could break it. They tried, but nature broke them.

Gaia remained watchful, checking the mirrors for anything behind and looking far into the road ahead. She was nervous of any movement, knowing an attack was unlikely, but taking nothing for granted. The Land Rover rattled on, the only sound in the white desert of silence. They would be heard and would attract attention, but hoped that whatever heard them, moved on. Few creatures would be so bold to attack in daylight, but there would be pockets of the Others who might. They had to keep moving. As long as they didn't stop until the cover of the forest they should be safe. All the while, they were leaving a trail that could be followed with ease. The snow was fresh and vehicles rare, but it was a risk they had to take. The forest was far, and abandoning the vehicle would mean leaving Ben too.

Freya drip fed water to her patient, who on occasion would mumble something, still delirious and slipping in and out of consciousness. His breathing had steadied and Freya had managed to stem most of the blood loss, but he remained weak, still clinging to the last few threads of life. Freya continued her vigil, focused and determined, refusing to be defeated. She embraced the preservation of those lives that mattered with the same passion and efficiency with which she took it from those that threatened. Gaia knew there was only a glimmer of hope, but if Ben could stay alive until they reached the forest there was a chance. There were trees, the bark of which could be ground and pressed, and the sap used as medicine. They could also use fire to seal the wound. Ben would need rest and plenty of it, time to recover, food and warmth to help build his strength. Gaia knew there was little chance of any of this. They were fighting the inevitable. Survival at all costs was their core instinct, even when all logic told them it was futile. Gaia looked back at Freya and caught her eye. She smiled.

'You make a better nurse than a killer. It suits you. How is he doing?'

'Surprisingly well. He's stabilised a little. It's still touch and go, but things look better now than earlier. He's stronger than we thought, and he doesn't want to give up. I can tell.'

Gaia nodded.

'Maybe it's Kali that's keeping him going,' she said.

'Well that's something we all have in common then,' Freya replied.

Gaia turned and stared at the road ahead, slipping into a half trance, mesmerised by the monotony and rhythmic hum of the journey. Her caution and fear remained, helping her fight the urge to sleep, but still feeling herself drifting at times. Her eyes would become heavy, her head would droop, then she would awaken with a jerk, looking all around, searching for danger. Aran leant his body over to hers.

'Don't fight it, Gaia. Get some rest,' he whispered.

'You too, Freya. There's little more you can do for him now.'

Freya stared down at Ben, then moved forward and put her hand on her sister's shoulder. Gaia looked behind and kissed her sister's hand.

'Are you sure?' Gaia said.

Aran's voice was tender and reassuring, his smile warm and comforting.

'I can rest when we get to the cave. It's no good us all being exhausted.'

Reaching out, she touched Aran's hand as it rested on the wheel. She left it there for a while, before he looked across at her and she let it fall. Closing her eyes, she allowed herself to succumb to sleep's spell. The motion of the vehicle and its robotic sway conducted the rhythm of her dreams as they crept further into the wilds of the north. The hum and rattle of the engine washed over her, smothering both Gaia and her sister in a deep blanket of sleep.

Gaia had a dream, not linear, but more a patchwork of flashing images, a montage of recent memories melting into one. There was the face of Ben covered in blood, and her frenzied attacker in the house in the hills. His mad eyes bore holes through Gaia as he squeezed her neck, crushing the life from her body. She saw images of the dogs, with thick saliva hanging from their jaws. Kali and Freya both appeared, the former laughing while she reached out a hand to save Gaia from falling off a cliff edge. Her sister stood behind Gaia looking on, nursing a baby wrapped in her arms, staring into its eyes, her expression a mixture of love and hatred. She dreamt of the rooms in the castle, the chambers of silent despair. The girl was there, hidden on the edge of the shadows, her legs hunched close to her chest as she rocked back and forth on the bed. She heard the desperate cries and moans, and tasted something acrid burning the back of her throat. The words of the girl's journal flashed into her head - *'She came later, told me The Community was proud of me, and that some day I would be rewarded.'* The images were vivid, so real Gaia could feel waves of emotion rushing through her - fear, horror, fury. It was as though she was walking through her past again, watching but unable to act, willing her legs to move and run away. Then there was a voice, a whisper at first, but growing in volume all the time. They kept chanting a single word, over and over. Gaia tried to hear what it was, but it was always just beyond her reach. She could see a figure mouthing it, but couldn't read their lips. Just when she thought she had it, the images dissolved and she was left with the lingering despair of not knowing what they had said. Her mind told her it was important and that she had to find it, but at the same time it played tricks with her and left it hanging. If only she could find the word.

14

They reached the forest and followed the main road for several miles, before Aran took a sharp turn and headed along a narrow track. The trees either side were packed close together, intertwined with bushes and undergrowth resulting from years of neglect. They pushed further on under the dense cover of the overhanging branches, the terrain becoming more and more uneven. The Land Rover bounced over bumps and obstacles hidden beneath the deep snow. Aran struggled to keep control, while Freya tried with increasing frustration to protect Ben. Gaia gazed out of the window at the wilderness beyond, scanning the forest for danger, still edgy after their escape and the attack of the dogs. She knew they were unlikely to encounter any dogs this time of day, but there were many other creatures lurking. She recalled the spiders in the woods when they fled the island, remembering how close they came to death.

'Is there much further to go?' Freya asked.

'We're almost there,' Aran replied.

Soon they came to a fork in the road with one route leading down a steep incline whilst the other headed higher up into the forest. Aran slowed, as though he was contemplating which direction to take, then followed the high road. Gaia noticed his expression, and felt sure there was something he was hiding.

'Do you know where we're going?' she said.

'Yes. We'll stop at the top of this hill and take it on foot from there,' he replied.

'You don't know, do you?'

Aran slammed on the brakes and both Gaia and he were thrust forward in their seats. He turned to face her, his face raging with anger.

'Do you want to take us there?'

Gaia didn't respond, wanting to bite back, but stopping herself and looking away instead. She knew there was little point enflaming the situation and Aran was right, she knew no better. They had to trust him, however unsure he seemed. They drove on in silence for a few more minutes, then Aran pulled over and turned off the engine. He paused a moment, staring into the forest; the only sound was their breathing, together almost in unison. Gaia looked back at Freya who lay by Ben's side staring up at Aran waiting for him to speak.

'What now?' Gaia asked.

Shaking himself from his thoughts, Aran replied.

'We'll hide the vehicle amongst those trees, cover it with branches as best we can. Then we need to make a stretcher for Ben. Are there some more blankets in the back?'

Freya rummaged through the assorted junk that littered the floor, looking under the seats either side.

'Yes, there's some here. There's also a shovel, axe, and a few other things that should be useful. How far will we have to walk?'

'The cave's a few miles from here, no more than an hour,' Aran replied.

'It isn't going to be easy carrying him over this kind of terrain,' Gaia said.

'We'll take turns and go easy. We don't have much choice. It's either that or leave him here,' he said.

'That's not what I meant. You know we can't leave him,' Gaia replied.

Freya scowled at them both, as Aran opened the door and stepped from the vehicle, walking a few yards away and stretching his arms in the air. Gaia climbed down from the passenger side, pausing a moment to take a deep breath of the crisp, clean, fresh air. It felt good to taste it again. It was so cold sharpness burned her lungs, but it was welcome after the bitter, smoke filled atmosphere of The Haven. She surveyed the area, listening deep into the forest, but there was only a deafening silence. Walking round to the back of the vehicle, she opened the rear doors and helped Freya to get out. Together they searched for two strong, straight branches and fashioned a makeshift stretcher using rope and one of the blankets. Meanwhile Aran gathered together their bags and packed away anything they could carry that would be of use. He lay on the stretcher to test for comfort and whether it was likely to hold Ben's weight.

'Let's hope it holds. Ben's a good bit heavier than you,' Gaia replied.

'It'll hold,' Freya said.

Aran drove the Land Rover behind a wall of trees, covering it with a mixture of fallen branches and snow, leaving a gap at the rear to lift Ben onto the stretcher. Gaia stared at his pallid features as they lifted him down. It was difficult to know whether he was sleeping or simply clinging to life. He showed no signs of responding or waking up, and they managed to lower him onto the stretcher with ease. Once they were sure he was secure and wrapped in sufficient blankets, they concealed the rear of the vehicle and set off on foot.

Aran led them along the edge of the road, until they came to a gap in the trees which took them deep into the still and silent forest. Aran walked ahead with Freya close behind carrying the front of the stretcher and Gaia at the rear. At first the stretcher was manageable, but soon became an ever increasing weight as they continued under cover of the trees. It wasn't long before Gaia began to sense an intense burning sensation in her arms, and her hands started to feel numb.

'Can we swap for a moment?' Gaia asked.

They stopped, Freya remaining faced forward, standing almost like a guard to attention, waiting in silence.

'Sure, I'll take over now,' Aran replied, as he moved to the back and took the stretcher from Gaia.

'It's heavier than it looks,' he said.

'It's probably best if we swap places, Freya, then I can lead the way and you can watch Ben.'

Aran and Freya swapped places, with Freya still not uttering a word. They set off again, snaking through the trees, up and down small ravines, often catching the roots and undergrowth that lay hidden under the snow. On several occasions, both Aran and Gaia lost their footing with Gaia slipping and stumbling to the ground. Freya was the only one that seemed immune to the obstacles, as though she had some sixth sense which allowed her to detect and avoid them.

They reached the brow of a hill and a break in the trees pausing a moment for a rest and to take in the breath-taking view. The sun hung low in the blue sky, casting a hazy golden glow across the tree-lined hills beyond. The white snow smothering the tops of the trees looked like an undulating blanket of cloud. Gaia stared at the others, each captivated by the scene, puffing icy vapour from their mouths with every breath.

'How did they not see what they had?' Gaia said.

'I know, it's hard to believe they could have been so stupid,' Aran replied.

'No, it isn't. It doesn't surprise me at all.' Freya said.

'Kali gave me a book in the castle, a gift for good behaviour. She told me it would open my eyes and show me the arrogance of the old society. She was right.'

Freya sighed and took a deep breath.

'It was about the old religions, full of stories of gods and goddesses, of plagues and destruction, of betrayal and revenge. They created gods that cast us in their own image, and gifted us this paradise, letting us rule over everything - land, sea, air, plants, animals. Earth was our domain.'

She paused a moment before continuing.

'They named it Mother Earth, and we were the keepers of the keys, the custodians. But we threw it all away, and before we realised what we were doing, it was too late.'

Gaia and Aran were shocked by Freya's outburst. She was someone of few words who preferred to act, but her words were coupled with a clear passion and emotion, her voice almost cracking as she spoke.

'We still have hope, Freya. We can build something better,' she said.

'You can bring your child up differently, away from The Community and the problems of the past. We can teach our children to love and respect everything and everyone around us.'

Freya moved away from them, taking a few steps forward. She stopped, lifting her head and scanning the view.

'First we must teach them to survive. Love and respect are for those with the luxury of comfort and time. We have neither, and nor will they. We just have to keep going, running away, always looking over our shoulder,' Freya said.

'I know it isn't going to be easy, but we can't keep running. We have to end this once and for all,' Gaia replied.

Aran nodded and moved beside the two sisters as he replied.

'We're not alone. There are others who want the same. If we gather together we can build something and put a stop to The Community.'

Freya turned, and shook her head.

'I want no part in it. I'll help you kill Kali, but as soon as I know she's dead I'm moving on. You're welcome to join me, but you'll need to find someone else to be a part of your plans.'

Freya gazed down at Ben, scanning the blanket for any sign of breathing. A look of concern swept across her face.

'Put the stretcher down!' she cried.

Lowering the stretcher to the ground, Freya crouched down beside Ben, placing her head next to his mouth. She sat up, and looked at the others.

'He's barely breathing now. We need to get him somewhere warm and sheltered where I can tend to him. I may be able to find some of the medicines I need in the forest, though it isn't going to be easy with the snow so deep. How much further is it?'

'It's not too far now. It should be down this hill and at the end of the valley. Maybe a couple more miles,' Aran replied.

'Should be?' Freya said.

Aran frowned.

'I've never been to this cave before, but Hannah gave me a map when we were in the village. I'm sure this is where we're supposed to be.'

'Let's get a move on then. He may not last that long,' Freya replied, jumping to her feet and grabbing the end of the stretcher.

Aran took hold of the other end and lifting together they continued onward down the slope of the hill. The going was even more awkward as they were struggling to keep a firm foothold. Gaia walked alongside the stretcher, trying to provide some extra support, but it was clear both Freya and Aran were tiring.

'Let me take over now. You've done enough, you need a rest,' Gaia said.

'No, I can manage,' her sister replied.

'Listen. I'm not taking no for an answer. Let me take the stretcher now. Aran, hold, it there.'

Aran pulled to a halt, the stretcher poised at a difficult angle. Gaia glared at Freya making it clear she had no choice.

'Don't move until she hands me that stretcher, Aran,' Gaia said.

Freya sighed and shaking her head shuffled round allowing her sister to take the two ends of the branches. As they reached the bottom of the ravine, Aran stopped.

'Do you hear that?' he said.

Gaia listened, at first hearing nothing but the gentle rustling of the breeze dancing with the forest, then a sound floated through the treetops. It was the faintest of sounds, but it was growing louder. It was voices, high pitched, filled with fear and panic. They were heading in their direction. Freya gave Gaia a stern look and began to scan the area for somewhere to lay down Ben. Spotting a gap in some bushes nearby, she shouted at the others.

'Over there in those bushes. Put Ben down and we'll hide behind. We won't be able to out-run them with the stretcher.'

They scurried over to the bushes, slid Ben through the gap and crunched down low behind them and waited. The voices were only a matter of seconds away now. Gaia couldn't make out the words, but there were screeches and hollers and it was clear they were running. As they approached Gaia heard one of them, though she still couldn't see them beyond the bush. It was the voice of a boy.

'They're still coming. It's no use we'll need to fight them.'

A young girl responded, the terror and hysteria clear in her voice.

'No. We can't. We won't stand a chance.'

'We can't escape. They're too fast and I won't split up and leave you,' the boy replied, sounding desperate.

There was another voice, a different boy this time.

'It's too late, they're here!'

Gaia heard a familiar sound, one she hadn't heard for some time, but it was unmistakable. A shiver of dread ran through her. She looked across at the others, seeing they had heard it too. Aran stared at them both, words unnecessary, pleading with his eyes for some sort of response. It was Freya who answered as she always did, not with words, but with her actions. Jumping to her feet, she pulled out a machete and ran past the bushes and towards the voices. Without thought Gaia and Aran followed, weapons drawn, and poised to attack.

They were about a hundred metres away, a group of five spread out with the rats upon them already. One lay pinned to the ground with two rats ripping at them, the razor sharp teeth Gaia had seen so many times, head's flailing from side to side. She made for them first, and with two swift blows had slain the attackers. She stared down into the face of a young boy, his face splattered with blood, his eyes open and full of terror. He was gasping for air, unable to speak. Gaia scanned him for injuries, seeing his throat was fine, though his hands were lacerated and his face had several bites.

'You'll live. Now wait here.'

She turned and ran towards another victim, fleeing into the trees, followed by two more of the rodents. Freya was to her right, only metres away, her machete plunged in the back of one of the rats, her knee pressed down on its head. She was staring down at it, checking to be sure it was dead. A boy and a girl were standing watching over her, the girl with an expression of disbelief, the boy with his head in his hands weeping. Meanwhile Aran was crouched by the side of another boy, the body of a rat lying alongside, covered in blood with jaws gaping and chest heaving, the last few gasps of air before dying.

Gaia sped after them, jumping over the branches and undergrowth, weaving and darting through the trees. She was gaining on the rats all the time, noticing the boy out in front was managing to keep a good distance between them. He was fast and agile, and it was clear he had no appetite for fighting the creatures and hoped to somehow get away. One of the rats stopped, and turning noticed Gaia in pursuit. It paused, it's black eyes peering back at her. Gaia didn't stop, knowing its intent, but not wanting to give the creature any edge. She hurtled towards it, machete drawn, as it began to run for her now. Only seconds separated them, the rodent leaping through the air like an arrow, bearing its jaws, shooting towards the target of her throat. Her instinct and training took over, all those hours of practice and programming, as Gaia arched her body to the side and whipped her arm across separating the head of the rat from its body.

Without pause she kept running, still in pursuit of the remaining rodent. The boy was showing no signs of tiring and was putting a safe distance between him and the creature. Gaia had never seen anyone run at such a pace, darting through the obstacles in his way with such skill. The rat continued to chase, unaware of Gaia on its tail. She was gaining, but it was fast and lithe, and she knew it would not be easy to catch. Though clinical in her response, the attack of the other rat had cost her vital seconds. Knowing the element of surprise was now unlikely, Gaia let out a holler in the hope of distracting the creature. At first it didn't appear to notice, but after another louder call, it began to slow and looked back at her. The boy also slowed and turned, watching as the creature changed direction and headed towards Gaia.

As with the other attack, Gaia didn't pause for thought, simply allowing her training to take over. With smooth, balletic precision she repeated the same manoeuvre as before. Waiting for the perfect movement to shift her body, and timing the sweep of her blade in a perfect motion. The blade of the machete sliced through the neck of the rat, the head falling a few metres away while the body continued in its trajectory smashing into the ground. This time she stopped running and gazed back at the severed body and head oozing crimson red blood onto the fresh white snow. The body flickered in its final, desperate spasms, while the eyes of the rat glowered at her. She gave the faintest of grins and whispered under her breath.

'Welcome back. I've missed you.'

Shifting her gaze through a gap in the trees and into the forest ahead, she saw the startled boy. He stood still, paralysed by his ordeal. Gaia began to walk towards him, wiping the blade of machete on the snow, before placing it back in its sheath. The boy remained still as Gaia approached, his body was quivering in fear, but she could see in his face the fear easing and his growing sense of relief. She spoke, her voice a soft, reassuring whisper.

'It's over now. Come with me and we'll find your friends.'

Reaching her hand out she took his arm and led him back through the trees to the opening where Aran and Freya were tending to the others. The group of four were standing huddled together, with shell-shocked expressions, covered in blood. Freya had her hand on the shoulder of a young girl, comforting her, while Aran was speaking to the others. As Gaia and the boy approached, the girl looked up and ran towards them, hurling her arms around him.

'You're safe! I thought I'd lost you,' the girl cried.

They remained wrapped together, as though they never wanted to part. They kissed, and Gaia walked on towards the others, leaving them to savour their joy and relief, together alone. Gaia put her arm over Freya's shoulder and Aran looked up and smiled.

'Just like old times, eh?'

'I guess so,' Gaia replied, smiling at the others in the group. They were all a similar age, probably in their early teens, little more than kids. She stared into the eyes of one of the boys. They were a bright, emerald green.

'Who are they?' she said.

'A group of others. They say their settlement was attacked by dogs a few weeks ago. The adults were killed and they've been on the road ever since,' Aran replied.

Gaia caught the eye of one of the boys, and gave a reassuring smile.

'Don't worry. You'll be safe for now. Have you any idea where you're going?'

The boy shook his head.

'We're been heading towards a village on the edge of the forest. Our elders used to trade with them. We thought they would take us in.'

'Do you know where it is?' Gaia asked.

'Not exactly, but we know it isn't far. Once we reach the lower part of the trees to the east we planned to follow it south. Where are you heading?'

Gaia exchanged looks with Freya and Aran.

'We're going to a cave. Do you know it?' Aran said.

The boy nodded.

'St Cuthbert's cave. Yes, I know it. No-one goes there. It's sacred land.'

Freya laughed.

'Nothing is sacred here anymore. Look around you: this place is godless.'

The boy lowered his head, remaining silent while Freya looked on waiting for a response.

'I know it was a special place in the old religion, but we need to get there. Is it far from here?' Aran asked.

The boy looked up.

'No,' he replied.

'Just follow the base of the valley and you'll come to an opening about a mile from here. You can't miss it. But be careful, it's protected by a colony of rats. There's a quarry nearby that's swarming with them. None of us go near there. It's forbidden.'

'How do you know, if you've never been there?' Freya replied.

'Our elders told us. A few of them had been there and told us to stay away. They spoke of a cave filled with walls of ancient drawings where the remains of the ancients had been buried. They said their spirits still haunted the cave, and the creatures had been placed there as its guardians.'

Freya shook her head.

'It's a good story, but I suspect they'd spun you a bit of a tale just to keep you away from the rats. What better way to protect you than fill you with fear?'

Gaia caught Freya's eye, her expression a clear warning to keep quiet.

'How old are you?' Gaia asked.

'Twelve,' the boy replied.

'Are you all OK?' she asked.

Both Aran and the boy nodded.

'Just a few bites and scratches, but they'll clean up and heal. They've been lucky. If we had been a few minutes later they'd have stood no chance,' Aran replied.

Another of the boys in the group spoke, his voice wavering and tears filling his eyes.

'Thank you for helping us.'

Gaia stepped forward and placed her arm over the boy's shoulder. Turning to Aran and Freya she spoke.

'So what now?'

Aran looked around the group, each of them dressed in tattered, filthy clothes, with fingerless gloves and woollen hats. Their faces were smeared with dirt, and speckled with crimson spots. One of the boys looked younger than the others, he'd remained silent since the attack, frozen with shock, still looking dazed. The first boy to speak looked the most confident, and seemed to have adopted the role of leader. The girl and the final boy had now joined the rest of the group, all five standing together, looking lost and helpless.

'We'll head to the cave as planned,' Aran said.

'What about these?' Gaia asked.

Aran shook his head.

'I guess that's up to them,' he replied.

'We can't leave them out here alone,' Gaia said.

Aran looked at the group.

'You're welcome to come with us, or continue looking for your village. We're going to the cave though, but I warn you, we face other dangers not just the rats. If you come with us, you need to be prepared for that.'

'You're from The Community, aren't you?' the boy asked.

'Yes,' Aran replied.

'We were warned about you. They told us we would know you by your eyes.'

'You're right to be afraid of The Community. Stay clear of others like us. Not everyone can be trusted,' Aran said.

'How do we know we can trust you?' The boy replied.

'You don't,' Aran said.

'Except we've just risked our lives to save you,' Freya spat out her words, struggling to hide her growing impatience.

'You don't have to trust us. It's probably a good sign that you don't. We've no fight with you or any of the Others. Our enemies lie elsewhere, and they're coming for us. The choice is still yours,' Aran replied.

The group looked at one another, waiting for their young leader to respond. He stared back at Gaia, Aran and Freya, looking unsure of what to say. After a long pause he replied.

'Thanks for your offer and saving our lives, but we'll try to find the village.'

'Are you sure?' Gaia answered.

The boy avoided her gaze, shuffling his feet in the snow as he spoke.

'I don't think we're sure of anything anymore, but we can't come with you to the cave.'

Aran reached out his hand, and the young boy shook it.

'Good luck. If you don't find the village you know where to find us. And if you come across anyone else from The Community, don't trust them. Trust no-one.'

They watched as the group gathered their things, gave thanks again and said their goodbyes. They headed up the incline, through the trees towards the brow of the hill. It was the direction Gaia and the others had come, destinies crossing, but on different paths. Gaia reflected on how fortunate the young group had been, and hoped their journey would be safe. Freya was right though. They were orphans abandoned in a godless world, with no-one to care but each other. Perhaps that was as it always was and should be. Gaia looked at Freya and Aran and realised the same was true. They waited a while until they were out of sight, then headed back to the bushes where Ben was still concealed. Lying still on the stretcher, his head was poking from the blankets, his mouth open and eyes closed. His complexion was as white as the snow, and Freya checked his breathing and pulse.

'He's weak. He's barely clinging on now,' she said.

Her face looked grave, and catching Gaia's eye she could see how worried her sister was. Sliding the stretcher through the gap, and throwing their bags on their backs, they set off along the artery of the valley, weaving through the trees. Freya and Gaia carried the stretcher, with Gaia at the front, while Aran walked ahead, leading the way, looking for any sort of natural pathway. They continued in silence, the only sound the music of the forest wrapped around them. Freya kept a watchful eye on Ben, while Gaia and Aran scanned the trees and bushes, watching and listening, jumping at any small sound or movement. Sunbeams burst through the branches overhead, catching Gaia's eyes and providing occasional flashes of warmth. Images of the rats raced through her mind, mixed with the words of the young boy, his warning about the creatures protecting the cave. She hoped Freya was right and it was all some tale conjured up to warn them. This was as it had always been; stories and legends fashioned to guide and maintain order. Part of her knew there must be more to it than just story. Every legend grew from a seed of truth, and stories were told for a reason. They would have to be on their guard. Unlike the nocturnal hounds, the rats hunted at all times, and where there were a few there were always more. It was unusual to encounter such a few rats in a single encounter. They would be from a larger colony, and it was only a matter of time before they found them.

15

They reached the end of the valley, and bursting through the edge of the forest they came to a wide natural avenue lined with trees. Continuing for about a mile up a slight incline, the avenue ended with a shallow wall of grey rock embedded in the hill, and peppered with snow-capped grass and moss. At its base, carved deep in the bank of stone over millions of years was a narrow, over-hanging lip, with a dark shadow stretching far within. The entrance to the cave was inconspicuous and the tree lined approach provided some natural defence. Aran stopped at the bottom of the final rise to the entrance and gazed ahead, silent almost in prayer. He then led them under the rock and into the shadows of the cave.

Removing his pack, he took out a sleeping bag, laid it on the floor and sat down. Gaia and Freya laid down the stretcher down between two boulders, forming a comfortable resting place for Ben. Freya gave Ben some water and checked his wounds, while Gaia sat opposite Aran. Soon Freya came and sat alongside her sister. They all sat in silence, light from outside casting a glow into the cave, just enough to see one another. Gaia and Freya wrapped themselves in sleeping bags and blankets and huddled together. Eventually, when they all seemed settled, Aran was the first to break the silence. There was a hint of a sigh in his voice as he spoke, most probably with relief.

'Here we are then. St Cuthbert's Cave.'

'I remember his name from the island,' Gaia said.

'Yes. We're not far from the island. If you head just a few miles to the east from here we'll find the causeway we crossed on our escape.'

Gaia shuddered at the memory of that night, the attack from the Night Birds, the rising tide as they scrambled across the narrow road, and the loss of Clara in the icy waters of the sea. An image from the beach, searching the waters for her body flashed into her head. She recalled her desperate screams as she combed the waters, and felt her hand that final time before she was dragged away from her by something in the water. A cold shiver ran through her as she thought of the black silhouettes she would see moving in the water when she sat alone on the beach. It all seemed like a different world, another person's life. Aran spoke again, breaking the dark thoughts in her mind.

'Cuthbert lived on the island, where they were the first to practice the old religion. It's claimed he brought it here, but the island was attacked by tribes from across the seas. They were warriors who raped the women, murdered and pillaged the area. Cuthbert's followers were no match for them and after years of attacks they fled the monastery on the island with his remains. One local legend is they sheltered here when they escaped. Others say Cuthbert himself lived here as a hermit.'

Freya laughed in a mocking tone and said,

'More worthless mythology and mindless nonsense. They fed them anything back then to keep them down. First they ruled with sticks and stones, then they replaced them with ideas. Why use violence when you can plant reverence and fear? Of course, The Community use both, but have a different way of brainwashing us.'

Aran shook his head, as Freya continued.

'Why are we here now? I don't see why we had to come all this way to escape.'

'You heard those young people earlier, even now everyone beyond The Community respects and reveres this place. The Community tried to wipe out the old ways, but they still have an appeal to those beyond. No-one comes here now, and the locals fear it which is why it works for us as a sanctuary and meeting point,' Aran said.

'A meeting point? Who are we meeting?' Freya asked.

'My people will come here. They'll take us somewhere safe.'

Freya looked at Gaia, both with puzzled looks mixed with concern.

'Your people? Who are they and why was there no mention of anyone meeting us here before?' Gaia demanded.

'Me...Hannah...others like us who have infiltrated The Community, but also others on the outside who have managed to hide and avoid The Community.

'What you mean the Others?' Freya replied.

'Yes, I suppose you could look at us like that, but we're different.'

'How?' Gaia asked.

'The Others get on with things, and for the most part are happy to co-exist with The Community as long as they leave them alone. The Community tolerate them. We're more organised and have come together with more of a purpose.'

'And that purpose is?' Gaia said.

'To destroy The Community.'

There was another moment of silence, Freya and Gaia exchanging more worried looks. Meanwhile Aran played with his dagger in the earth in front, prodding and twisting the point of the blade carving out small, random holes. Gaia broke the silence.

'And you just expect us to come with this group of your people?'

'You don't have to. You're both free to do as you choose, but it's best for all of us. We can rest and recover for a while, and Freya will be able to have her child in safety.'

Gaia was becoming more furious, finding it difficult to contain her anger. She sat forward, spitting out her words.

'Why just mention this now, Aran? That wasn't what we talked about. When I spoke of escaping to the island in the North you asked if you could come. Why not tell me then?'

Just when Gaia had started to trust Aran again this felt like another betrayal. How could she have been so stupid? Trust no-one. Nothing is as it seems. Those were the words she had been told time and again, and they were the only words that held any truth. Aran looked embarrassed, his discomfort growing along with his fear. He knew he was no match for Gaia and Freya together and would need to work hard to convince them this wasn't a repeat of what had happened with the escape. He spoke, his voice trembling with emotion.

'I agreed to help you find Freya and free her from The Haven. I kept my side of the deal. But you're forgetting there was another part of that deal. Remember we were meant to rescue Cal too, and I've had to deal with not knowing whether he's still alive or dead.'

'It wasn't my fault Cal wasn't there. If we could have found him I would have helped you free him too,' Gaia replied.

'I know it's not your fault. I'm not saying that, but all I'm saying is I kept my side of the bargain even though he wasn't there,' he paused, sighed and took a deep breath.

'If we managed to get out of The Haven I'd arranged with Ben to bring me here. You didn't have to come. I was going to explain when we returned to Ben's and let you make the choice. Everything was done then, and we were free to go our separate ways. I was going to leave it up to you and Freya to decide what you wanted to do next, but things didn't turn out as I planned.'

Aran waited a moment, allowing the others to digest his words, hoping it was beginning to make sense and was calming them. He surveyed them both, trying to gauge their mood. Freya was difficult to read at any time, but Gaia still had a troubled expression and anger and resentment in her eyes. He continued.

'When we got to Ben's it was clear we had to get away as quickly as we could. There was no time to stop and discuss things. On the road up here I was going to mention it, but I thought the best thing was that we just got here and then we could talk about it.'

There was another pause, again studying their faces, this time waiting for them to respond. When it was clear neither would he continued once more.

'You don't have to come with me. You're free now. You can go wherever you want. You're together again and have each other,' taking a moment to clear his throat.

'I have to go with my people. I have unfinished business and I need to settle this.'

'We can end this, Aran. Just walk away,' Gaia said, her voice reflecting her growing understanding.

'We can't run forever, Gaia,' he replied.

'We have to stop them or Kali and the other leaders will continue to destroy the lives of young people like us. It'll go on and on.'

Aran moved closer to Gaia.

'Think of those young girls back at the castle. What future is there for them? I can't just walk way. You might be able to, but I can't,' he said.

'And what about, Cal?' he continued

'I can't just leave him to rot on the island. I have to try and save him.'

Gaia caught Aran's eye, before looking away. They knew what the other really thought and felt, and Aran knew despite her words Gaia cared. He had seen her growing love with Ruth and Mary, and her selfless determination to save Freya. The survival instinct and programming of her youth was still strong, but even killing the young addict in the school at The Haven was an act of mercy. It was a form of release for the boy, an act of kindness, a gift of freedom, from pain and suffering, and a world without hope. Gaia couldn't just walk away. She wanted the same thing as Aran, something beyond happiness. She wanted the freedom to become whatever she wanted to be, not a path determined by others. She wanted to build a future of her own making, with Freya and her baby. She wanted Aran to be a part of that future, more than anything. This was Gaia's awakening. In a world with The Community she could never be free, and she could not think of living in a world without Aran. He saw the look in her eyes, the softening of her expression, as she accepted the truth and the realisation that whatever happened next it had to be with Aran. He spoke.

'You're right, Gaia. We have to end this, but not by running away. We have to face them and fight them. With both Freya and you we stand a chance.'

Gaia looked across at Freya.

'So what's the plan?' Gaia asked.

'We're building support across the area, working with the Others. We're trying to gather as many together as we can. The plan is we build an army to attack The Haven and overthrow The Community once and for all. Some of us will head to the islands and the nurturing centres and free the young there. I'm heading for the island to find Cal,' he said.

Aran paused a moment before continuing.

'It's time for a new beginning. The day of reckoning is coming and I want you to join us.'

Gaia was still struggling to take everything in. This sounded like madness, but in the whirlwind of the last few days anything made some kind of sense. It was clear Aran was not the only one. First there was Hannah and the revelation of the hidden eyes, and there must have been others within The Haven - Aran's contact had revealed as much before abandoning them. None of which filled Gaia with any hope about this clandestine group. He was right about the last few hours though, the escape from The Haven and discovering Ben injured had been intense, the sequence of events spiralling beyond anyone's control. None of them had found any time to stop and think, let alone discuss or plan their next moves. She could see why Aran had brought them to the Cave. At least he knew there would be others coming and there would be somewhere for them to go. At least Aran felt he had a purpose, rather than wandering the frozen wilderness in the hope Kali didn't find them. Gaia spoke.

'So what do we do now? Do we just wait?'

Aran nodded.

'They know we're coming here, or at least they know Ben and I were. We just have to hope they get here before Kali does.'

Freya replied, her voice calm, taking everything in with the usual clinical indifference and acceptance.

'Let's hope it's soon then. We've left a clear trail for Kali to follow and it won't take her long to find us. She won't pause for thought and will be heading this way now. I can guarantee it. We've got something she wants and she won't stop until she gets us again.'

'How long do you think we've got?' Gaia asked.

'My guess is they'll attack tonight under cover of darkness. If your people don't arrive before then we'll need to be ready, but the three of us alone won't stand much chance,' Freya said.

Freya and Gaia both looked at Aran. He thought a moment then replied.

'Freya's right. We've got to hope my people get here before sundown, that'll give us a bit of a head start.'

'And if they don't? Do we just wait here and fight, or do we run?' Gaia replied, the frustration clear in her voice.

'We run! If we stay we'll die,' Aran said, giving Gaia a stern look, as Freya looked back at Ben still wrapped in blankets clinging to life.

'And what about Ben?' Freya asked.

Aran lowered his eyes and shook his head.

'I don't know. I really don't know.'

The last remnants of the morning dragged by with dark clouds descending bringing with them another violent blizzard. The cave protected them from the fresh deluge of snow, but soon a white wall lined the entrance, sheltering them from the gusts of icy wind. Freya kept a watchful eye on Ben while Gaia and Aran prepared for the attack they hoped would never come. Hidden in the back of the cave, in a casket buried in a concealed underground chamber were a number of weapons. Some Gaia was more than familiar with - machetes, axes, swords and daggers. There were also a couple of crossbows complete with a small armoury of metal tipped bolts. All three had used crossbows on the island and had been given training. However, such weapons were used sparingly and seldom given to the young for fear of their lethal potential and the difficulty in defending against them. Every leader knew they had the upper hand in one on one combat, and most likely could overpower a small group of rebellious youths. Crossbows swung the balance, giving whoever was armed with them a critical upper hand. This was a risk the leaders would not take. These weapons were rare, and the ammunition to arm them even more so. Gaia knew that having them was a major boost to their chances of fending off an attack. The cave provided some natural defence and the avenue made it difficult for anyone to surprise them. However, at some point they would be drawn into a face to face fight and they would need to eliminate or wound as many leaders as possible before this happened. There were three of them, but there would be more leaders with Kali and Gaia knew they would be outnumbered. As Gaia stared down at the weapons lined on the ground before them, Aran peered out through the thin gap between rock and snow. He spoke, almost under his breath.

'This is good. It should cover our tracks and make it harder for them to find us.'

'At least it'll delay them. It won't be easy getting through this blizzard,' Gaia replied.

'We need to expect them regardless. If we've learnt one thing it's never to underestimate, Kali. She's coming for sure. We all know that. It's just whether she finds us tonight, or not,' Aran said.

Playing with the crossbow in her hands, Gaia looked across at Aran, knowing he was thinking the same thing as her.

'Did you know these were going to be here?' she said.

'Yes. I asked for them, especially.'

'We'll need them, and we'll have to take Kali out first,' Gaia replied.

Aran nodded.

'I know. You and I will have both bows on her. As soon as we get the chance at a good shot then take it. Aim for her neck. It's the best chance of killing her. Hopefully, she won't be expecting us having these and that's our main element of surprise.'

Gaia continued to roll the crossbow, running her hand up and down the smooth wood.

'The only problem is they won't attack us in the light. They're bound to leave it until nightfall and that's going to make any shot much harder,' she said.

Aran spoke, his voice becoming more animated as the thought of attacking Kali began to pump the adrenalin inside him.

'When it happens, we just need to be ready. We'll only have a few seconds, but if we can eliminate Kali we stand a chance. The other leaders will feel weakened without her and that gives us an edge. We take down as many as we can with the bows and then face them one on one.'

All three took off their belts and laid them on the ground. Aran and Gaia arranged the weapons on each one so they were ready when they needed them. They loaded the crossbows with one bolt and placed them by Aran and Gaia's belts. Then they sat and waited; Aran with his back against a rock, Gaia resting on the back wall of the cave while Freya remained sat alongside Ben. Aran dozed and Gaia sat watching as his head bobbed back and forth. Seeing him asleep made Gaia drowsy too and soon she drifted off too. While she slept she dreamt. It was the same dream from the night before, with the same people, and ending with the image of Kali. Once again there was the chanting of the single word, the message, the warning, but still she couldn't make out what it was. Just when she thought it was within reach the dream faded and she awoke feeling empty and drained. Echoes of the images lingered, as did the bitter taste of frustration at still not knowing what the voices were trying to tell her.

When Gaia woke the blizzard had stopped and the sun was beginning to seep through the thinning clouds. The faint yellow orb was low in the sky now, well on the downward arc of its descent towards the horizon and beyond. Only a few hours of light remained. Gaia scanned the cave and saw Freya beside Ben, continuing her vigil, but she couldn't see Aran. Shuffling over by Freya's side, she placed an arm on her shoulder and whispered.

'Where's Aran?'

Freya looked up, almost in a daze.

'He said he had to go and check on something. He said he wouldn't be long,' she replied.

Gaia frowned and looked over to where the weapons had been laid out, noticing the crossbows remained, but Aran's belt had gone.

'How long has he been gone?' Gaia said.

'Maybe ten or fifteen minutes.'

'Did he say where he was going?'

Freya shook her head.

'No, but don't worry.'

Gaia looked down at Ben, his face drained of all life and colour.

'How is he?' she asked.

Freya turned to face her sister, and with the gravest of expressions shook her head. They both watched as Ben lay there. He seemed to have aged a decade in the hours of the journey, his skin looking wrinkled and worn. His breathing was faint and shallow now, with the occasional croak as a few remaining gasps of air were forced from his parched lips. Gaia put her arm around Freya and pulled her close. Leaning her head on her sister's shoulder Gaia spoke.

'We haven't had much time to talk since the escape, but I just wanted to say how good it is to have you back.'

Gaia felt Freya's head press close to hers as her sister replied.

'Thank you for saving me. I knew you would try.'

Gaia took her sister's hand.

'When this is all over, we can make up for all that lost time. It's hard to believe we spent all those years as enemies and now we're sisters.'

Freya laughed.

'Isn't that how it's supposed to be? I thought siblings were meant to be rivals.'

'Maybe you're right, but not quite in the way we were.'

They sat in silence for a moment, Freya stroking her sister's hair as they continued to hold hands, running their fingers through one another's. Gaia thought of the future, way beyond the next few hours, dreaming of them being together somewhere on an island in the north. After a long wait, both of them buried deep in their own thoughts, Freya spoke.

'If we don't make it, I want you to know that I love you. Maybe neither of us really know what that word means, but when I think of you it's the only time I feel like it's worth going on. The thought of us being together again was what kept me going.'

Gaia sat up and stared into Freya's deep, blue eyes, her face burning with emotion.

'I love you too. Don't ever forget it. When Kali told me, it seemed to all make sense; it was almost as though deep inside I'd always known. When I was recovering in the village I knew I had to save you.'

Fighting with her own emotions, Gaia could see tears running down Freya's cheeks. Reaching out, she wiped the teardrops from her sister's dirt-stained face. Leaning forward she wrapped her arms around her and whispered in her ear.

'We will get through this Freya and then we'll find somewhere safe where we can be together, and bring up your child. We have something else worth living for now.'

'What about Aran?' Freya replied.

Gaia thought for a moment. Deep down she knew she wanted to be with Aran. She loved him in a way she hadn't loved anyone else, not even Freya. No-one made her feel so frustrated and angry, but neither could anyone melt her heart as he did. Even now her mind had been racing with thoughts of where he was, if he was safe, and at the same time fears that he had run off and betrayed them once again. She had no idea where she stood with Aran, and was never sure if she would fully trust him. However, she could not picture a future without either him or Freya. She wanted both of them in her life. Gaia answered her sister, choosing her words with care.

'I need Aran as much as I need you,' she said.

'Have you told him how you feel?'

Gaia sat back, lowering her head and staring at the earth.

'No, he doesn't know, and you mustn't tell him.'

Looking up at her sister, Gaia continued.

'Promise me!'

Freya nodded, looking slightly dazzled at Gaia's response.

'I won't. But you have to let him know.'

Gaia gave her sister a faint smile.

'I will, as soon as this is over.'

Freya looked concerned, and taking both her sister's hands in hers she replied.

'We might not get through this, Gaia. It could be our last night together. Do you want to risk that without Aran ever knowing how you truly feel?'

Freya's honesty struck Gaia hard. There was a truth she was burying and refusing to face. Her sister was right. The sands were falling ever closer to the end, and she couldn't stare into the face of death leaving any regrets behind. She had to tell him.

There was a shuffling sound from the far side of the cave, just beyond the entrance. Both Gaia and Freya reached for their weapons, but Aran appeared, brushing snow from his jacket and trousers and kicking his boots against a rock. Crouching low he approached, smiling, his face flush with the raw red of a cold winter's day.

'Is everything OK?' he asked.

'Where've you been?' Gaia asked, struggling to hide her simmering anger at his disappearance, but also relieved at his return.

'There was something I wanted to check nearby.'

'Like what?' Gaia replied, still bubbling with relief and rage.

Freya caught her sister's eye, her expression making it clear she thought Gaia should back off and calm down. Aran gave her a confused look of someone who felt they had done nothing wrong.

'There's a small quarry near here. It's just over the top of the hill behind us. I needed to make sure it was exactly as I was told.'

Gaia frowned.

'What about it?' she asked.

Aran replied, looking uncomfortable.

'The rats from earlier, well didn't you think it was a bit unusual there were only three of them?'

'Yes, we know they usually hunt in much larger groups. So what?' Gaia said.

'One of the other reasons none of the Others will come near the cave are the rumours that it's guarded by rats. The locals think it is sacred and the rats protect it. When I was told to meet here they warned me about the quarry beyond the hill. They said it was swarming with a huge colony of rats.'

'And is it?' Freya asked.

'Oh yes, hundreds of the things. You can only just make them out under the trees, but you can hear them.'

Gaia got to her feet and approached Aran.

'So you thought it was a good idea to go alone and see if this colony was there?'

Looking concerned as Gaia drew close, Aran shrugged his shoulders and nodded.

'Yes, why not?' he asked.

'What if you were attacked? What chance would you have stood on your own? Are you an idiot, didn't you think about us?'

Gaia spat out her words, all her anger and frustration clear to see. Aran looked shocked, both by her words and the intensity of her anger. Struggling to respond he looked across at Freya his eyes pleading with her to help him out.

'Just tell him, Gaia,' Freya said.

'Tell me what?' Aran asked, now looking even more confused.

Gaia looked back at her sister, then lowered her head. Freya spoke again.

'Go on. Get it over with. We're running out of time.'

There was a long pause, and then Gaia lifted her head and stared back at Aran who still seemed bemused. Her voice was soft and calm now.

'I was worried about you because I care.'

She paused for a moment, searching for the right words. Meanwhile Aran continued to look on, his expression softening as the words hit him. Gaia continued.

'What I mean is. I can't get through this without you both. I want us all to be together. You, Freya, me.'

Gaia looked up at Aran, and Freya watched as they stared at one another.

'What she's trying to say is she cares for you. A lot. Am I right?'

Gaia nodded, struggling to hide her embarrassment.

'Yes, that's what I mean,' she replied.

Aran smiled and clearing his throat he replied, his voice wavering with emotion.

'I think you know my feelings for you, Gaia. I've made that pretty clear.'

Gaia stepped forward and put her arms around Aran, clinging together as though they never wanted to part. Then raising her head, she stared into his eyes, smiled and they kissed. It was a long, lingering kiss, both of them knowing it may be the last one they ever shared. Freya watched them with a sense of warm relief. She was resigned to whatever fate held for her, but wished this was only the start for them. As she sat stroking her stomach, she had other worries. Staring out of the cave, Freya gazed into the sky beyond. It was the hour before twilight, when a veil of gold sometimes descends upon the world, and birds sing their sweetest chorus, heralding the darkness to come. Above the trees a magnificent spectacle was unfolding. Thousands of tiny black birds were locked together, swirling and dancing in wondrous formation. Wave upon wave, they rolled and twirled through the sky, twisting this way and that. Dipping low then sweeping high, all in one majestic motion. A murmuring of starlings together as one.

16

The sun had set and darkness enveloped the cave. Aran's torch was the only light, casting a silvery glow as all three sat huddled together, with Ben lying by their side. Gaia had her head resting on Aran's lap as he sat cross-legged on the ground. He stared into space, deep in thought, while Freya crouched nearby, watching over Ben. His face was still, barely moving for what seemed like hours. Every now and then a wave of panic would sweep over Freya, and feeling sure his breathing had stopped, she would lower her cheek against his parched lips. Only the faintest of sounds could be heard, the gentle purring of his throat as he clung to the tattered threads of life. She would ease her head back, feeling a mixture of relief and the sadness of knowing it was only a matter of time. As the light from the torch touched his grey features, Freya looked on, watching and waiting. They all knew death would call sometime tonight.

As she stared at Ben, his eyes opened. At first there was nothing but an emptiness, but then a look of panic swept across his face. She leant forward trying to calm and reassure him, but he began licking his lips, seeming to be desperate to speak. Freya gestured to Gaia to pass the water bottle and began feeding him cold, refreshing water. They waited as he swallowed, spilling most of it as he spluttered and spat. His eyes remained open, blinking and searching the darkness, as if he was looking for someone he couldn't see. He began to speak, forcing the fractured words from his lips, his voice dry and frail. At first it was difficult to fathom anything he said, as each word seemed random and aimless. Then the words were more frequent, developing a structure, and becoming clearer. They were still fragments, but Gaia listened as they began to form some meaning.

'Kali... Careful... She won't stop.... No heart,' he said.

His eyes blazed with an alarming ferocity now, begging Freya to listen, hoping she would understand. She eased forward as Ben continued to force out the words.

'Killed her mother... Wife... Dead.'

Freya took his hand in hers and began to mop his brow. Icy cold sweat was running down his forehead, but he wouldn't settle, ignoring all her attempts to calm him.

'Sshhh, just take it easy, Ben. Don't worry about her. I promise I'll make sure she pays for what she did.'

Ben's eyes were raging, a look of manic terror etched across his face as he replied. It was as though he was slipping into a kind of delirium, so desperate was he for Freya to hear his words.

'No! No! Can't... Mustn't...'

Leaning forward, Freya tried to stroke his cheek, her voice quiet and measured as she spoke, but still it had no impact.

'I thought that's what you wanted. We know she was your daughter, and what she did. But Kali is someone else. She's a monster now. She has to pay for her crimes.'

'Yes, yes. A monster. My daughter. Dead. Kali too. But not you. Can't! Mustn't! Please. Not you. No...'

Ben's back arched upright as though a bolt of lightning had shot through his body. He became gripped in a spasm of pain, looking paralysed, and no longer able to breathe. His face was wracked in agony, and began to change from pale white to an intense red. Freya held his arms, trying to push him back on the stretcher, growing in desperation. Gaia grabbed him, and together with her sister they tried to stop him reeling from the spasms. Aran looked on, knowing there was nothing they could do. After a few minutes the spasms eased and Ben's body fell limp, his eyes still open, staring far beyond them, an emptiness within. Freya continued to hold his arms, gazing down at the serene and gentle expression now on his face. She felt dazed, fighting new and confusing emotions she had never known before. Gaia fought back tears as she stared first at her sister's pain and then down at Ben's still, lifeless body.

Aran placed an arm on Freya's shoulder and whispered.

'It's over, Freya. You did all you could.'

She remained still, her eyes fixed on Ben, hoping they would spark with life once more, willing him to breathe again. After a long pause, she began to shake her head, and loosening her grip on his arms, her head dropped and body crumbled towards the floor. Aran reached forward and closed his eyelids, while all three sat in silence around the body. Gaia's mind drifted away, recalling some of the words from the song on her trip from the village. Closing her eyes, the melody echoed through her head as the words unfolded in her mind:

'Yet when the trumpets ring,
The thrust of a poor man's arm will go
Through the heart of the proudest king!'

Gaia thought of what Ben had said, how even in his final moments he wanted to protect them from

Kali. The words were broken, but the meaning was clear. He wanted them to stay away, maybe even run, knowing how dangerous she could be. However, it was too late for that. Even clinging to those last fragments of life, all Ben could think about was her, the woman who had taken away everything he had ever loved, even his daughter. She had no doubt dominated his thoughts, plagued his days, with the hunger for revenge eating him up inside. Even though she was no longer a part of his life she continued to ruin it. Gaia knew what it meant to be free now. Picturing Kali's face in her mind, a surge of hatred shot through her body, her chest aching with the desire for revenge. She could choose to forget her and run, but then she would always be running and would never be free. She could not allow Kali to destroy her life in the way she had done to Ben and so many others.

Gaia knew her purpose now, her one goal above all else. She had to confront Kali and kill her. Only then would it be over, and she could stop running. Only then would she and all the others be free, and they could move on with their lives. The image of Kali continued to burn in her mind, she could taste the bitter feeling deep inside. Her features were crisp and clear, the menacing blue eyes staring back at her. There was a wry, mocking grin on her face, taunting Gaia, inviting her to come closer, willing her to attack. Her arms were placed on her hips, poised, ready and waiting. Kali knew Gaia was no match for her, or least her arrogance told her so. If Gaia was to kill her she would need to outsmart her. She had to find another way. The image of the deadly smile began to fade and Gaia could feel what was about to come. Something inside spoke to her, and she knew it was only a matter of hours before Kali and her would meet again. She had never been more sure of anything.

....

Wrapping Ben's body in the blankets, they lowered him into the underground chamber at the back of the cave. Aran and Gaia had looked on, heads bowed in silence as Freya said a few words. There were no prayers: only thoughts and kindness. Gaia watched the way Freya conducted these last goodbyes. She was so gentle and delicate, different from the girl she had known on the island. Her time in captivity had changed her, but while she had gained she had also lost. It struck Gaia how taken Freya had been with Ben, an old man she had never known, yet tended to with an almost obsessive determination and care, willing him to survive. It was a strange connection. Perhaps she thought that in saving him she was saving herself, making amends for all the killing that had gone before. Maybe the thought of motherhood had changed her focus and unlocked an inner caring. Nature found what nurture had buried. Even in death Freya shone, sprinkling drops of water on the body, and whispering a few final words.

'Rest in peace old man. You're free now,' she said.

'Free from the terror, the pain, and this time of monsters.'

She paused a moment, closing her eyes, before continuing.

'You were one of the good, and however hard they've tried to destroy it, kindness will come again.'

Closing the lid of the chamber, they concealed it once more, then heads bowed they each remained for a few minutes in silence. Lost in their own private thoughts. Gaia closed her eyes and pictured Ben's smiling face, the warmth and kindness of his welcome. She recalled them laughing and joking over supper, the stories he told, the lively animated air, his joy in their company plain to see. She felt Aran take her gloved hand, gripping it tight. Opening her eyes she turned her head to see him weeping, tears running down his cheeks. She pulled him close and comforted him. She knew how he was feeling. There was guilt at knowing their appearance led to this moment, and the sense of loss they all felt at seeing another good man die. How different life would be if they could only see the outcomes of their choices. As with their escape they had looked to Aran to lead, but he was no leader. His heart ruled and his conscience was strong, and that was one of the reasons Gaia loved him. She had grown to see that all his choices had been made for others. He was loyal to those who were closest; even in his betrayal he was trying to save his brother. Gaia knew she would do the same thing if it meant saving Freya. The bonds of blood run deepest and are the hardest to break.

After they had said their goodbyes, they sat by the entrance spread out across its long narrow stretch. Peering into the blackness of the night they waited. They could see nothing but the dark silhouette of the trees as they reached the skyline, the gentlest of breezes slipping through the branches as they swayed high above them. The blanket of darkness beyond was peppered with millions of tiny flickering lights, some clustered together in familiar shapes.

Gaia recalled ancient Greek stories, told from the earliest days of the nurturing, each one linked to a pattern in the sky. The Greeks had told many myths with hidden morals and warnings. The Community chose these stories with care, always telling ones that reinforced the values they wanted to maintain. She saw the distinctive shaped 'W' of Cassiopeia, the vain queen who boasted of her beauty and was forced to sacrifice her daughter, Andromeda to a sea monster unleashed from the depths of the ocean by Poseidon the god of the seas. Perseus saved Andromeda and they were married, both also immortalised in the stars. She tried to remember some of the other names. Orion, the Hunter, another who was made into a constellation with the distinctive belt and bright dog star at his feet. The big and little bears, each shaped like a plough. There were other great tales of many who didn't make it to the stars: oracles and monsters, one-eyed creatures and horses with wings. It was a world where the gods made lovers of their mortals creating demi-gods on Earth. Where men went on epic quests and adventures, seeking lost treasures and rescuing kings daughters captured or in distress.

One story had fascinated Gaia more than all the others, a tale the leaders told them many times. It was a myth Kali herself would often tell. It was the story of Oedipus, the boy who was born to a king and queen with a prophecy that he would murder his father and marry his mother. Through a series of well intended actions, each meant to avoid his destiny being fulfilled, Oedipus killed his true father, the king unknowingly, and earned the hand of his mother, the queen in marriage. The story reminded her of Ben's tragedy, he knew his daughter and had to live with the horror of what she had done. Like Oedipus she had murdered a parent, all for what she saw as the greater good. The Community was everything, they were nothing. Gaia's was different. She had no parents, and had never known who they were. The Community had always been her family, her parents, her life.

As her mind wandered, and she played with the myths and legends of her childhood, a tense melancholia descended on Gaia. The emptiness of time and endless waiting filling her mind with dark thoughts. She tried not to think of what was to come, but with each passing hour the failure of Aran's people to arrive meant a showdown with Kali was ever likely. Every now and then she thought she saw a flash of light somewhere in the distance. Noises came from deep within the trees, rustling sounds, the crack of a branch, but nothing and no-one appeared. She stared at the others; Freya sitting between Aran and herself, each guarding their own part of the entrance. A torch was perched on their laps, the glow lighting up their faces. Both looked alert, scanning the black wilderness outside, looking as far into the night as they could, concentrating on the narrow avenue leading to the cave. They knew this is where they would come. Kali would not lower herself to surprise. She was too confident and arrogant for that. She wouldn't even attack at first. Kali wanted them alive, and would try to persuade them to give up and return. She would be sure they numbered few, and know they could be overpowered and captured again. What she didn't know was they had their own element of surprise. They had the crossbows.

The hours passed long into the night, with nothing but the monotony of the darkness and silence, broken only by the occasional noise from the nocturnal forest. Then Gaia sat, feeling sure she had heard something else. It came from her left, a few hundred yards from the cave. It was a rustling sound, as though something was moving in the snow, not running, but searching, isolated to just one spot. She strained her ears, trying to make out the movement of the sound, and its direction of travel, hoping it was heading away from the cave. More sounds came. A flurry of shuffling, followed by the faintest of unmistakable squeaks. Soon it was much louder, as more and more of the creatures scampered through the snow. Gaia couldn't see them, but she didn't have to. She would know their distinctive sound anywhere. The rats had returned.

Gaia made a silent gesture to Freya and Aran, but both had heard the sound and were looking back in alarm. They all turned off their torches, plunging the cave into an intense darkness. Gaia's eyes struggled to adjust, and a feeling of disorientation swept over her as she grasped for anything in the black emptiness. She remained still, knowing they couldn't move. The rats had the acutest senses and would hear the sound of any movement, which they would investigate or attack. They had to wait for now, and hope they moved on. Gaia listened as the scurrying continued outside. There was more and the noise was getting nearer. She tried to slow her breathing, conscious even the faintest of sounds might be picked up by the creatures. Her eyes began to adjust, and she picked up some movement in the shadows, It was just the slightest flicker of something in the dark, but soon there was more. Coupled with the steady rise in the sound of the rats footsteps, and the occasional shrill, sinister screech, she knew the rats were moving closer to the cave.

She saw the eyes first, two small dots burning a bright fiery red. It was just a few yards from the entrance, head lowered, its nose pressed against the snow. Gaia held her breath and reached down to feel the machete in her belt. She grasped the handle and waited. The creature raised its head and paused, eyes peering straight at her. She waited, poised for the moment to attack, not wanting to react unless she had to. If she killed one the others would follow and then it would be wave after wave, an onslaught they might never survive. Still the creature waited, staring, but not moving. Then it came.

In the distance, from within the trees lower down the valley, there was a howling. The terrifying sound echoed far through the night, seeming to hang in the air before fading. It came again and again, joined by more with layer upon layer of howling in a cacophony of blood-curdling sound. Gaia watched as the rat shifted its head, the red eyes disappearing as it turned and ran off. In the gaps between the howls Gaia could hear the sound of the creatures scurrying away into the night, until only the howling of the dogs remained. Still echoing in the distance, it didn't seem as though they were on the move yet.

The torches lit up and Freya and Aran huddled next to Gaia.

'Saved by the dogs. Who would have thought it?' Freya said.

'That was close. I was a second away from slicing one of their heads off,' Gaia replied.

'It's good you didn't. We'd have had hundreds of the things on us. The quarry is infested,' Aran said.

'What now?' Freya asked.

'Hopefully, the dogs will find something to distract them,' Aran said.

'Where are these people of yours?' Freya asked.

Aran sighed.

'I thought they'd be here by now. Maybe they think it's safer to wait until first light.'

'Is that what they told you?' Gaia asked.

'The instructions were just to get to the cave and wait until they arrived. They'd come as soon as they could. Ben was meant to tell them the night he dropped us off. They knew we would be in and out by dawn.'

'How do they know we made it? They might think we've been captured and won't come,' Freya replied.

Aran shook his head.

'The plan was to come anyway. They won't leave those weapons here. They're too important to them.'

Gaia and Freya exchanged looks, then Freya spoke.

'Listen. The howling has stopped.'

Aran peered into the darkness, as Gaia sensed his growing anxiety.

'Let's get back to our positions and wait till dawn. If they haven't come within an hour of first light, we'll decide what to do next,' he said.

They each returned to the areas from which they were keeping watch, Aran and Gaia at either end of the entrance with Freya in the middle. The forest had returned to its quiet nocturnal mystery and calm. Their was no sign of the rats or dogs who had gone now, scattered back to their lair, or continuing the hunt for victims. Any other creatures that could brave these conditions remained hidden, buried within the shadowy world of the dark. Their only preoccupation was to find food and avoid predators, a cycle of secret survival played out night after night.

Another hour or so passed, and Gaia was struggling to stay awake. Her mind was drifting in and out of a strange, sleepy stupor, the world between dream and reality. She watched and waited, her thoughts reaching into the darkness of the forest, picturing the creatures lurking beneath the fallen branches and undergrowth. She thought of the spiders in their escape from the island. She could almost smell them again, and saw the multitude of tiny bulbous eyes staring back at her. She heard the sound of a crack or rustle, and imagined the creatures that made it. At times it felt as though she was there, foraging in the frozen snow-lined belly below the trees. More images flashed through her head from their journey, the faces of those they had slaughtered; some sneering, others laughing: it was a world of endless death. Kill, or be killed. She had come so far, but still she was nowhere. Every day she was changing, but still she didn't know what she was becoming. She had no idea what the future held, where she would go. She was tired of running. It was time to move on, but things were beyond her control.

As the vacuum of the waiting played with her mind, Gaia recalled something she had read somewhere: 'The old world is dying, and the new world struggles to be born: now is the time of monsters.' Looking into the blackness of the frozen night, waiting for the sun to push through beyond the horizon and the trees, the words kept rolling in her head over and over again. Who were the monsters now? When and how would this new world be born?

In the distance something pierced the darkness, a flicker of orange light. At first, Gaia ignored it, her mind telling her it was another part of the charade playing out between her sleep and dreams. She saw it again, at the start of the avenue of trees, followed by another and another. She sat up, alert now, and gazing deep into the blackness for the dancing lights. There were several bright flaming torches. She counted ten, spread out across the narrow stretch of open land leading up to the cave, moving closer. Gaia looked across at the others who were watching the torches too, concerned looks on their faces, each gripping their weapons.

'Do you think this is them?' Gaia asked.

Aran looked back, a grave expression revealing far more than his words.

'Best be ready, just in case,' he replied.

'You don't think it could be Kali, do you? Surely, not even she would announce her arrival,' Gaia said.

'If it is Kali, she's capable of anything. She won't be afraid of us,' Freya answered.

They all crouched low to the ground. Gaia had carved out a small gulley in the snow in front so she could lie flat. Gaia and Aran loaded the crossbows and lay with them pointed down the hill, along the avenue, ready to respond to the approaching shadows, and the first signs of any attack. The flames were spaced out in a horizontal line, edging closer all the time. As they neared, Gaia noticed the one in the centre was in front of the others. A few hundred metres from the entrance, at the foot of the final rise to the cave, the flames stopped moving. Only the one in the centre continued ,still pushing forward towards them. Gaia remained focused on the flickering light, concentrating on the shadow below, straining her eyes to see who was holding the torch.

As the flame neared, the light grew more intense and its warm glow began to reveal brief glimmers of what lay beneath it. At first Gaia thought it was just one person holding the torch, but then she noticed there were two silhouettes in front of someone else. The two in front were shuffling forward with less purpose and intent, as though they were being ushered ahead by the one behind. They stopped moving, paused and waited. Though the flames were brighter, Gaia still couldn't see who was holding the torch. She could feel her heart racing as the adrenalin began to flow. Pressing the butt of the crossbow handle into her shoulder, she peered down the eye of its sight. Focusing on the flame, she lowered the centre point of the bolt to the area below the heart of the flame. She could just make out the grey, shadows of the two figures in front, one a touch taller than the other, the silhouette behind taller again than both.

After a long silence, with only the sound of her heart thumping in her chest, Gaia heard a voice. It was loud, clear and one she recognised in an instant. The unmistakable sound sent shivers through her, as the words echoed into the emptiness of the night. Her instinct took over and she felt her finger tense, pressing hard against the trigger of the crossbow.

'I know you're in there,' Kali shouted.

Gaia looked across at Freya and Aran who were both staring down the hill at the shadows beneath the flames. Their tension and uncertainty was clear as both shuffled and fidgeted on the ground. Gaia looked back down the sight and barrel of the bow, trying to lock onto the shadow, but struggled to get a clear line of sight due to the figures in front. She felt sure which of the silhouettes was Kali, but couldn't risk taking a shot for fear of hitting the others. As she wrestled with her thoughts and tried to line up a shot, she heard the voice again.

'I know what you're thinking, but I would put the bows away if I were you. I'm sure you wouldn't want to lose these girls again.'

As the words hit Gaia, she lowered the bow and lifted her head. She still couldn't see the faces of the figures, but images flashed through her mind. She ran over the words again, and the same two faces kept appearing. Her heart fluttered with excitement, refusing to believe it was real until she saw their faces. She tried to steady herself, focus her mind. Maybe this was another one of Kali's tricks. Looking across at Aran, she could see his crossbow pointed forward, his head still pressed against the handle, and eye trained on its target. She tried to attract his attention, but it remained fixed on the shadows and the voice outside. She spoke, as loud as she dared, hoping the sound didn't carry through the echo of the cave.

'Put the crossbow down, Aran. Put it down.'

As Aran heard Gaia's pleas, both he and Freya gave her quizzical looks.

'Don't shoot. It's too dangerous,' Gaia said.

It was Freya who seemed to realise first, the puzzled expression lifting as she made the link between words and faces. Aran still appeared confused and reluctant to carry out Gaia's request. This was their chance, the first shot was critical he had said. They couldn't waste the opportunity. What puzzled him more was how Kali knew about the crossbows. There was no way she could see them, and these were not weapons common enough to assume would be in their possession. She had to know they had them and how was worrying Aran more than the shadows she was using as human shields.

'We have to take a shot. It's our only chance,' Aran said.

Gaia glowered at him, the menace clear to see and hear in her voice.

'No, Aran. Drop it. I won't risk killing them. I think she has Ruth and Mary,' she replied.

It was then Aran understood. He had been so focused on Kali's knowledge of the bows he'd not heard the repeated reference to the girls. As the realisation hit him, he lowered the crossbow and shook his head. Then all three of them stared into the night and the torch, waiting for the voice again, none of them daring to speak and confirm they were here. Kali spoke again, her voice loud and commanding.

'There's been enough bloodshed already. I don't want to see any more. I'm hear to do a trade.'

She paused and continued.

'I've no interest in the boy; he's served his purpose and can go. Gaia, Freya. It's you I want. Hand over the weapons, give yourselves up and come back to The Haven with me and I'll spare Aran and the girls. I'll give you five minutes to make up your mind then I kill the girls and we're coming in for you.'

Aran crawled closer to Gaia and Freya.

'We can't trust her. She won't let us go. Either way, she'll kill us,' he whispered.

'What choice have we got? There are ten of them. We can't fight that many. Kali would be difficult enough alone,' Gaia replied.

'We've got the bows. They'll take a few out before they get close. We can take Kali out as planned,' Aran said.

Gaia scowled at him as she answered.

'No! I won't risk killing the girls.'

'You thought they were dead anyway. And do you honestly think she'll let me go with them? As soon as you hand yourselves over - that's it: we've got nothing to bargain with and she'll have all the weapons too,' Aran said.

'What about you, Freya? What do you think?'

Gaia looked at her sister, watching as she pondered over her response. She was in no hurry, making sure she chose her words with care.

'Kali doesn't care about you or the girls, Aran. It's Gaia and me she wants. We've got to try and stay alive. As long as we survive, there's a chance. We have to go with her.'

Aran shook his head.

'It's madness. Let's stall her. My people might arrive and we can attack then. We'll have more numbers. For all we know they could be watching.'

Freya frowned and placing her arm on Aran's shoulder she spoke, her voice measured and calm.

'Your people aren't coming, Aran.'

There was a look of disappointment on Aran's face, as though he knew what she was thinking, but was begging her to tell him he was wrong.

'There's still time,' he said.

'How do you think they know about the crossbows? Is there anyone else who could have known?' Freya replied.

Aran knew she was right, and the thought had crossed his mind already. Kali wouldn't take any risks and if she knew they had come here to meet them she would have waited and ambushed them before they arrived. The Haven was riddled with spies, deceit and betrayal, and Aran thought back to their encounter with his contact. His behaviour had been suspicious and he had given them no help, despite the assurances Aran had received that he could be trusted. He sighed, and lowered his hands.

'There's no other way, Aran. It's over. She's too strong for us. Maybe this is how it's always meant to end,' Gaia said.

Freya held her sister's hand, and gave her a reassuring smile.

'We still all have each other. We'll live to fight another day.'

Gaia returned the smile as she felt Freya's grip through their thick gloves.

'Are you going to tell her, or should I?' Gaia said.

'Maybe, it's be better coming from you,' Freya replied.

Reaching her arms out, Freya wrapped them around Aran and her sister. They huddled close, heads pressed together in silence, knowing once again this could be another journey's end. As they clutched each other for what could be the final time, Aran whispered.

'This isn't over. I'll come and find you. I'll bring others. Remember what I said. We're gathering and the reckoning is coming. Just make sure you stay alive. Do you hear me? Don't give up.'

He pressed his lips against Gaia's and she lost herself in the tenderness of his kiss. She wished they could remain like this forever, that the darkness that enveloped them would remain, snuffing out all life around them. She was losing the will to go on, growing tired of surrender. Only the thought of Aran, Freya and the baby kept her going. If she no longer wanted to live for herself, then at least she owed it to them. A voice called from beyond the entrance.

'I need a decision,' Kali cried.

Releasing her lips from the warmth of Aran's, Gaia turned towards the entrance and shouted her response.

'We'll hand ourselves over, but let the girls go first.'

There was laughter, followed by Kali's reply.

'It's good to hear your voice again. You had us worried running off like that.'

There was moment of silence.

'I'm glad you've seen sense, but here's how it's going to work. You're both going to walk out slowly, hands in the air with the bows unloaded and strapped to your backs. When I say you'll stop and throw them to me. Then I'll let the girls go to the cave. They wait here with Aran while we leave.'

'How do we know we can trust you?' Aran shouted.

There was a loud, raucous laugh before she composed herself and replied.

'You don't know if you can trust me, but you haven't got much choice, have you? I give you my word, if that is worth anything to you.'

'Your word means nothing. You've shown that to all of us many times,' Aran replied.

'Either you do it my way, or you all die. If my word isn't good enough, how does that sound. I know how Gaia feels about the girls and she wouldn't want that to happen, would she? So let's get this over with, shall we?'

Gaia looked at the others and frowned.

'Leave it Aran. We have no choice. Pass your bow to Freya.'

Aran hesitated, fighting with his anger, searching for some other way. Knowing Gaia was right he picked up the bow and threw it at Freya. Strapping it to her back, she removed her other weapons and laid them on the floor. Gaia did the same, then climbing to their feet, they both turned to face the entrance. Aran grabbed hold of Gaia's hand.

'Remember what I said. Stay alive and I'll come for you,' he said.

Looking down at him one final time she began to walk forward towards the light of the torch, Freya by her side. They both had their arms raised above their heads. As they neared, the light from the flame began to unveil what had only been silhouettes and a voice for now. Gaia noticed the children first, the youngest Ruth still looked frail and timid and had lost her long blonde hair, now cut much shorter. Mary had also lost most of her distinctive fiery red hair. As Gaia approached, she felt a wave of joy and relief to see them, staring into those beautiful, bright green eyes. Mary's face lit up as they approached, the broadest smile upon it. Ruth held her hand, pressing close to her sister's side. Gaia began to walk faster and lower her arms. It was then she heard the sharp voice of Kali.

'Keep your hands in the air,' she shouted.

Raising her hands again, Gaia stared into the eyes of Kali once more. Her look was as piercing and menacing as before, the marble blue eyes almost mesmerising in their terrible beauty. Her head was shaven to the bone, her skin taut, and a wry grin on her skeletal face. Gaia stopped, only a few metres away, desperate to hug the girls. She could sense Freya, by her side, and could feel the tension. Kali smiled.

'Hello again. It's good to see you both,' she whispered.

Gaia and Freya remained silent, and Kali continued.

'Throw the crossbows onto the ground, then I'll let you speak with the girls.'

Gaia removed her bow first, hurling it to the side of Kali. Freya followed, neither saying a word. Kali looked down at the weapons by her feet.

'And the bolts,' she said.

They both took the bolts from their jacket pockets and thrust them to the ground by the bows. Kali nodded, a sinister look of satisfaction on her face.

'Good. Now you have two minutes with these, before they go off with the boy.'

Ushering Ruth and Mary forward, Gaia dropped to her knees and wrapped her arms around them both. She felt their bodies pressed close to hers, their heads resting on hers. Tears fell down her cheeks as a wave of emotion swept through her. She had never felt this way before, the relief at seeing them once again mixed with an overwhelming feeling of love. The girls had been so helpless, victims of this cruelest of worlds. Gaia only ever wanted to protect them, and losing them felt as though she had let them down, something she had never forgiven herself for. They were alive and safe, and there was a chance she could save them once more, make amends. Whatever the future held for Gaia and

Freya, there was some good that could come out of this day. As she hugged the girls, she heard Kali's voice.

'You didn't think I would release them to the dogs, did you? What do you take me for? No, I knew how precious they were to you. I couldn't let myself do that.'

Freya spoke, her voice calm, but filled with venom.

'You're a fucking bitch and I'm going to kill you.'

Kali let out one of her chilling laughs.

'You're not in much of a position to threaten me, Freya. I would watch your mouth. You need to stay calm and think of that baby of yours.'

'Fuck you!'

Freya lunged forward to attack Kali, but as she reached out for her the leader jerked her body to one side and struck her on the side of the head. Freya fell on her knees, head bowed, spitting blood into the snow. Gaia jumped to her feet, her instinct to attack and protect her sister, but she saw Kali draw her dagger. They exchanged looks, the leader waiting to see how she would respond, Gaia knowing it would be madness to attack.

'Don't do anything stupid like your sister. You're a lot smarter than she is. Now say your goodbyes and come quietly,' Kali said.

Kali looked down at Freya still on all fours in the snow.

'Put your hands behind your back,' she commanded.

Freya looked up, and still on her knees she lifted her body and placed her hands behind her. Taking off her bag, Kali removed some cord and passed it to Gaia.

'Tie her hands up. And do it properly.'

Gaia bound her sister's hands then knelt in front of the girls. Staring into the eyes of each in turn she wiped away the tears from her eyes as she spoke.

'Go with Aran. He's in the cave. He'll take care of you. Stay safe and I promise I'll come and get you. I won't let you down again.'

Mary grabbed Gaia and burst into tears.

'Please Gaia. Stay with us, please,' the young girl pleaded.

'I wish I could, but I can't. Don't worry, everything is going to be fine. Aran will look after you. You're safe now.'

Gaia placed Mary's face between her hands, pressing them against her tear soaked cheeks. Leaning forward she kissed the young girl's lips, then did the same to Ruth.

'Go now,' Gaia whispered.

Climbing to her feet, the girls remained clinging to Gaia, desperate not to let go. Both were sobbing, as Gaia wiped tears from her eyes. The elation she had felt just minutes before was now replaced by a hollow emptiness. She had known this feeling before, it was the same as the last time she had to let them go, never knowing if she would see them again. It was the bitterest cruelty to have them back in her life again, only to be wrenched apart once more. She tried to push them away, but they continued to hold her tight, still trembling as they cried in desperation. Gaia looked up and saw Aran walking towards them, a ghost lit only by the orange glow of the flames from the torch. He approached without speaking, a gentle, loving smile on his face, then taking the girls by the hands he led them away towards the cave. They walked either side of him, each holding his hands, disappearing into the darkness, leaving only the echo of the crunch of their feet in the snow, mixed with the girl's quiet sobs. Then they were gone, and for a moment Gaia sensed this would be the last time she saw them.

Taking a deep breath and composing herself, Gaia turned to see Kali standing before her, the flaming torch in one hand, a dagger in the other. Freya was on her feet, hands behind her back a look of defiance on her face. Kali looked at them both.

'Here we are then. Just us, together again.'

Freya sneered.

'Don't you want to see where we buried your father while you're here.'

Kali's expression changed, and for a rare moment the cold, hard exterior slipped.

'What did you say?' she replied.

With cool composure, taking great pleasure in twisting this knife, Freya continued.

'Your father, Ben. Remember him? The one you abandoned after you killed your mother. We brought him here after your henchmen attacked him. He died in the cave a few hours ago.'

Kali looked shocked, almost wounded, a vacant expression drifting over her face. She seemed lost for words, her lips were moving, but she was unable to speak. Gaia moved towards her.

'You see where all this has led to, Kali,' Gaia said.

Something seemed to click inside Kali's mind, a realisation of where she was and who she was with. The wall came down again and the emotion drained from her. Shaking her head, Kali was mocking in her tone as she answered.

'I have no father, only the Community. Family is nothing, the Community is everything.'

Gaia looked back at Freya, unable to disguise her disdain.

'You don't really mean that, do you? It's just what you're meant to say. They were your mother and father,' Gaia said.

She stepped forward towards Kali and continued.

'It isn't a weakness to care.'

Kali snarled at Gaia.

'They meant nothing to me.'

Freya could hold her silence no longer, the simmering anger bursting from her.

'Is that what you tell yourself? You murdered your mother. You can't just brush that aside and hide behind the greater good.'

'I can, and I will. Don't judge me. You of all people.'

Both Kali and Freya moved toward each other, as Gaia placed her body between them. As they jostled and pressed against her, Gaia feared the leader was about to strike her sister down. She looked down as Kali played with the handle of the dagger in her hand.

'Let's leave,' Gaia said, hoping to somehow break the tension. Kali stepped away from her and nodded.

'It's time we were moving. There's somewhere we need to be, and we can't miss the tides,' she replied.

Gaia and Freya exchanged puzzled looks.

'Tides?' Freya asked.

'Yes, tides. We're going back to the island.'

17

The dawn was upon them and light was beginning to creep through the gaps in the trees. Gaia and Freya walked just ahead of Kali, their hands bound behind their backs. The other leaders walked in front, in a straight line as they snaked through the narrow paths. The numbers included Savas and Joe, the former just ahead of Gaia and wearing a patch over his eye. Both had given Gaia a cold reception when Kali led them down the hill. Neither had spoken to her as they made their way through the forest. The leaders continued to carry the burning torches as they led the way back to the road, though there was now just enough light to see.

The sisters walked behind in silence, watching and listening all the while, heads lowered pretending to be concentrating on their footing. They were both making mental notes, looking for any opportunities, sizing up their captors, thinking of potential plans for escape. Gaia knew this was her mind going through a drilled programme. They had been brainwashed to do this, over and over again on the island. Look to survive, find the weakness, but she knew it was futile. They were outnumbered and Kali was there. She would be well aware of how they were thinking. She had trained them, programmed them to think in this way. She would always be a step ahead, knowing their every move before they got a chance to make it. Aran was right. Stay alive at all costs. Hour by hour, day by day. That was their best chance of getting through this. Kali wanted them alive, or they would be dead already. She came a long way to capture them again. Whatever it was she wanted, it was important to her.

The repetitive monotony of the march saw Gaia's mind drift, and it wasn't long before her thoughts moved to the return to the island. When she left, she never thought they would return, and during her time recovering in the village there was a part of her that missed it. However, she knew that the island was a prison and once they had returned there would be no chance of another escape. She had deliberated for years how to break free, and it was only when Aran told her of the tides and the causeway that she realised there was an opportunity. The leaders would be more wary than ever now and Kali would make sure that route was no longer possible. As Gaia pondered the situation something began to trouble her - Aran.

Once again he had led them somewhere with the promise of escape, only to lead them back into the arms of Kali. Where were these people he spoke of? Why had he persuaded them to wait until morning with the hope they would arrive? He knew Kali would follow, but perhaps he knew more than he had said. How had Kali known about the crossbows? What if they were a decoy, simply there to give Gaia and Freya a false sense of hope? Why had Kali agreed to hand over the girls to Aran and let him go? Why had Aran led them here when it was so near to the island? She recalled something he had said about the island being near, and how at the time she had thought it worrying they had returned so close again. More and more questions began to build in her head. Part of her wanted to believe this was just fatigue, feeding a paranoia compounded by her capture. Perhaps she was just looking for someone to blame, and Aran was an easy target. The truth was they all made mistakes, and she and Freya didn't have to listen to Aran and stay. Then another part began to question this, remembering all that Aran had done before. As she walked on, her head spinning with these conflicting thoughts, one question kept appearing time and time again. It was a question she could not let go of, and had thought about many times since her torture in the village. Could she ever trust Aran again?

From the corner of her eye, Gaia noticed Joe slowing and edging back towards her until he was about a metre away. Still facing forward he spoke.

'I bet you're surprised to see us again after that stunt you pulled the other night.'

Gaia remained silent, marching step by step behind him, keeping the same distance. her head looking to the ground all the while. Joe continued, his voice calm and quiet, making no attempt to hide the conversation from Kali or the other leaders just in front.

'You're trap didn't work though, did it?. Your friends thought they had us, but they underestimated us and paid for it.'

Eyes fixed on the snow, Gaia replied.

'They weren't friends of mine. There was no trap. I was attacked just as you were. I would have been killed if Aran hadn't rescued me. It was either stay and die or run. You know they weren't working with us though, don't you?'

The leader's voice became louder and more agitated, hoping the others would hear.

'Do you think we're stupid? You and Aran planned this all along. You and those other traitors back at the village. That old witch we had to feed to the dogs. You were all planning this together. Well, they got what was coming to them.'

Gaia heard his words about Hannah, each one pricking at her like razor sharp needles.

'It looks like they took a piece of you with them,' she said.

Joe stopped and turned to face her; lunging forward he pressed his face close to hers. She could taste his stale breath as he spat out his words.

'That's right girl. Look closely. Lost because of you. Don't you worry - you'll get your turn soon. You'd better watch your back from now on.'

Kali's voice came booming from behind them.

'Keep moving you two, and take it easy, Joe. You heard what I said before. No-one touches them, but me. They're mine. Lay one finger on either of them and I'll have the other eye. Do you understand?'

Looking up at Kali, then back at Gaia the wounded leader began walking towards the others. Gaia turned to see both Freya and Kali just a few metres behind. Kali scowled at her, the menacing blue eyes set deep within her sharp features.

'Come on girl. Move it,' Kali said.

They walked on in silence again, the forest beginning to reveal brief flourishes of the hidden life buried deep within. Two magpies flew down from a tree, perching on a nearby bush. One let out a repeated harsh call, appearing to watch as the train of strange creatures slipped by. Somewhere in the distance Gaia heard the rattle of a woodpecker as it hammered at a tree, the sound echoing through the sky overhead. There were other noises, the crack of a branch, the cackle of crows, and the soothing trickle of running water.

They forged ahead, winding through the trees, sticking to what little pathway remained. Then Gaia sensed a change in the mood, as though all the sounds had been smothered from around them. An uneasy and eerie tension swept over the forest, and she had an overpowering feeling they were being watched. She scanned the trees searching for any sign of movement, but there was nothing. Looking ahead at the leaders, they carried on walking as before, unaware of any change around them. Pretending to lose her footing, Gaia fell on one knee, pausing for a moment to glance back at Kali and Freya. Neither seemed unnerved, though Kali was annoyed at her stumble, and hastened her to get up and continue.

Climbing to her feet, Gaia focused on the forest again. There was something there, though she began to doubt herself more and more as they moved on. Rationality rode over instinct as her brain grappled with what she thought and how she felt. It had been a long night, and she was tired. Though she trusted her senses, this seemed different; an odd feeling she had seldom had before. She also knew it was just a feeling, with no evidence and all the other indicators suggesting it was only in her mind. Still, she was edgy, and the odd sensation remained. Her eyes and ears were alive now, picking out even the smallest movements and sounds, zipping this way and that, searching through the trees for anything untoward.

Then she saw it. Just for the briefest of moments, something appeared to flash by, to her right, across a gap in the trees. She looked again, but told herself it was nothing, a bird in flight, or an animal in motion. It happened again. This time it was something larger, probably human, perhaps she had even caught a glimpse of a face. She was convinced this time, as her heart began to race. Still the leaders pressed on, none of them showing any sign of concern. Gaia slowed her pace to let Freya gain on her, then pausing a moment she glanced over her shoulder catching Kali's eye.

'Keep moving,' Kali barked.

'I think there's a stone in my boot and it's cutting into my foot. Can we stop a moment while I sort it?' Gaia asked.

Kali waited a moment, then shouted at the other leaders.

'Take five minutes everyone.'

Kali untied Gaia's hands.

'Don't try anything stupid,' the leader said.

Gaia lowered herself on one knee and began to undo her lace. She watched Kali and the other leaders as they huddled together exchanging idle chatter. Scanning the trees again, she searched for any sign of movement but could see nothing. Removing her boot, she pretended to search for the stone, all the while taking as much time as she could without arousing suspicion. From the corner of her eye she noticed Kali had broken away from the other leaders and was also surveying the forest, her hand placed on her dagger. Gaia looked on, holding her breath, watching the leader's every move, hoping Kali had not seen the same thing. She looked across at Freya who seemed lost in thought. Gaia coughed hoping to attract her attention. When that failed she flicked a small stone in her direction. Freya seemed startled, and stared at Gaia with a puzzled look.

Looking across at the leaders first to see if they were still chatting she raised her eyebrows hoping it would urge Freya to approach. There was another quizzical expression. Gaia repeated the gesture, but this time with a frown too. Freya began to shuffle towards her, moving within comfortable earshot without appearing to be too close. Gaia kept her head lowered fumbling with her boot. She whispered, just enough for Freya to catch her words.

'I think there's someone following us.'

Freya tried to look relaxed, all the while looking across at Kali and the other leaders. Kali had stopped scanning the forest and appeared to be giving some instructions to the others. Freya spoke, trying to move her lips as little as she could.

'Do you think it's, Aran?'

'Maybe, but I doubt it.'

'What about the group coming to find us at the cave?' Freya replied.

'Do you think they were ever coming?' Gaia said.

Freya looked down at her sister.

'Why wouldn't they?'

Freya paused for a moment, a look of realisation creeping across her face. Then she noticed the pain and anguish in Gaia's eyes.

'It's possible,' Freya said.

'Who knows who to trust in this fucked up world, but if you ask me I think Aran's genuine. There's a lot that doesn't add up, but why go to all this trouble to bring us here. They could have just captured us at The Haven. That was the time to get everyone.'

Gaia thought for a moment.

'Why here, so near the island when that's where Kali wants to take us anyway? Why let him and the girls go so easily? There's something not right about this,' she said.

Freya frowned.

'I understand why you don't trust him, but maybe it's about something more.'

'What do you mean?'

Freya avoided her sister's uncomfortable gaze, looking back at the leaders. She was still trying to avoid Gaia's stare.

'It's clear you have feelings for each other. Perhaps that's what's messing with your head,' Freya replied.

Gaia put her boot on, and got to her feet, ignoring her sister.

'I'm ready,' she called.

Kali approached, and after tying Gaia's hands behind her back she ushered Freya and the other leaders forward.

'We need to get a move on or we'll miss those tides,' Kali said.

As they followed the path again Gaia began to slow her pace hoping to open up a bit of a gap between Kali, Freya, herself and the other leaders. She continued to look into the forest, but other than the sights and sounds that had become familiar and expected, she saw and heard nothing more. The sun was rising, beginning its slow, shallow rise across the winter sky, and Gaia sensed the weather may be changing. The bitter chill in the wind had eased and there were moments when she thought she could feel the warmth of the sun breaking through. Her heart told her the thaw was coming, her head kept looking for more assurance. The snow clinging to the branches was beginning to melt, and the drops of water that fell to earth were forming icicles no longer. Gaia thought of her spot by the stream in the village, of the icicles she had gazed at for hours there. They would be melting too, disappearing, changing, their only footprint in her memory and the moments of joy they had given her when she was alone.

She could feel Freya on her shoulder, just metres behind, Kali had dropped back a little and was now working someway behind them. Gaia heard her sister's whispering voice.

'I saw something in the forest. I think you could be right.'

Gaia kept moving forward, twisting her head towards her shoulder when she give her hushed reply.

'We need to get ready. They might not be friendly, but if they attack it could be our chance to run.'

'Keep your eyes on the leaders, I'll see to Kali if need be. As soon as one falls get their weapons. We need to cut ourselves free or we'll be as good as dead.' Freya said.

Unsure of whether it was Freya's confirmation, or her own growing tension, Gaia began to sense the same ominous feeling of impending threat she had earlier. As she shuffled through the snow she was aware of how vulnerable both Freya and her were. With their hands tied they would need to act as soon as there was any sign of an attack. But for now they could only walk, watch, and wait.

The attack came moments later. A flurry of bolts flashed through the air striking a number of the leaders. Gaia heard the swishing sound as they zipped towards their targets and in a split second several leaders lay on the floor. Some were clutching at wounds, others were in the final twitches of death already. All the bolts had struck them in the neck, each accurate, true and devastating. Gaia sprinted toward the nearest dying leader, dropped to her knees by his side, crouched low and grabbed his dagger. Twirling the blade, she cut herself free, picked up a machete and looked towards Freya and Kali.

Wincing with pain, the leader had one hand clutching a bolt lodged in her shoulder. In the other was a dagger which she was using to fend off Freya who, with hands still tied behind her back was trying to find any opening to attack. Kali was wounded and both Gaia and Freya knew this was their chance. Gaia saw the flashes of movements within the trees, and was trying to take cover. There was the sound of more bolts and another few leaders fell to the ground. In desperation they charged into the trees trying to locate the attackers. After each flurry of bolts there would be the briefest of pauses and the bodies in the trees would disappear, only to reappear to launch another wave of attacks. Gaia crouched low behind a tree. It was clear, this group were well orchestrated and drilled, minimising the risk to themselves and picking off their targets with clinical accuracy. She watched as several more leaders were hit and fell into the undergrowth. Only a few remained and still none had managed to reach those delivering the bolts for one to one combat.

To her right, Freya was also hiding behind a tree, and just a few metres away Kali lay on her back still holding her injured shoulder. Gaia shouted to her sister.

'If I get a chance I'll cut you free, but I can't risk it yet. Whoever they are, they're good.'

Freya nodded.

'Throw me the dagger,' she shouted.

Gaia peered out from behind the tree, unable to see any of the attackers hidden in the forest. She threw the dagger to Freya, landing just behind her. As it hit the ground, Kali rolled over, jumped to her feet and began to run. Gaia called to her sister.

'Quick. She's getting away.'

Despite the danger, instinct took over and Gaia sprung to her feet in pursuit. She reached her sister, who had managed to cut herself free already, and was upright and turning ready to run. Without pausing, Gaia kept up the chase of Kali who was darting through the trees ahead at a swift pace.

'Split up or we're an easier target,' Gaia cried.

As they pursued the leader through the forest Gaia realised not a single shot had been fired at them when they made their first move. If any had been, they had not come anywhere near to either Freya or herself. Even the bolt that had hit Kali had only wounded her, at odds with the deadly efficiency of the other shots. Whoever was leading the attack, they wanted the three of them alive.

They hurdled undergrowth and fallen trees, and ducked under low hanging branches. Gaia kept Kali in view, though was struggling to gain on her. To her left, weaving a parallel path through the forest, Freya was also maintaining the chase. Kali's wounds would have weakened her, and though her strength and determination were sustaining her at the moment, this would fade and she would be theirs. Gaia knew all they had to do was keep her in view, and not let her hide. If they lost her she could stay concealed for days in this barren environment. The last thing they could do was let her escape.

Gaia became aware of a sound behind her. It was a similar crunch of snow, shuffling of bushes, and the crack of breaking branches. She was being followed, and whoever it was they were close. After several minutes of running there was still no sign of Kali tiring. All her training and athleticism were proving more than ample in overcoming the pain and weakening from her wounded shoulder. Bursting through a gap in the forest, Gaia realised they were at the base of the avenue of trees leading up to the cave. Kali was sprinting up the hill, with Freya now ahead of Gaia and close behind the leader. Her sister had managed to lift her pace and gain on Kali and it was only a matter of moments before she would close the gap. Hearing the rustle of bushes behind her, Gaia continued her chase up the hill towards the cave. She knew there was a risk in losing time by looking behind, and allowing her pursuer to gain even more. Whoever was chasing her, they were getting closer all the time.

Kali approached the long, narrow opening to the cave, veering off to the left, and clambering up the steep, slippy incline leading to the lip hanging over the entrance. She headed up the hill beyond the cave, with Freya almost within reach of her. The leader was heading for a copse of trees that topped the hill, and Gaia recalled Aran's warning this led to the cliff overlooking the quarry infested with rats. Reaching the entrance, she followed the path laid out in the snow by the other two. It was heavy going and she could feel the burning in her legs as they pounded the snow step by step. The hill was steeper than it looked and she could feel her footing slip as she pressed on. Kali and Freya had both entered the cover of the trees, and Gaia could hear the panting of whoever it was behind her.

As she entered the woods Gaia took a sharp right and dived behind the cover of some bushes. Crouching low, she tried to steady her breathing and make as little sound as she could. She looked at the opening in the trees she had entered as her pursuer burst through. Without stopping, they kept up their darting run through the trees. Gaia got to her feet and followed them, keeping a steadier pace, reassured that whatever threat she though they were under it was less so now. Whatever Aran was up to she would find out soon.

18

Reaching the edge of the treeline at the top of the hill, Gaia saw Freya first then Aran standing close behind. Both had their daggers drawn and were staring at Kali at the edge of the cliff. She too was armed, but it was obvious her injury and the chase had taken its toll as she looked exhausted. The leader was panting, struggling to recapture her breath, and the arrogant snarl that so often accompanied any threat seemed dampened as she fought with the pain. She looked unsteady on her feet, rocking and swaying as she clutched at the icy air. Freya was focused on Kali, and she didn't even acknowledge her sister when she appeared from the trees. Aran looked on, avoiding Gaia's scowl.

A chill wind was blowing, and without the natural protection of the trees and the exposure of the higher ground, Gaia could feel its razor sharp bite against her face. Kali looked at Gaia and spoke, her voice sounding cracked and frail, but still with the customary edge.

'Well, here we all are again. What are we going to do now?'

Freya stepped forward as she spat out her reply.

'We're going to kill you.'

Aran edged towards Freya, reaching out his arm.

'No Freya. Wait! No-one is going to get killed. Let's just take our time and think this through,' he said.

'Think what through? This is what we wanted. We have her now. It's time we ended this,' Freya replied.

'She's right, Aran? As long as she's alive this will just keep going. Let's finish it now,' Gaia said.

Aran turned to face Gaia, his expression was almost pleading with her.

'You don't want to do this, Gaia. Neither of you. I can't explain now, but it's important you listen to me, please.'

Gaia shook her head, snarling in disbelief.

'Listen to him, Gaia. He's talking sense. Killing me is not going to solve anything. It means nothing to me, but you'll end up regretting it,' Kali said.

'You shut the fuck up!' Freya replied, lunging towards the leader with her dagger, but pulling back as Kali thrust her own knife back at her. It was clear Kali was not going to give up without a fight.

'She's right. Both of you need to listen. Let's just tie her up and take her back with us. We can decide then what to do with her. I'll explain everything,' Aran said.

Gaia gave him a puzzled look.

'Back where, Aran? Who were those people back there?'

Aran took a few steps towards Gaia, reaching out an arm in reassurance. Looking down at it she brushed it aside, then returned her accusative stare. He lowered his gaze.

'They're my people. The ones I told you about,' he replied.

'They arrived soon after Kali took you. They'd been following them for a while, but were reluctant to attack until they were sure I was safe. They'll wait for us in the forest. We have somewhere in the hills we can go. We'll take Kali there.'

'Where are the girls?' Gaia asked.

'Someone is watching them. They'll be there when we return to the forest. Don't worry about the other leaders, they'll all have been taken care of. Kali is the one we wanted,' he said.

Gaia exchanged looks with her sister, then stared at Kali. The leader was struggling to hide the pain, but still had a mocking grin on her face. For a moment, Gaia saw the briefest flash of weakness, a softening that took her by surprise.

'I know what we've all been through and how tempting it is to take out your anger and revenge on her,' Aran said. He paused, waiting for Gaia to respond, but she looked away instead. He continued.

'No-one wants to kill her more than I do, but my people need her. She'll get what she deserves in good time, but not this way. Trust me, please.'

The word 'trust' was all that Gaia heard. A word she had heard so many times from everyone she came in contact with. She recalled the warning Hanna had given her to trust no-one. It had proven good advice so far, and she saw no reason to discard it now. While she thought about what would be the best next move, her sister spoke.

'Don't listen to him, Gaia. He has his own agenda. They want Kali so they can get to The Community. That's not our fight, it's theirs. Think of what she's done to us. What she's done to others. She'll never change.'

Kali laughed and shook her head.

'Listen to you. Are you so different? Remember I made you what you are, all of you. I know you better than anyone. I know what you've done and what you're capable of. Who are you all to judge me?' Kali said.

Freya frowned and continued her attack on the leader.

'We're only like you because you made us into killers so we can do the dirty work for The Community and you,' she said.

'We know what you are and we're not your slaves anymore. The Community is over as far as we're concerned. We're starting again away from all that. You deserve all that is coming to you for what you've done.'

There was another mocking laugh from the leader.

'You can run away, but you'll never change who you are. Believe me I know. It's who you are,' Kali replied.

Gaia stepped towards Kali, her anger at both Aran and the leader had been simmering, but hearing these words meant she could contain herself no longer.

'We're nothing like you, and whatever we were we'll leave behind. You're the lowest of the low. You killed your own mother and father. What does that make you?'

Kali's expression changed, the grin disappeared and was replaced by something more serious and sinister. Her voice was calm and more controlled, little more than a whisper as she responded.

'Kill me and you'll be no different. Don't you see?'

Gaia listened to the words, struggling to understand their full meaning. As she stared back at Kali, trying to unpick and fathom her words Aran took hold of her arm and spoke.

'Don't listen to her, Gaia. She's trying to get inside your head,' he pleaded.

Kali turned her stare to Aran.

'Are you afraid to tell them? You know the truth, don't you? And you've known all along?'

Gaia gave Aran a puzzled look.

'Known what?'

'Go on tell her, or I will,' Kali said.

Aran thrust a menacing look at Kali.

'Leave it, Kali!' he snarled.

'No, Aran. Tell me. What's going on?' Gaia asked.

There was a silence, everyone looking at Aran, waiting to see if he would reply. His head was lowered, staring at the snow on the ground, struggling to think of what to say, looking into an abyss he couldn't see a way of escaping. After a long pause, it was Kali who broke the silence. Her voice was calm and clinical as she uttered the words, cold and devoid of all emotion.

'Kill me and you're just the same,' she said.

Kali paused, waiting for a response. She continued.

'Haven't you worked it out? Come on, you're smart girls. Why do you think I've taken so much interest in you both? Why all these second chances?'

There was another pause, but only silence.

'I'm your mother.'

At first the words seemed to hang in the air, floating and unwanted, waiting for someone to grab them. One by one those final powerful words seeped into Gaia's mind, their full meaning unfolding, flowing through her veins, and piercing her heart. She felt a stabbing pain in her chest as if Kali had thrust her dagger between her ribs. She looked across at her sister, who seemed to be in a daze, her eyes glazed and vacant. The tone of her sister's expression began to change to frustration and anger.

'Liar!' Freya cried.

She lunged at Kali, but with one deft move the leader stepped to one side, tripped Freya, then struck her on the back and watched as she fell to the ground. Freya lay still in the snow, head bowed, hunched on all fours. Gaia looked down at her sister, then at Kali, before she shifted her gaze to Aran.

'Is it true?' she asked.

Rather than reply, Aran lowered his gaze, and avoiding Gaia's eyes he nodded. Dumbstruck, the look of bemusement returned to her face. Shaking her head in shock and disbelief she continued.

'Have you known all along?'

There was a pause, Aran building up the courage to respond.

'I've known for a long time,' he replied.

'How long? Did you know on the island, during the escape? I mean are we talking months or years, Aran? How could you have kept this from me?'

There was no reply, instead Aran kept his eyes fixed on the ground, wrapped in shame. Gaia turned to Kali, still trying to appear calm and in control, but the injury was taking its toll. Looking at her shoulder, Gaia noticed a large, dark stain on Kali's jacket. The leader's eyelids looked heavy, her lips parched and dry. Her body still swayed as though she might collapse at any moment. Gaia looked the leader up and down, still in disbelief, but also with a mixture of sorrow and disdain. Her emotions were racing now, and she was fighting to remain calm. Steadying her breathing, she tried to focus on other thoughts, and distract her mind from the enormity of what she was trying to understand.

'So what now?' Kali asked.

Gaia thought for a moment. Everything before had led her to this moment. Everything she had told herself was about now, how she would confront Kali, and end it all for good. She had told herself so many times that she would only be free once Kali was dead. This was how it was meant to be, but now things had changed. Nothing was as it was before. Kali was still the feared leader of old, but she was also something else, something more. Whatever Gaia thought of her, she was her mother. An image kept flashing into her mind, the dream she had with Kali in it. There was one word she could never recall when she awoke. The word that was chanted over and over again, but had proven so elusive. She could hear it now, playing in her head. The word was *'mother.'* Shuffling forwards, Gaia approached the leader.

'Drop your dagger, then turn around, and face the other way,' she said.

Kali looked puzzled, and just as she was about to speak Gaia barked at her.

'Just do it. Now!'

The leader paused, in two minds whether to obey. She was the one used to giving orders, and every fibre of her was trained not to take orders, especially from the young. However, Kali was well aware of her predicament and was weighing up her options, hoping to drag out the time as long as possible. She threw the dagger at Gaia's feet, then turned her back to the others, taking a couple of steps forward to the edge of the cliff. Gaia approached her, moving just behind.

'Put your hands behind your back.' Gaia said.

Kali obeyed, wincing as she moved the arm with the wounded shoulder. The leader stood upright, looking across the quarry, now overgrown with a thick canopy of treetops, dusted in speckled, white snow. Gaia took some cord from her bag, and bound the leader's hands together. With each twist of the cord she pulled it extra tight, taking pleasure from the winces of pain Kali tried to conceal. Gaia looked down at Freya, still on all fours but watching her sister along with Aran. Exchanging glances with both, she nodded and turned back to Kali.

'This is where it ends,' Gaia said.

Kali cleared her throat before answering, her voice the faintest of whispers.

'Remember this. Everything I have done was to protect you and your sister. You may not think it, but it was only ever about securing what was best for you both.'

Finishing the words, Kali stepped forward and plunged off the cliff into the trees below. Gaia sprang forward, trying to grab her and prevent her from falling, but it was too late. Staring over the edge at the body as it fell below Gaia screamed.

'No!'

Freya and Aran scrambled by Gaia's side, all three looking down at the carpet of white snow and green foliage. They all stood in silence, aghast at what they had seen. The biting cold of the wind nipped at their cheeks as they stared in horror. This was what she had always wanted, but now the moment had arrived there was a feeling of complete emptiness. Reaching down, Gaia took both her sister and Aran by the hand. As they gazed below, images flashed through Gaia's mind, pictures of the dream, and the memory of its ending. Kali was falling into some dark, bottomless abyss, and then she heard the constant chanting of *'mother'* in the background. This was the word she was always grasping for and struggling to remember. It was the word that kept dissolving and stayed beyond her grasp when she awoke. In the dream Gaia reached out, trying to save her, but she was helpless and could only watch as Kali disappeared into the darkness. This was how the dream ended, and maybe this was how it was always meant to be.

19

Gaia couldn't believe she was gone. She sat in the forest on a fallen tree stump, Freya on one side, Ruth and Mary on the other. Aran stood nearby, speaking with some of the group that had led the attack on the leaders earlier. She was tired and confused, dazed and numbed by the events of the past few hours. The sun still hung low, but burned much brighter in the sky, and the heavy, snow-laden clouds of recent months had all gone. There was a subtle warmth in the air, a glimmer of spring breaking through. The treetops were clear, all the snow and icicles that had clung to them for so many months had melted. As Gaia listened to the sounds of the forest, she felt sure there was more birdsong than before. Perhaps it was only her imagination, or the dawning of an optimism and hope, but the forest seemed to have changed, with a calm, gentle buzz and the promise of new life.

Staring at the ground by her feet, Gaia's mind drifted as her eyes searched for patterns and faces in the snow. She thought of what might happen next, what the future held for Freya, the girls and herself. Here they were together again, which was more than she could ever have hoped for. Kali was gone and they were free. Yet, every time she pictured Kali's body falling into the trees she flinched with pain, and felt an emptiness inside. This was what she had wanted, but not how she imagined it, another broken dream. Aran was having discussions with his people, planning the final part of the journey, their trip to safety in the hills. Where did the future lie with Aran? Would he be a part of her world?

There was a gentle slope just down from where they sat. At the base was a small frozen pond, peppered with brown reeds and rushes, dead, but waiting to flourish again. Something caught her eye on the edge of the icy water, a swan waddling across the frozen surface, its head hung low as it shuffled and slid towards the other side. Gaia watched as it stumbled over the ice, looking tired, jaded, and alone. As it reached the far edge of the pond the bird paused and raising its head high into the air began to sing. It was the most beautiful and haunting of melodies, laden with sadness, and a dark, mournful quality. Gaia looked on, enchanted by the mesmerising sound. The other sounds of the forest seemed to melt away, as the tune cast a spell over her. As the song floated through her, all the sorrow and regret she was feeling seemed to evaporate, her mind emptied of all the recent woes. All she could hear was the majestic song from this regal bird, standing proud for one last time. The song ended and lowering its head the swan shuffled into some nearby reeds and disappeared.

Freya took hold of Gaia's hand.

'How are you feeling?' she asked.

Gaia looked at her sister and smiled.

'I don't know. Shocked, confused, relieved. How about you?'

'Pretty much the same, I guess.'

Freya paused and pointed down the hill to the pond.

'It's beautiful, isn't it?'

Gaia nodded.

'I've never heard any bird sing like that before,' she said.

'*Hark, canst thou hear me? I will play the swan. And die in music.* It's from a play written by one of the ancient writers. They read it to us during the nurturing. The old stories spoke of a swan song, or the final melody from a dying swan.'

'I hope they were wrong, and the swan doesn't die.'

Freya smiled.

'The stories were wrong about a lot of things, but right about so much more. If it's better, we can tell ourselves that it isn't dead, and it will live to sing again.'

'Yes, that's how I want to picture it,' Gaia replied.

'Then we will. Think of the swans spreading it's wings and flying off into the sunset. Free to go wherever it choses.'

Freya squeezed her sister's hand and laid her head against her shoulder.

'So what now, sister? What next for us?'

Gaia looked across at Aran as she replied.

'We need to speak with Aran, see what their plans are. Then we'll have to decide what's best for us and the girls.'

Freya leant forward and stared at Ruth and Mary. The older girl had her head leant against Gaia, while the younger huddled in close against her sister. Freya spoke.

'What about you, girls? Do you want to stay with us? I don't know where we'll end up, but at least we'll all be together, and you'll have a sister or brother in a few months time.'

Freya looked down at her stomach, then at Gaia. Mary raised her head and nodded.

'You still don't say much, do you?' Freya said.

Mary smiled and shook her head, and Freya and Gaia laughed.

Finishing his conversation with the others, Aran approached and crouched opposite. Picking up a small branch, he began to play with the snow, etching random patterns.

'We're heading for our hideout in the hills soon. Have you made your mind up what you want to do?' he asked.

Freya squeezed the hand of her sister, who after a long pause replied.

'What are you going to do with The Community now Kali's gone? If she's gone, that is.'

'She's gone. I doubt anyone can survive that, not even Kali. If she survived the fall, the rats would have gotten her. The quarry's swarming with them.'

Aran paused for a moment, his expression changing as he realised his cold, and heartless words and tone.

'I'm sorry. I forgot. You must be feeling pretty mixed up at the moment,' he said.

Gaia recalled his secret and lies, and as he caught her eye he looked down at his etchings on the ground.

'I know none of this is easy for either of you, but you have to look at Kali's death as you always would. It's a good thing for all of us,' he said. Still peering at the ground, he continued.

'She was never a mother to you, or a daughter to Ben and his wife. She changed. The Community poisoned her. It's what they do. The Poison destroyed one society and another poison came along. You've lost nothing, but gained your freedom from her. Finally, we're all free. We can move on and build our lives again.'

There was a silence while they each thought about Aran's words.

'Was this all planned? I mean, did you bring us here because you knew Kali would follow us?' Gaia asked.

Aran nodded.

'We had to get away and I knew my people would come for us. Kali was bound to follow us. She wanted you and Freya too badly. The plan was once her and the other leaders arrived they would attack.'

'They were here all along?' Gaia said.

'Yes,' he answered.

Gaia shook her head in disbelief, fighting back tears of rage.

'We're safe and Kali is dead. Isn't that what we always wanted?' Aran said.

Unable to hold back her anger any longer, Gaia replied, her voice wavering with emotion.

'You knew this all along and never told us. And you knew that Kali was our mother and kept that from us. Is there anything else you're hiding?'

'I told you my people would be here and that Kali would come. I didn't mention the trap or that Kali was your mother because I knew it might upset things. I wasn't sure how you'd both react and I couldn't put the ambush at risk,' he replied.

He paused a moment before continuing.

'I'm sorry, but there were bigger things at stake than us.'

Both Gaia and Aran gazed at the ground, and Freya was the first to speak again.

'We have to decide what's best for us now. Gaia, me and the girls. That's all that matters,' she said.

Aran looked at Freya and nodded.

'I understand. If I could have made this happen any other way I would have.'

'What about your plans to attack The Haven?' Freya asked.

Aran frowned.

'We're still planning to go ahead,' he replied.

'Kali's death doesn't change anything. The Community will be weakened now. They've lost Kali and a lot of prized and well-trained leaders. We've killed some strong fighters, and there's never been a better chance to destroy them. We can be better than them. We have to be. The day of reckoning is coming.'

Aran paused for a moment, then continued.

'I'm heading to the hills, then I'll lead an attack on the island. Come with us.'

Gaia was filled with doubt, while Aran looked on, pleading with her to say the words he wanted to hear. What now? She had thought about little else since Kali had plunged to her death. They had a child to think of, and the girls to care for. Life wasn't just about themselves anymore. They had responsibilities, and while their futures had been determined by The Community and the leaders, now it was bound by love and a commitment to others. Gaia knew this all too well, and the weight of responsibility hung heavy on her heart as she pondered what to do. Should she walk away and end this, or join Aran and fight on? As the silence lingered, Aran spoke.

'What's it going to be?'

Gaia looked at Freya, then felt the girls pressed against her. Clearing her throat, she gave her answer.

'We'll come with you to the hills, then we'll decide.'

Aran nodded and rose to his feet. He reached out a hand to Gaia.

'Let's go then. We only have a few days.'

ABOUT THE AUTHOR

Chris is a married father of four boys. After graduating in the early 90s he became an English language teacher living in Turkey, Portugal, India and traveling beyond. He returned to the UK to study an MA in International Politics and worked at Warwick University. He then moved into policy research and implementation. Currently, Chris is a Partnership Manager for the National Citizen Service, delivering outdoor activity and social action programmes for young people across the North East.

A keen musician, Chris plays solo horn for Jayess Newbiggin Brass Band in the village where he grew up, and the setting for his second novel 'The Storm.' Chris loves running and in addition to a couple of marathons has run many half marathons and 10Ks. He currently lives in Monkseaton, near Newcastle upon Tyne.

Chris' dream was always to write, and his journey began in August 2015 when he took voluntary redundancy from his role in education policy. His first novel 'Becoming' was published in September 2016 to widespread acclaim. 'Becoming', the first book in the Gaia Series, is a dystopian story about a teenage girl called Gaia and her attempt to escape a brutal community on Holy Island in Northumberland. His third novel 'Awakening' is the sequel to 'Becoming.'

When he isn't working on new story ideas, Chris writes regular articles for a blog, and his work has appeared in local newspapers and magazines. As well as delivering readings at local author events, he had visited schools across the country to give talks on writing. In 2017 Chris was commissioned by Woodhorn Museum to write a series of passages in support of their 'Wonderfolk' interactive family experience.

Further information on Chris and his work can be found at:
http://chrisord.wixsite.com/chrisord
or on Facebook at:
https://www.facebook.com/chrisordauthor/

Printed in Great Britain
by Amazon